SECRETS

SECRETS

JOHN FLOYD MILLS

FRANKLIN
SCRIBES
PUBLISHERS

SECRETS
©2013 by John Floyd Mills

Published by Franklin Scribes Publishers. Franklin Scribes is a registered trademark of Franklin Scribes Publishers.

Franklin Scribes books may be purchased in bulk for educational, business, fund-raising, or sales promotional use. For information, please email SpecialMarkets@ franklinscribes.com.

Publisher's Note: This novel is a work of fiction. References to events, establishments, organizations, locales, and real people living or deceased are intended merely to equip the fiction with a sense of authenticity and color. They are used factiously. All other names, characters, places, and all dialogue and incidents portrayed in this book are the product of the author's imagination.

Library of Congress Cataloging-in-Publication Data
Mills, John Floyd
Secrets/ John Floyd Mills
2013954831

Summary: Tommy Townsend, a young author and English instructor from the University of Washington has come to the panhandle of Oklahoma to interview his aging grandfather for his next book. The long-promised interview is to discover the secret surrounding a mining accident in 1968 which buried Tom Howard, his "Papa Tom", alive. Tommy Townsend becomes exposed to more than just secrets—a woman, a dangerous criminal, and truths that will both inspire you and break your heart.

ISBN 978-0-9886433-3-8 (soft cover)

Secrets is the sequel to Buried, ISBN 978-0-9886433-2-1

Printed in the United States of America

To Buddy, my Tommy Boy.

Setting my drink down on the table between us, I rock back and smile, shaking my head. I hear chuckles around me. Several others had quietly gathered on the porch to listen to my grandfather's story.

Chapter One
The time has come.

*M*y cell phone plays a familiar ringtone, the selected one which announces my mother calling. Its vibration sends it shimmying across my night stand. With each dance step, it moves closer to the edge. Before it falls to the floor, I reach across the empty space of my too large bed, a sad testament to my self-imposed single life. I capture it and slide it to answer, ending the repetition of Beethoven's deep opening notes, pum…pum…pum… pummmm. Rolling over on my back, I struggle to focus on the time; 4:31 AM glares in the darkness.

Still half asleep, I mumble, "Good morning Mom."

"Goooood morning, Sweetie!" She sounds full of life, as if she just finished a short stack of pancakes and a tall order of Pilates. "I wanted to catch you before you left for class."

"Not to worry, Mom. Still on summer break, although I always appreciate the opportunity to see the sunrise—and, of course, talk to you."

"Hmmph," she exhales.

"You don't work, Mom. Don't you ever sleep in?" I flip over and peer through my window overlooking Puget Sound. The ocean, the hills, the sky—all blend together in near darkness except for the reflective lights of Seattle dancing on the bay's black water. "Did you forget Seattle is three hours earlier than Atlanta?"

"Tommy Lee Townsend, stop your whining."

I hate it when she calls me that. My book jackets refer to me as Thomas L. Townsend. My students call me Mister Townsend. My colleagues—Townsend. Only my mother calls me Tommy Lee.

She continues, "I've been up for over an hour. Your dad has been at the studio since five—he's on the air now if you want to catch him. Anyway, we found out last night and thought you would want to know..."

"What's wrong, Mom?"

"Doc Watson called us from the nursing home in Divine. If you still want to interview your grandfather for your next book, you need to get out to Oklahoma—soon."

Purchasing a ticket at the counter is by far the costliest way to travel, especially when you're trying to get booked on the next flight out. Don't have a clue how long I am going to be gone. Got a one-way ticket. Eight-hour travel time with a plane change in Memphis—add drive time of three to four hours from Oklahoma City to Divine. I've learned to travel light.

The ticket agent smiles and asks, "Checking any bags, Mr. Townsend?"

"No, Ma'am."

"Your flight begins boarding in one hour at gate 22-B. Have a pleasant trip."

Today is one of those times when being married would be a good thing. If I had a Mrs. Townsend she could have taken me to the airport,

2

I wouldn't have to deal with long-term parking. A wife could have done my packing while I showered. She could have made the calls to clear my calendar, revised my schedules and appointments. If married, I could have a dog—always wanted a dog—can't just pick up and go at a moment's notice with the responsibility of an animal. And plants, live plants would be nice but no one to water them when I'm gone. Plastic ones just get dusty. When I get back, I think I'll work on getting a wife. Thirty-one is a good age to get married.

The incessant clicking of the broken wheel on my travel bag is really annoying—not only to me but apparently to everyone on the concourse. I assume everyone is staring at me because of the clattering of the cracked plastic roller—not because I'm wearing a pin-striped suit with a pair of obnoxious neon orange running shoes. And, of course, my favorite blue and yellow striped rugby shirt.

I never travel without my Armani book-signing suit. A shameless self-promoter, I never miss an opportunity to grab the spotlight or the microphone to hawk or talk about my books. Can't pack it inside a small carry-on for fear permanent wrinkles would be left by travel trolls residing in small bags appropriate for storing in the overhead bin or on the floor beneath the seat in front of me.

And my running shoes? I would never wear my Italian leather Donald Trump wingtips in a hostile environment like an overcrowded airliner or a bustling airport where children and rolling travel bags run wild. No fear of being recognized here—although once I did get mistaken for that guy who played Ferris Bueller.

You'd think I was waiting in line for the most popular ride at Disneyland. I slowly trek toward security personnel, x-ray machines and endless grey plastic tubs gliding across rollers in and out of the scanning tunnels. I anxiously long for the other side of security, where shoes go back on and the fear of missing your flight subsides. The other side is only yards away now—yet more than a hundred faceless fellow travelers wind through the narrow pathway, shifting and shuffling toward freedom—forward, on to the gates!

"Please have your photo I.D. and boarding pass out…If you are carrying a laptop, please take it out…Excuse me, sir. Sir…" His voice dropped an octave and his left eyebrow went up. "Place your shoes in a separate tub."

And then, on my first attempt at the metal detector—BEEEEP! Behind me, I hear a chorus of frustrated fellow travelers exhale deeply and in perfect harmony.

"Sir, please step back and place your watch and anything else in your pockets into the plastic dish."

I comply and re-enter the security portal. No beep. I'm cleared. Triumphantly, I retrieve my bag, my computer, my backpack, my watch, keys and coins, and slip on my Nikes. Laces trailing behind, I consider raising my hands victoriously and declaring loudly, Free at last—thank God almighty, I'm free at last. I only consider it.

Having passed the gauntlet of airport security, I'm cleared to travel the corridor to the gates. At long last, a Starbucks. Within sight of my gate, I plop down with a dark roast venti and a too sweet and not-on-my-diet cheese danish. What to do till we board?

Displaying my value to the world and significance in society, my laptop comes out, pops open and lies on my tightly joined knees. I'm sure I look like a preening peacock. Just resting my fingers on the keyboard gives me a rush of my being in control once more. I'm in my element now—prepared to take charge now that I have evaded Homer Homeland Security. Now while Seattle and the rest of the world are at their desks, I check my calendar, begin placing the calls and making the changes on my schedule that need to take place to accommodate my being in the remote panhandle of Oklahoma for the duration until… Until he tells me the secret. Or, he dies.

I can't believe I actually consider that thought—him dying. My grandfather. My Papa Tom. The hero of my youth. Certainly there exists a person more famous than he, but none greater in my eyes.

The first call goes out to my editor, Bill Sims. Bill published my first book. We have a great relationship—a little rocky at first, but only because he failed to recognize just how much writing talent I possess. I didn't realize until much later just how much knowledge he had about the publishing industry. Last year, I pitched him the idea of a book about my grandfather. I've already spent the small advance.

Next, I need to let my grandfather know I'm on my way. I hadn't even considered the possibility Papa Tom would not be ready for me to come and interview him for my book. He had made me a promise—when I was eleven—to tell me the secret about him and Mr. Morton Podus. Seven years ago, Podus became the subject of my first book, *Biography of a Criminal*. Convicted for fraud, conspiracy, and attempted manslaughter, he masterminded a mining accident designed to free his company from a supply contract—the accident caused my grandfather to be buried alive. And then, Podus stepped in to prevent his rescue. He said because it wasn't safe for the rescuers to go back into the mine but he meant until the supply contract became invalid.

Papa Tom's mysterious secret comes from a statement I've heard whispered since my childhood—*considering what Tom Howard did for Mr. Podus, I can't believe he would just let him die.*

When I interviewed Mr. Podus, he told me a great deal. I wrote about his life, his trials—both in and out of court—his successes and his failures. He discussed his motives and his regrets. But, when I asked him the question point-blank, he never answered—he only told me to ask my grandfather. And, when I did, Papa Tom told me as long as Mr. Podus and his son, Jake, were still alive, he wouldn't tell me. Until then, it would remain a secret.

Morton Podus died in 1999, at the age of 92. Jake Podus died three years later. There are no living siblings, children, grandchildren or spouses. Papa Tom is the only person alive who knows the secret and the only living person who would even care, I guess.

I scroll the phone's directory and the newly entered Wildflower Nursing Center in Divine, Oklahoma comes to a stop. Papa Tom seems genuinely excited to hear from me and tells me to come see him anytime. But, don't wait too long, he warns. I tell him I'm at the airport in Seattle and on my way. He doesn't seem surprised.

Next call: After a disconcerting number of rings, a summer intern in the English Department at the University of Washington picks up. I ask her to cancel all my appointments indefinitely and that I'll keep in touch through texts and emails.

At last, time to board. The plane climbs through the clouds, away from the airport, and leaves the Great Northwest for Memphis and then back to Oklahoma.

Flaps up and then, wheels down. I arrive at Will Rogers Airport in Oklahoma City. By the time I get my rental car onto Interstate 40 and head northwest to Hwy 270, it's beginning to get dark. And, although it's another hour or so to Divine, the small city of Woodward seems a good place and a good time to call it quits for the day. The GPS shows nothing exciting for the next 75 miles, my tail bone is sore from sitting all day, and my stomach thinks my throat's been cut. Man can't live on peanuts alone. The very next *Dairy Queen* gets my food order and a pillow at the first motel in Woodward has my name on it.

Chapter Two
Our first sit down.

've dreamt about this day for twenty years; perhaps that is why I got so little sleep last night. I check out of the Travel Lodge in Woodward and arrive in Divine at 8:30. I regret not stopping for coffee earlier but look forward to eating breakfast at the Pitt Stop Café—if it's still there.

There are now three places to eat breakfast in Divine—the Pitt Stop isn't one of them—it's now a resale shop. When Mom worked there in the late 60's it was the only place in town to dine, unless you ate at home or in neighboring Woodward. The town has grown. There are now three traffic lights, all on Main Street. Where once there were none, now there is a choice of two motels.

For breakfast, I chose *The Spot!*—a good choice. And, for a place to stay while I'm here—The Antelope Lodge. But first things first, I hit *The Spot!*.

I ponder the breakfast menu choices—the Rough Neck, the Rancher or the Coal Miner's Plate? All three more than adequate to satisfy the appetite of a behemoth of a man prepared to work dawn to dusk with his back. My duties for the day will be to listen and take notes. I order the oatmeal, wheat toast and a mixed fruit cup.

I pull up to the front of the Antelope Lodge. Should I have made a reservation? Not exactly a 5-Star accommodation. I am greeted by a rural icon. She is sixty-plus, pleasantly plump, and wearing a bright flowered housecoat. Her expression is neither pleasant nor bright.

"Good morning, can I get a room?" I inquire with a non-committal smile.

"Do you have a reservation?"

"No, Ma'am. I apologize for not making a reservation. I just flew in from Seattle and rented a car in Oklahoma City. I just got the call yesterday morning."

"Call? An emergency?"

"I hope not. I'm visiting my grandfather out at Wildflower Nursing…"

"Who's your grandfather?"

"Tom Howard." Now her face shines as bright as the flowers on her outfit. Then it goes dark again and she puts her hands over mouth.

"He all right?"

"Yes, Ma'am. I'm just here for a visit—maybe a week or two."

"Wonderful." She brings out a registration card and hands me a pen. "How will you be paying?" I hand her my credit card. "You must be Annie's child. How is she doing? Where does she live now?"

"See's fine. She and my dad live in Atlanta."

"Please tell her Mildred Ahr says hello. Wait… Ahr is my married name. Tell her Mildred Blackburn. Your mom and I went to high school together."

"I'll be sure and tell her. In fact, you can tell her yourself. She plans on coming here in a week or so. I'll be talking to her tonight and I'll tell her to be sure and call you—to make a reservation."

"She won't need a reservation. But, tell her to call just the same—so we can talk."

A red-letter day—twenty years in the making. I drive to the outskirts of town, past the Divine Coal Mine and then up the long winding driveway to my grandfather's current residence, Wildflower Nursing Center. The extended care facility has an expansive covered porch along the front and down one side. The shaded veranda is lined with large white wooden rockers and small tables that can be folded quickly and disappear inside when prairie gusts come up unexpectedly, carrying dreams and outdoor furniture away. Or, so I've been told.

Endless fields of bronze wheat ripple outward to an almost flat horizon dotted with idle windmills and active pump jacks. Four-strand barbed wire fences crisscross the gentle slopes in the far off distance and divide the land into precise sections of 640 acres each.

Inside the front door, a kindly elderly woman greets me, "Morning sonny, what can I do for you this beautiful day."

My watch confirms I am right on time. "My grandfather is expecting me."

"You must be Tommy Lee Townsend." She beams and grabs my hand with both of hers. She doesn't shake it— she just holds onto it as if we were standing in front of a minister. She looks sincerely into my eyes. "Mr. Howard has been telling us all about you. Welcome, welcome. Your grandfather was among the first to eat breakfast this morning and has been anxiously waiting for you. He wants to visit with you outside on the front porch. Why don't you go out and have a sit in one of our rockers and I'll have someone bring him to you?"

"Thank you. I'll do that. You know, I apologize, when you first walked up I thought you were a resident."

"Oh, I am." She chuckled and seemed to puff up a bit with pride. "But don't none of us just sit around crocheting pot holders. We—well those who can, you know—we like to stay busy. If they had to pay someone to sit here and say 'Howdy' every time someone came in those doors, we couldn't afford our big screen TV in the lounge." She beamed with pride.

"I understand. You do good work too." I smile and move out to the porch and choose a group of rockers that still sits in the early morning sun.

Fidgeting with my recorder, I flip it on and hide it in plain sight on a small side table—it is disguised as a leather-bound Day-Timer. It's small, the latest technology and what I consider a little pricey. I've learned from experience that recording devices make many people nervous— especially guilty people, people hiding a secret, and many of the generation prior to the baby-boomers—well, just older people. Papa Tom just turned eighty-four.

People with integrity are more consistent with what they tell you. Those without, their stories tend to ramble and their facts seem like shadows from low clouds racing across an open field—constantly changing. I know my grandfather's story won't vary. Papa Tom is a man of God who stands as a bulwark against the winds of evolving times and eroding values. With feet firmly planted in his faith, he always speaks the truth—gently and in love.

Why is Papa Tom stuck in a nursing home? Numerous family members and countless friends have offered to take Papa Tom into their homes and look after him. For more than fifty years, Tom Howard has served the people in and around Divine. He never held or had an office—didn't have a title. He seemed to search out people with needs. Sometimes, they found him. If something broke, be it windmills, fences, or people's hearts, he set about mending them.

I understand from Mom that although physically fragile, his mind and memory perform flawlessly, and his quick wit often will catch you off guard. His physical strength is abandoning his body. But, his fierce independence and his desire to serve others drew him here to Wildflower. Papa Tom chose—no, demanded—to be here. He has taken on the role of in-house pastor, welcoming committee, grief counselor, entertainer, friend to all, and resident of Room 237. With a full schedule and so many callers on a daily basis, regardless of your status in life, you must make an appointment to visit him. On his last birthday, Mom said nearly the entire town stopped by to wish him happy birthday and share some cake.

The staff seems to delight in fighting for the privilege of rolling him out onto the porch. From the custodian to the facility's administrator, nurses and occasionally the doctors, Mom said everyone looks forward to spending a few moments with him.

Today, Martha, head of food services, wins the honor. Beaming and bending over to whisper private exchanges in his ear, she pushes his wheel chair parallel to the rocker across from me. She places a brightly colored cushion on the rocker's hardwood seat. It has been needle pointed especially for him by an admirer. Martha gently, but firmly, assists him into the rocker and spreads a small handmade quilt across his lap, smiles, straightens the back of his collar, and gently kisses his balding head.

"You two play nice," she says and returns back inside.

My appointment is from 10:30 to 12:30. Today, I can eat lunch with him on the porch provided the wind doesn't get too strong. There are subsequent 2-hour appointments with me penciled in on his chart: three times a week—Tuesdays, Thursdays and Saturdays—until he finishes his story or God calls him home. He looks very frail compared to the last time I saw him. I'm embarrassed at how many years have passed since I saw him last.

"Well, how are you, Tommy Boy?" he says with a broad, warm smile.

His bright eyes open wide; the deep wrinkles around them disappear and reappear at the corners of his mouth. He holds his arms straight out—his silent request for a big, lingering hug. Papa Tom considers handshakes too formal and chooses to give a warm embrace to everyone he encounters. It's difficult not to be immediately drawn to him.

"I'm fine, Papa Tom. You look great today." I can't help but lie. His arms are light, almost limp. Gone are the muscles that used to lift me up, high off the ground. Gone are his thick thighs that propelled him off the scrimmage line and gave him the strength to block men twice his size away from his teammate with the ball as they thundered like wild horses down field. His smile engages you and his eyes still sparkle but they are now hauntingly sunk back in his face and encircled with dark rings.

"I feel great. Written any good books lately?"

"I'm looking forward to writing yours."

"I know you've wanted this sit-down for some time."

"You got that right."

"Well, I've been going over my life all week—trying to put the important things up front in my mind so as not to bore you with the mundane. Trouble is, I've had such an exciting and richly blessed life—don't think any minute of it wasn't worthwhile to remember. But, it might not be interesting enough for someone to want to read about it. A few times were painful…" He closes his eyes and seems to reflect for a second. When he looks up, his soft grey eyes are glistening. "…some more challenging than others. Still, not sure it deserves a book."

"I'm not sure my dad, let alone your daughter, would agree with you. Dad says covering the mine cave-in story about you not only made him a successful journalist but more importantly made him a success in life. Finding you, God, and my mother all on the same day—he claims that day will always be the most important day of his life."

"I would have thought when you and your sister were born must have been pretty special days in his life too." Papa Tom took a great deal of pride in his son-in-law, my dad, and the role he had in turning his life around.

"He mentions that, but he claims all the blessings in his life were made possible because of that day."

"Well…if we're going to get this done, we better get started. You ready?"

I take out a binder and write Tom Howard at the top of the first page and put "April 1, 2006" in parentheses. My stealth recorder is on and its hidden microphone faced toward him. Recording the entire interview word-for-word while jotting notes of what I consider to be the important parts has made my job a lot easier. It makes my subjects more comfortable when they can talk freely and openly and I make only a casual note or two.

"Where would you like me to begin, Tommy Boy? You were only ten or eleven when I promised to tell you what I had done for Morton Podus. I said when you…"

"Yes, yes. You promised when I became a writer like dad, you would tell me the story. But, you've been stalling, putting me off up until now. So…what did Morton Podus owe you?"

"Remember first, Tommy Boy, I never said—or even thought— Mr. Podus owed me anything. I still don't. I visited him while he sat in prison…told him then I never blamed him for the accident… even though he confessed…well, I forgave him…told him right then."

"Remember, Papa Tom, the cave-in wasn't an accident. When I interviewed him seven years ago—just before he died—he admitted what he had done. He told me you had visited him in prison and that even you forgave him—although he never forgave himself for abandoning you. He emphasized, 'Especially in light of all your grandfather did for me.' But, he wouldn't elaborate on what that meant." I look up into Papa Tom's face and ask, "Especially in light of what?"

He clasps his hands at his chest, lowers his head and rubs his chin with his entwined fingers. He inhales deeply and exhales after what seems like a long time, so long, I think he has stopped breathing. I reach to touch his blanket-covered knees—he startles me as he suddenly and resoundingly continues.

"Well…now that everyone is dead and gone…except for me, of course." He smiles and laughs quietly. "I guess you can write the story. The truth can't hurt anyone now."

"So, what was it?" I can't believe I just blurted it out and it appears Papa Tom can't believe it either. One eyebrow goes up and his mouth drops open. I take a breath and start over in a slower, less excited speech. "What did you do for Mr. Podus…?"

Chapter Three
A cord of three strands.

didn't get an answer to my question. Instead, I got a request from Papa Tom for iced tea— which I promptly fetched.

With my back against the front door, I push it open. A corresponding buzzer sounds at the front desk. The person in charge looks up and notices it's only me, holding two large plastic glasses of iced tea and backing out to the porch. I carry them to the far end of the veranda where Papa Tom sits, his feet resting lightly on the white weathered planks. He sits as a statue, erect, posture-perfect, his gaze fixed on the horizon. Far away thoughts seem to reside in his cloudy grey eyes. With his pale appearance he could easily be mistaken for a wax figure.

"Here's your tea." I say, startling him. "Deep in thought?" I ask, putting my hand on his shoulder. Papa Tom retrieves his drink, his hand trembling. After a small sip, he places it on the table, closes his eyes, lowers his chin to his chest, and rubs his balding head; his fingers trace a long jagged scar which runs from above his right eye to the middle of the top of his head. He finds a patch of thick silver hair and stops there and strokes it, smoothing and straightening the remnants of his once flowing waves. He seems far removed from the front porch and the row of mostly empty rockers. The muted breeze wanders across the lawn and gently lifts fallen rose petals and inspires the large American flag to unfurl and pop like a whip when it reaches the end of its rolling stripes. Papa Tom is not here, he is somewhere else.

After a moment, he begins a narration, sounding very unlike himself, more like a voice I've heard on archived black and white newsreels. "It was early January, 1945. We struggled to maintain our momentum, moving against the German front lines just north of Bastogne under cover of the cultivated forest of Bois Jacques. I had seen the stand of pines before the artillery fire began. Christmas cards were made from such scenes as those. Row upon row of tall straight timbers thick with snow, before the blanket of white on the ground had hidden all of the earth's imperfections—now pock-marked with craters, fractured trees, abandoned weapons and soldiers' gear, along with the wounded and the dead amidst patches of crimson snow."

He took a long, deep breath and continued. "Less than half a mile separated our battle line from the Germans. The campaign had begun a week ago, with E Company, 2nd Battalion moving into the forest, up the rail lines and on northwest toward the village of Foy. The snow fall limited the visibility and muffled the sounds of life, making it difficult to determine where the enemy hid. Exploding shells shook the ground as well as our confidence. We were equally afraid when the quiet returned—we were always afraid."

Papa Tom tightly closes his eyes and takes in another long breath. It first seems he is resting—his eyes remain closed—and then his lips come together. He looks like he is preparing to whistle and instead empties his lungs as if half-heartedly blowing out birthday candles. His thoughts return, only this time from the midst of a battle.

"BAM!" He shouts, his arms explode out, hands rocketing into the air, fingers extended like a burst of 4th of July fireworks. He isn't just telling the story now, he's living it.

His voice continues in quick cadence and with urgency. "It started again—the enemy's artillery had found its range. To our left, the crack of bursting light and then the thundering sound followed on its heels. The next, a hundred yards closer, then another, and another. Closer and closer. Now the explosions and the reports came together. Bright, searing white light temporarily stealing our vision. For almost an hour afterward we couldn't hear anything but the ringing in our ears. We rejoiced at our still being alive—our only comfort—still being alive. We would have welcomed heaven. Perhaps even hell wouldn't have been this bad.

"Jake Podus ran past and dropped face down in the snow, ten feet in front of me. I thought he had been hit but he quickly grabbed the spade from his pack, rolled over, and while lying on his back he began clearing the top layer of fresh snow—about six inches of it. The thick, cold, shiny crystals he stacked in front of him to hide himself. The wall of wet white didn't offer any protection from the 170mm shells dropping around us or the machine gun fire that would soon come again. But, at least it would keep him from being a visual target. I had fallen in a crater left from an earlier explosion—already a high berm around it, the snow and top soil removed by the blast. What were the odds of another shell falling in the exact same place—you know, like lightning striking twice and such?"

I am caught up in his recounting the frightening experience. I am lost, entranced in the telling of his tale. When he would tell me stories as a child my mind would race and catch the visions he created, chasing after them and embracing them as if they were real. Papa Tom stops abruptly. He reaches over and slaps the back of my hand.

"Why aren't you writing this all down? I have been conjuring up these old experiences for you to put into your book," he snaps.

I realize I haven't made even a mark in my binder since he began.

"Papa Tom, please don't think I'm not getting all of this." I'm ashamed of my deception. "I must tell you the truth. I've recorded each and every word you have spoken since we first sat down together. See here…" I open my Daytimer and reveal the recording device and the microphone. "Forgive me for the ruse but I don't want to miss a word and I couldn't possibly transcribe everything you've said. I don't want to miss anything."

He looks as though he's considering having me sent away and then he flashes a brief faint smile. "It's okay. I guess you know what you're doing. Your dad never recorded any of our interviews. He wrote down everything. I mean everything! They didn't make those contraptions that small and sneaky back then. But, I guess I wouldn't have blamed him for using one." He leans back and folds his hands. "Shall I continue my story?"

"Yes. Yes, please go on."

"Well, fifty yards to our right another shell bursts in the trees. Bark splinters, limbs snap, and sail aloft spraying sparkling powder, the ground shudders and fresh fallen snow flutters and drifts back to earth. Someone behind me hollers in pain, 'I'm hit!' The next round falls behind us and off to the right. Jake scampered from his hastily fashioned foxhole to retrieve fallen branches to pull over him. The grim reaper had passed over us."

It dawns on me Papa Tom is no longer recalling the past but he is recounting it as if it is actually happening now.

"When Jake returns, a piece of tree as big as a horse glides behind him in the snow. He drops it in front of his shelter. 'God, it's cold—colder than I'd ever been in my life,' he mutters. Clouds of steamy moisture bellow from his mouth like a steam train climbing a grade. 'Jake, you okay?'

"Jake shivers so badly he is barely able to speak. His rapid breathing is punctuated by puffs of smoke. Not sure if fear caused his tremors or the cold. Trudging through the snow with full gear, ammo, rations and such completely exhausts a body. We sweat and then our wet clothing quickly freezes and becomes stiff."

A chill comes on me just from listening to Papa Tom's saga. My shoulders tighten and I rub my arms to chase away the goose bumps that have manifested themselves in the middle of this warm spring day.

Papa Tom glances up. "Gives me the shivers too, just talking about it." His eyes fix again on his hands which are knotted in his lap. He continues. "Jake's eyes told on him. They were wild and desperate. He raised his head as much as he dared and surveyed north into the forest. The shelling stopped as quickly and suddenly as it had started. The Krauts would begin working toward our position. He looked back at me and caught me watching him. His eyes pleaded for me… I knew what he desired—he wanted Bobby Joe and me to run interference, to block for him, to clear a path—through the enemy. He pulled the blanket of branches and needles over him, curled into a fetal position and trembled with fear—or maybe because of the cold. Whichever. I saw his boots shake uncontrollably. Before the quiet stopped and the machine gun fire started again, I heard him crying.

"We hadn't seen Bobby Joe for two days when a barrage of artillery fire sent us scrambling in different directions, when the quiet finally came and the chaos ended—he couldn't be found. We looked—asked every medic that passed our way. No word about Bobby Joe."

Papa Tom sits straight up. I don't know if his eyes had been open before, but now they are open wide—mine too. It is quiet and peaceful on the porch. For a moment it is deathly silent. The wind is still, the trees take a rest from the breeze.

He clears his throat, wipes his mouth with the back of his hand, and folds his arms tightly. "Let's come back here later. Too many, too much…" His body language screams he doesn't want to revisit this part of his past—at least not now.

I change the subject. "Tell me how you first met Jake Podus."

"Oklahoma University, Norman, Oklahoma—football try-outs at Owen Field. Late summer of…hmmm, nineteen and forty…yes, nineteen-forty. Me, Jake…and Bobby Joe."

Papa Tom shifts his weight back in the rocker, grips both arms of his chair and pulls himself forward, putting his rocker, and him, into motion. He grins, gritting his teeth together and smiles, showing two fully populated rows of perfect pearly whites. Now, in a perfect rhythm, his slippers sweep the porch as they glide forward and back, mimicking the sound of a drummer's brush on a tightly stretched drum skin.

He continues now in a voice that seems to recall a happier time. "Bobby Joe Hampton and I were like brothers—born just one day apart, and in the same house. Actually, in the same room—almost the same bed. Their farm sat on the other side of our east fence. With no doctor around for miles, Mr. Hampton and Daddy arranged for a midwife to come up from Lawton and stay at our house until the birthing was complete. Daddy put a small bed in Mama's room for Mrs. Hampton. The two women could reach out, holding hands, sharing their pains, and then sharing their dreams when the pains subsided.

21

"After Mrs. Hampton gave birth to Bobby Joe at 11:30 on the evening of February 3rd, 1922, Daddy took Mama for a walk around the barn. Mama said it was more like a forced march and that she nearly froze to death. Before the roosters started crowing the next morning, she had seen all four sides of that barn nearly a hundred times. She paraded into the bedroom a little after four, plopped down on the bed and just spit me out. It would have cost Daddy another dollar and a half for the midwife to stay on another day."

Setting my drink down on the table between us, I rock back and smile, shaking my head. I hear chuckles around me. Several others had quietly gathered on the porch to listen to my grandfather's story. He often told tales, mostly morality plays but some with no point—just light humor.

A huge burly man silently rolls his wheel chair up behind me. He has a shaved head and a week's worth of white beard poking out from his puffy red cheeks. A young man, an orderly I guess, stands behind him resting on the porch rail. A middle-aged plump lady in a white uniform leans against a porch column. I can't see her name tag—can't tell if she is management or worker bee, but for now she is engrossed in Papa Tom's tale like the rest of us.

Papa Tom hands me his half-empty glass. "Put this on the table, will ya?" He scratches his chin. "Now, where was I? Oh, yeah, trying out for the Sooner football team with Bobby Joe and Jake. Coach Stidham scrutinized us rookies like a buyer at a big cattle auction—fresh meat for the team of '41. Because of his special God-given abilities, Bobby Joe became a shoo-in to make the team. He shined at football. For years we had played ball in the wheat fields—just he and me. He could throw, kick, tackle and run faster than a jack rabbit. Always trying to get away from him, I would be run down and tackled from behind by him again and again.

22

"Bobby Joe and I played football only one year in high school, our senior year. That was the only year there were enough boys to field a team. By the time we graduated from Lincoln and got to college, the two of us shared a special ability. After years of summers spent running through the wheat fields, we developed strong legs and quick reflexes. The taller and thicker the wheat got the higher and longer we jumped, hurdling stalks and successfully side-stepping the occasional cow patty. Dodging the defensive back field became our specialty. The local newspaper sports reporter saw to it that everyone in the state knew about our special abilities. It was a different story for poor Jake.

"Jacob Benjamin Podus—the brightest guy I ever met. Bobby Joe and I met him for the first time at football try-outs. He had attended some hoity-toity college prep school in Oklahoma City. He came from a well-to-do family in a tight knit Jewish community. Before I met Jake, I… do you know what the name Jacob Benjamin means in Hebrew?"

I shake my head, thinking to myself this is getting me further and further from discovering Papa Tom's secret, and I make the mistake of putting down my pen and reaching for my glass, preparing to just sit back and listen for a while.

Papa Tom immediately stops rocking grits his teeth and sits forward. His eyes narrow and an unfamiliar and uncommon scowl flashes across his usually smiling face.

"Tommy Boy, this is important—as important as anything else I might end up telling you. Are you making a note of this?" Papa Tom said, looking directly at my pen as it lay idly on the table next to my recorder. "Jake's problems started with his dad naming him Jacob Benjamin."

"Sorry, sir—why is that?" That is the first time and I hope the last time I ever address my grandfather as sir. I should have never put the pen down. I suddenly feel ten years old, four-foot tall and about to get the whipping of my life. I'm 31 years old, over six-feet, and I've only been spanked once. I put down my drink, wishing I had taken a quick slurp, and pick up my pen.

"Jacob means usurper. And, Benjamin means son of my right hand. Morton Podus just had the one kid, Jake. Morton Podus spent his entire life usurping everything he could get his hands on—other people's money, their property, their sweat and their dreams. He wanted it all, and he wanted it all for his son too. But you know, I think he really wanted it more for his family name, Podus, than for Jake.

"You see, when Morton was just a little kid, he woke up one morning in New York City's Hebrew Orphan Asylum. The night before Jake's father had gone to sleep in his own bed and awoke alone the next morning in the strange and unfamiliar surroundings of an orphanage. It was maybe 1910, and Podus three or four years old. He arrived during the night with a piece of cloth pinned to his shirt and his name, Morton Podus, scribbled on it along with the Star of David drawn next to his name. Rejected and bitter, he ran away from the orphanage at the age of 12, looking everywhere for someone, anyone, with the same last name. Living on the streets, he became obsessed with finding someone named Podus. One day he asked a man, as he shined his boots, if he had ever heard of a family named Podus. The man said he once knew a family named Podus and they had headed out to Oklahoma to take part in the free land give-away. Either he didn't tell him the land rush had been twenty-years earlier or Podus didn't hear him, but Podus immediately made up his mind to leave for Oklahoma—wherever that might be."

I am more than a little disappointed. How did Papa Tom know all this about Morton Podus? When I interviewed Podus, he didn't want to talk about his childhood. Papa Tom now sat enlightening me about a man whose life story I had researched and later even wrote his biography. I only hope my publisher doesn't find out how much I hadn't uncovered. "Can I stop you to ask a question here?"

"Sure, Tommy Boy."

"How did you come to find out all this information about Morton Podus' life? He never went into his childhood with me. He didn't just sit down and tell you all this. Did he?"

"Nope. What I know about old man Podus, I learned from his son. Jake told me his father's stories over and over again. Accounts of how rough his childhood had been, how hard he had struggled to get to the top, and how many adversities he had to overcome on the way. He continually reminded Jake how good he had things, the privileges his dad had given him, and how much Jake owed him for providing him with a good name. Jake had a responsibility to honor the name Podus…at any and all costs."

He stops and licks his lips, reaches toward his tea, stopping midway. He straightens himself in his rocker and leans forward, placing his hands on his knees and widening them like a catcher squatting behind home plate. He closes one eye and looks at me hard as if he is going to give me a signal to throw a fast ball, rubs his nose and mouth and then shakes his finger at me to alert me to the importance of his next statement.

"Old Man Podus took advantage of everything and everybody. The very day he set out to locate Oklahoma and his heritage, he stumbled onto a devastating tragedy—for others, an opportunity for him. A New York City train derailed right in front of him, killing more than a hundred people and injuring countless more. It may have been very bad fortune for the dead and injured passengers but the young Podus wasted no time climbing through the carnage, scavenging for their money and valuables. He even came away with a new pair of shoes. Podus bragged to his son that the owner of the shoes struggled fiercely to keep them for a while, and then passed out from loss of blood.

"The next day Morton Podus traveled to Oklahoma City aboard a passenger train along with his new found fortune. He never located anyone with the name, Podus. He himself had no birth records, no papers, no past—only a future. Rather than change his name, he started his own legacy with the name pinned to his shirt and he would make the name of Morton Podus known to everyone. He put a great deal of pressure on his son to become a part of that legacy and to continue it."

Papa Tom pauses and seems to be considering where he'll go next. So I jump in. "You know, I wanted to interview Jake for background on his father's biography but his father threatened to withdraw from the project if I contacted him. In fact, he swore if I used any information from Jacob or even about Jacob—he would sue me and my publisher and get a restraining order to prevent the release of my book."

"That sounds like the Morton Podus I knew." Papa Tom looks at me. I mean he really looks at me—right through me with a deep questioning look. I sense he thinks I'm bored with his tales and philosophies. Truth is, I am fascinated with his stories. But I don't seem any closer to the answers I have been looking for. "But, I'm guessin' this book you're writing isn't about social studies, is it? I'll try to stay on task. I know what you're really after." Papa Tom leans forward, reaching for his iced tea. His chair tilts and teeters on the front edge of its rockers—for a moment it looks he might be up-ended. Being right behind him, plump lady in white rushes to the rescue, grabbing the back of the rocker with her right hand, and with her left she deftly snatches the tea glass from the table and delivers it to Papa Tom's outstretched hand. Catastrophe averted.

"Thank you, Sandy. But it really wasn't necessary. I've learned how far I can go." He smiles and takes several grand gulps. There is very little ice remaining in his glass. The day is starting to warm. He takes the quilt from his legs, and hands it across to me. "Put this on the porch rail, will you?" He turns and asks her to kindly refill his glass. She asks if I want more. I shake my head and look back to Papa Tom for him to continue. I jot down a reference about Morton Podus.

"You're probably wondering how a couple of farm boys from poor families in rural Oklahoma got to go to college."

"No offense, but it does seems unlikely the two of you would have gotten academic scholarships and with just one year of high school football, it would have been difficult for both of you to receive football scholarships."

"The reason Bobby Joe and I became like brothers wasn't just because we were born in the same room. We were raised as brothers from the time we were two. We didn't find out we weren't brothers until we were almost fourteen years old."

"Huh? How can that be?"

"One morning, Bobby Joe's momma took him with her to milk their cow. Mr. Hampton had stumbled home in the middle of the night after drinking and playing cards and she must have been afraid to leave the toddler alone in the house with his dad passed out in the parlor. The cow's hobbles must have come loose during the milking and she may have been spooked, gotten bit by a horsefly or something— anyway she kicked Mrs. Hampton in the head. Later, midmorning, the baby's bawling awakened his father. He found Bobby Joe hanging from his overall straps, dangling from a hook on the barn door—where evidently his momma had secured him to keep him out of mischief while she tended to the milking. He found Mrs. Hampton in a pool of blood, a gaping wound to her head and near death. Without ever regaining consciousness, she passed before the week was out.

"Mr. Hampton, grief stricken and full of remorse, brought Bobby Joe over to our house after the funeral. He told my folks he couldn't hold the child or bear to look at him for the shame he felt. He begged my momma to raise him as her own and gave Pa the deed to his farm to pay for Bobby Joe's upbringing. He left the next day and never looked back. We didn't know where he went. We never heard from Mr. Hampton again.

"Pa and the two of us boys worked both farms as one until we turned fourteen. We had begun asking questions about why—if we were twins—why we didn't look anything alike? Pa figured us old enough and strong enough by then to handle the truth. Several years later, after we graduated from high school, he sat down with us and told us he wanted us to go to college. And, to accommodate the expense as well as cut back on his work load with running both farms, he sold the Hampton farm. He kept the livestock and put the money from the land, the house, the barn, and the equipment into a bank account for Bobby Joe and me. We didn't stop being brothers when we discovered the truth. I think we became even closer. We had become brothers because we wanted to, not because we were born into it."

"A college freshman too like Bobby Joe and me, Jake was younger than us by a full year or more. He appeared to be almost two years behind us in growth but wiry and quick. An only child, he had no siblings to chase after or to run from. Extremely smart—book smart and street smart. He knew when to side-step to keep from getting

28

run over. And, he knew when to cut and run rather than face certain disaster—a perfect broken-field runner with a healthy dose of fear, dogged determination and an instinct for self-preservation. Jake soon became a third brother in our tribe.

"On the football field, Bobby Joe and I saw to it that Jake found a path to the end zone relatively free from defenders. When Coach Stidham sent in a play that had Jake reverse and run the ball on the opposite side of the field, Jake would panic and run for the sidelines. He didn't trust anybody else to look out for him. I don't think Coach ever caught on. But eventually Stidham yelled enough at our offensive linemen on the other side of the line to step it up. Eventually Jake became a champion running back with all of the glory and attention that goes with it.

"In appreciation for our blocking efforts, Jake became our benefactor. Bobby Joe and I had no money, no car, and no charm. Jake had all three—especially the charm. Like three nuts in a peanut shell, we stayed together every minute we weren't in class. We were a strong team both on and off the field—something about a strand of three cords being tough to break.

'While Bobby Joe and I shared several classes, we rarely saw Jake during the day. Jake's courses were more advanced, higher learning, and more highbrow. We took Ag 101 and Animal Husbandry—he took English Literature, Political Science, Economics and Latin. After the first several weeks, Jake grew tired of trying to round Bobby Joe and me up, dropping us off, picking us up again in the mornings, so… he asked us to do him a favor and move in—his dad had provided a house for him. It came with a cook and a lady to do our laundry and pick up after us. How could we refuse?

"Every Sunday morning I would plead with Jake to attend church with Bobby Joe and me, and he would counter with, 'My father would rather find me in a brothel than in a Christian church.' Bobby Joe and I had been in church nearly every Sunday morning of our lives. We certainly didn't know brothels would be open then."

My elbow slips from its rest on the arm of my rocker. My chin falls to my chest. Plump lady in white scolds Papa Tom with a correcting cough. The young man standing behind bald sleeping giant snickers. Papa Tom flashes a broad grin.

"Just kidding, Tommy Boy. Wanted to make sure you all were listening. Anyway, it was obvious Jake didn't want to risk Mr. Podus finding him in church or even associating with poor Gentiles.

"His dad was overly generous with his son but miserly when it came to the common class—that would be us. He didn't mind hiring us to work in his businesses and paying us as little as possible, but he would have pitched a fit if he knew his money—hard-earned or not—was feeding, housing and often clothing us. Sometimes Jake preferred to take us out to dinner where our clothes weren't considered proper attire.

"On the other hand, sometimes Jake would dress like us and ply his charisma on the young Christian women who found our company, country charm and rugged good looks appealing. I told him God's law, both in his Torah and in our Bible, instructed us not to be unequally yoked. He said he understood. I laid down the law—as long as he kept it platonic he could mingle with our women friends from church. It wasn't long after Jake met Sally Yarborough that he broke with his father's traditions and followed her into church Sunday morning and sat right down in a pew behind her. The following week he escorted Sally to the church picnic where he woofed down five hotdogs before he discovered they contained a variety of forbidden pork parts. He knew he would be struck dead for sure. When he awoke alive the next morning, Bobby Joe and I convinced him that the dietary laws of Leviticus had claimed him, and now he was a born-again Christian."

"Humph." Plump lady in white scoffs, turns and walks back to whatever duty she is supposed to be performing. The young man laughs so loud that bald sleeping giant comes to life. He turns and barks at the young man, ordering him to take him back to the lunchroom—more hungry than offended. Papa Tom's eyes twinkle, his eyebrows raise, and the corners of his mouth turn up. He pushes his tongue against one cheek looking like a baseball pitcher with a full mouth of tobacco about to choose his next pitch. He so delights in luring his audience in and then pulling the rug out from under them with his humor. I jot down a few more details in my notebook, reach over to my once-disguised recorder and re-adjust its position on the table.

"Tommy Boy, you can edit that story out of your recorder if your editor thinks it too colorful or just plain inappropriate." His smiling eyes go from looking at me, to looking down at my hidden recorder and back again. "It's all right. I understand. Forty years ago, when your dad interviewed me in the hospital, it annoyed me—him always writing down word for word everything I said. I got so preoccupied trying to see what he had written; I sometimes forgot what I had been talking about. But then, the entire interview for his story took less than two hours."

"That's because he spent many more hours interviewing other people about you. What they told Dad about you literally saved his life. You actually led him to Christ before you met him, without him meeting you—while you were still trapped in the mine."

"Tommy Boy, God just used my life to point the way." Papa Tom sits up, straightens his back, and gazes out across the fields. He grabs a deep breath. "Would ya take me for a spin around the parade grounds? We can go inside for lunch after that. I'm getting a little bit hungry."

"Parade grounds?"

Papa Tom looks beyond the porch, waves his arms, making large circling gestures. "The sidewalk—it runs out and circles round the flag pole and the rose bushes and then goes around the parking lot and ends at the back door of the dining hall. On mornings, when the weather permits, a half dozen or so folks line up with their walkers and march single-file around the property. When I could still walk, I would lead the parade. Anyway... fold my quilt and put it over the back of my chair, will ya?"

CHAPTER FOUR
The Prognosis

While Papa Tom and the residents of Wildflower enjoy their lunch, I go in search for answers about his condition. No one wants to broach the subject of how much time is left of someone's life. It doesn't seem right to ask, let alone to know—especially if it's someone else's life you're curious about.

I locate Mrs. Martin, the head nurse on his wing, and introduce myself. "Thomas Townsend. Mr. Howard is my…"

"Yes, how are you, Tommy?" She grabs me, encircling my shoulders with her long arms and gives me a hug as if she hasn't seen me since the reunion. "Mr. Howard has been telling us all about you. Many of the staff here, most of the residents who can still see well enough to read, and many of the visitors have taken the opportunity to read all your books. You'd be surprised how many people would rather read a chapter of one of your books than watch TV—unless there's a Sooner game on."

"I'm flattered, quite flattered. I've never heard of anyone putting down a TV remote to read one of my books."

She smiles and points to a large library of books and magazines along a corridor wall. "Your grandfather has filled a shelf of our bookcase with several copies of each of your books. We're excited you're writing one about Mr. Howard. We can't wait to read it."

"He is an interesting person, but you already know that." I want to get to the point while I still have the courage. "Listen, Mrs. Martin…"

"You want to know how long he's got, don't you?"

Did she just say that, out loud? "Well, I…"

"You should ask him, Mr. Townsend. He is completely aware of his disease and his prognosis. Dr. Watson has discussed it at length with your grandfather. He isn't afraid of dying, Mr. Townsend. He knows he made you a promise, and he regrets it has taken so long for you to come see him. He would have called you himself but I think he wanted your mother to ask you to come."

"I thought he was just getting along in years. He hadn't started using a walker when I saw him last and now… now he's in a wheelchair."

"He's not as fragile as you might think—physically or mentally. He's weak. His appetite has disappeared. I should say his appetite for food has disappeared. Mr. Howard still has a hunger for life, living it, and wanting to share his joy with others."

"But, how long…"

"I told you, Mr. Townsend. Ask him."

"Yes, Ma'am. Thank you. Thank you for…" The words lodge in my throat and a knot forms in my stomach. This is humiliating. I'm not usually this emotional in front of people—especially strangers. "Thank you…" I turn and hurry down the hall, going the wrong way, but as long as I'm moving away from people it is as good a way as any. Getting to the end of the hall, without noticing the red-lettered warning sign on the push bar, I bolt out the exit into the sunlight, my eyes blurred by tears, and my ears burst with the clanging alarm signaling someone wandering off or attempting to escape.

Too late now. I've made a real spectacle of myself. All eyes are focused on me now. They seem to know it's the kid from the city and not to pay him any mind. I'm outside now and I lean on the backside of the door. I can see the equipment yard of the Divine Coal Mine down the hill about half a mile away. I step out into the sun, away from the building, turn and notice the row of windows. They are full of residents with questioning faces—what idiot went out the emergency exit?

Making my way back around to the front porch, I sit, rock, and consider my next embarrassing move.

"Mr. Townsend? Mr. Townsend?" The lady I mistook for a receptionist walks up to where I'm sitting.

"Ma'am."

"Your grandfather asked me to find you and let you know he has finished eating and is going to his room to take a nap. He asks that you come back at your scheduled time, Thursday morning at 10:30. Will that be okay with you?"

"Yes, Thursday at 10:30. Thank you."

She smiles and leaves. I return and collapse back into the porch rocker.

The difference between the pose of Rodan's Thinker and mine is that Rodan's sculpture appears to be contemplating life—I must appear like I am dreading it. I almost want to be back in Seattle. Or, even Atlanta, at my parent's home where I could curl up on Mom's couch and pretend I was... maybe ten years old again and I had never grown up and this day was not part of my life but maybe someone else's tale of...

"Is everything all right? Can I do anything?"

I look up from my daydreaming and self-indulgent pouting and there she is. The early afternoon sun is being eclipsed behind volumes of brilliant red hair. Streams of searing light radiate from above and behind her, creating a silhouette of a—gasp—an angel. The blinding bright rays conceal her facial features, but I surmise from the soft sultry tones in her seductive voice that rather than a heavenly angel she is just as likely one of Odysseus' sirens luring me to destruction.

"Excuse me?" I ask.

"You look like you can use a friend—an ear—a shoulder perhaps?"

"Excuse me?" Excuse me? I said it again. I blink and try to focus my eyes—and my mind.

"That's quite a vocabulary you have. Are you hard of hearing? Lost in thought—or just lost?" she inquires.

I start to say excuse me again but a part, albeit a small part, of my brain kicks in. Now, with a clear vision and almost a clear mind, I see the person in front of me is both real and striking. I am losing it. The students in my creative writing class would lose all respect for me if they caught me using just one of the clichés I am considering right now. Instead, I pitch out a curve ball.

"Mom's on the roof and we can't get her down." I say excitedly, like a frightened little boy.

"What?" she says.

I say it again, only this time I speak each word slowly, dryly, without contractions and with perfect enunciation, "Mom is on the roof. And, we cannot get her down."

"Are you a resident here?" She says with a puzzled look. But, I suspect she is still a step ahead of me, rather than trying to catch up.

"Depends—are you a caregiver here?"

"Do… you… require… help?" She, in turn, speaks slowly, deliberately and directly with exaggerated lip movements. Perhaps she thinks I am hard of hearing or that I read lips. Time to pitch a slow ball right over the plate.

"When I first went away to college, I missed my pet cat, Lucille, something terribly. I called home every week to check on her. One day when I called, my little brother answered the phone 'How's Lucille?' I asked. He blurted out, 'She's dead—the mailman ran over her.'

'You should be more sensitive. Have a little compassion—you should have broken the news more gently.'

'Like how?' he said.

'You could have told me that Lucille was up on the roof and we can't get her down. Then later when I called back you could have said the firemen are here now, and they have put a ladder up against the house. Then, next time you might say, Lucille jumped out of the fireman's arms and fell to the ground, and we took her to the vet. Then, finally, you could tell me, Tommy, the vet did everything he could—she died peacefully. Do you see how much better that would have been? My brother said he was sorry and he would try to be more sensitive in the future.

'So, how's Mom?' I ask. 'And he said…

And, we both said, in unison, "She's up on the roof and we can't get her down."

Her grin is somewhat larger than mine but no less welcomed.

"Is there a place, away from here, where we can grab some coffee, lunch, and I can start over?" I say in a pleading tone.

"You're not from around here, are you?" She says, shaking her head.

"What gave me away?"

"The electric orange Nikes. The local western wear slash feed & seed store doesn't carry that brand—at least not in that color."

37

"Seattle—that's where I'm from, Seattle. And, by the way, I'm Tommy, uh, Tom Townsend."

"So, you're Tommy Townsend. Pleased to meet ya. Let's take my car.

I follow her to a monstrous crew cab pickup with a fifth-wheel trailer hitch in its bed.

"Do a lot of haulin', do ya?" I say with an unnatural country drawl.

She slows, hesitates and then comes to a complete stop on the driver's side and looks across the truck's bed at me. "Listen. This whole flirtation thing has been exciting and all, but we've got to get a few things straight before this goes any further—and certainly before I let you in my truck."

"Okay. I'm for that."

"I didn't just get home from kindergarten, didn't fall off a turnip truck, and this ain't my first prom."

"Three clichés in one sentence—my students will never believe this." I take my notepad out and begin jotting them down.

"What are you writing?"

"Your wonderful use of platitudes and remarkable grasp of the English language."

"Listen Tommy Townsend, I think maybe you should climb back on that porch and rock your troubles away, and I'll just get on down the road."

"Whoa, whoa. Let's not let a potentially great opportunity to get to know each other get trampled by my immaturity and temporary lack of good taste. My grandpa is resident of this place and I'm an associate professor of literature. I really am from Seattle. That's my rental car." I point to my car. "And, I'm here writing a book about my grandfather and..." And then the reality of what his nurse said hits me—hard. "And, he's dying." It's not a playful scene anymore. "This whole bantering with you, it's just—just a diversion to keep me from the realization that he's, that I'm…" I look down and kick one of the huge tires on the back of her truck. It hurts. If she thinks I'm crying, I'll tell her it's my toe. Great! I am crying.

"Okay then. My name is Hannah Harrison. I'm divorced, no kids, a physician's assistant from Portland, Oregon . This is my dad's truck, my mom's at home—on her knees praying—about fifteen miles from here…" She hesitates. And now, she appears to be tearing up. "And, my dad is lying on his back in a bed across the hall from your grandfather. He doesn't move or speak but he blinks twice to acknowledge he knows I'm there."

She looks like she must have kicked a tire too.

"Hi, Hannah. Nice to meet you. Would you like to have lunch with me?"

CHAPTER FIVE
Getting to Know Hannah

The big farm truck rumbles down the winding road from Wildflower Nursing Center and Hannah and I both take a break from the snappy repartee and the realities of our respective family member's health.

For a brief moment we sit in silence. As for me, I need to sort out thoughts about Papa Tom's future and memories of our past together. The summers during my teens I always managed to get down to Divine, spending a couple of weeks away from my zero-tolerance mom, my over-committed dad and my pesky little sister. I was overwhelmed with the excitement of being free in the country. Free to run and play. Free to experience becoming a man, learning to drive, holding my breath and squeezing the trigger, dropping a mule deer at 200 yards. Papa Tom and I became more than sidekicks during the summers, we became best friends. He became my mentor and spiritual guide. I learned the things a boy needs to know. I learned things you don't learn in school. I watched things being born, things growing, and things dying. I learned how to be dependable, how to tell truth from a lie, tell fact from fantasy, and how to trust in yourself, in God and which people in your life you could trust—and which you couldn't.

Tired of introspection or perhaps afraid of too much, I turn to Hannah and start a new dialogue. "Where did the time go? And, why did it have to end at all?"

I evidently have caught her by surprise; she must have been doing some quiet introspection herself because she seems to be startled by the sound of my voice.

"What? Oh, I'm sorry I was thinking of my dad. His work gloves are here on the dash. They smell like him and the work he did around the farm. What were you saying?"

"I was just commenting about how time got away from me since my last visit with my Grandpa. I remember now—the summer between my junior and senior year in high school I decided to stay home in Atlanta. I let go of my youth, my innocence, my grandfather—and my faith. I told myself I was growing up. Truth was, on the inside I stopped growing and started decaying. The longer I stayed away from Papa Tom, the more I became interested in me."

"What would you like for lunch?" Hannah breaks my train of thought. Maybe she's uncomfortable with my vulnerability?

"Oh, yeah—lunch. Sorry, I was thinking about when I used to visit my grandfather when I was a kid. I had some great times around here."

"Why did you quit coming?" Hannah asked.

"I guess I was looking for something else."

"Ever find it?"

"I found a lot of things, but looking back, I think I gave up a lot more than I got."

"I grew up here and couldn't wait to get to a big city. This is the first time I've been home for more than a weekend in five or six years. Everything good that's ever happened to me happened here." She looks over at me for a moment, smiles, and looks back down the highway and the silence returns.

The next few miles creep by as did the minutes, exaggerated by our silence. She startles me when she speaks—louder and more upbeat than a moment before. "Well, what's it going to be? We've got three choices—*Dairy Queen*, hamburgers and pizza —at *The Spot!*, fried chicken, fried catfish—or just 'bout anything you want fried at *Jerry's Café*. Oh, wait—if you want Mexican food we can drive 15 miles to…"

"Mexican sounds great! Seattle may be known for seafood but it is short on enchiladas."

"Mexican it is. Hold on to your hat." She puts her foot down and black smoke bellows from the truck's exhaust. She speeds through Divine and takes Highway 23 South. Both traffic lights in town give her the green. The *Dairy Queen* on Main Street is surrounded by pickup trucks and large Suburbans—a string of cars loop around and through the drive-thru. Down a little and across the street, *The Spot!* is not nearly as busy. Passing *Jerry's Café* on the way out of town, the smell of everything fried wafts in the air.

"Where are we headed?" I ask—not because I want to know but because I want to get the conversation re-started.

"*Las Carretas*. It just recently opened. Wasn't here last time I visited. It's right next door to Love's truck stop at the intersection of Highway 270—about 15 miles south of here. Mexican food isn't a big deal to folks around here, but the truck drivers sure seem to go for it."

"You like it?"

"I like the peace and quiet. I like that it's away from Divine. I don't run into all the people in town that I know and grew up with."

"That a problem for you?"

"I don't like answering everybody's questions. The people in town all want to know 'how you been, where you living, whatcha doing, got any kids yet?' Or, they ask about my dad."

"Divine is a pretty small town isn't it?" I don't want to ask her any personal questions—at least not just yet.

"There's nothing but small towns around here—small people and small town thinking. Back in Portland, when I'm not at work, I can go for days and not see anybody I know—or have to answer any questions other than 'you want fries with that?'"

"Don't you have any friends? Don't you go out?" Didn't I just tell myself not to ask any personal questions?

She growls, "Did someone in Divine give you a list of questions?" She lowers her head slightly, glaring, gritting her teeth and appearing to squeeze the life out of the truck's steering wheel.

"Whoa. I'm just trying to get to know you—get to know who you are and…" I swallow and change my direction quickly like a skilled sailboat skipper tacking and crossing the wind on Lake Washington. "What kind of Mexican food do you like, Hannah?" Good—she looks back at me with a smile, even appears a little embarrassed about going for my jugular and seems happy that I've changed my interviewing technique.

"You know, I really don't like Mexican food all that much," she admits. "I miss salmon, crab, mussels and the Pacific Northwest, tall trees, misty afternoons and cool breezes off the ocean."

"I can't wait to get home either." Finally, we both seem to be on the same page. "Do you want to talk about your father?"

"No. Let's talk about Portland… or Seattle, if you prefer. I love Seattle. What part of the city do you live in?"

"Not far from the University of Washington—that's where I teach. I live across Portage Bay from the campus."

"I know exactly where that is," she says excitedly. "That's such a beautiful campus with all its tall pines. I miss the trees back home. I work in Portland for a group of doctors but I live in Beaverton."

"I go to the Seahawk games when they're in town. I've got season tickets."

"I'm not a big basketball fan," she says, scrunching up her nose and shaking her head. Her mouth turns down and her eyebrows furrow and almost run into each other.

"No, the Seahawks are NFL, professional football." Now, I've got a stern look on my face and she's wearing a huge grin. Her eyes sparkle mischievously and she winks.

"My doctors are always offering me Trail Blazer tickets. Maybe you could drive down and go to a game with me?"

"Okay…" I say with too much uncertainty in my voice as if even I question my enthusiasm.

Silence. Her expression seems to indicate she is a little tentative about continuing this dialogue, too. Her brow is furrowed again. Back to square one.

"Listen, Hannah, I know what this is"

"What what is? What is this, exactly?"

I've got the hornets riled up again. My voice softens and I try to pick my words more carefully. "We're rushing head-long into a pseudo relationship because we aren't comfortable with the reality of what's happening around us. Let's slow down. We're strangers who are both a thousand miles away from home. We're dealing with devastating news about people we love and we have no one to share our anxieties with. Getting to know you better is an exciting prospect for me. I need a friend here in Divine—would you be my friend?"

"Does that mean you're not going to pay for my lunch and then meet my mother afterwards?"

She is wonderful. Is it just my melancholy that makes her seem so... so... did I already say she's wonderful? And she's funny... in a dry sort of way. I am drawn to her like a moth to a flame. Please, God don't let me get burned.

We arrive back at the nursing center in the middle of the afternoon. She pulls the big truck up to the front entrance. The taste of the Pescado de Ajo a Mojo, baked fish with garlic gravy, still lingers in my mouth, the creamy garlic-infused oil, a fragrant reminder, blotted not only in my memory but also in my blue and orange rugby jersey. My appetite for Mexican food is satiated but my hunger to take in more knowledge of Hannah remains.

Once we had gotten past the awkward posturing that make up a typical first date in the city, we settled into an enjoyable conversation. Our shared Great Northwest anecdotes drew us together and seemed to form a common bond between us. We avoided talking about her father, her past life in Divine, and my grandfather. The time will come, and I hope it's soon, when we share those things as well. But now, as Humphrey Bogart's character said in the last scene of Casablanca, "I think this is the beginning of a beautiful friendship."

"Thanks for the wonderful afternoon and delightful lunch." Hannah leans over and it appears like she is going to kiss me... but my anticipation disappears as her hand goes up to the top of my left shoulder and she gives me a pat. A pat? It feels like she is trying to control a large friendly dog from jumping up and pawing her. If she says, "Good boy..."

"This has been the first genuinely good time I've had since I got here. When do you see your grandfather again?"

"Not till the day after tomorrow. My visits are restricted to two and a half hours each on Tuesdays, Thursdays and Saturdays. Today was my first visit."

"I don't understand. Why can't you see him whenever you want, for as long as you want?"

"It was his request. I'm interviewing him for a book I'm writing and he is giving me the time he's set aside for that particular purpose. He evidently has a full schedule of activities he is involved in and most of them take priority over my book." She still rests her hand on my shoulder. Like a conditioned dance partner, I anxiously await her lead. Will she lean in more, draw me to her, or push me away?

"Well, you apparently have a lot of free time on your hands. Here is my card; my cell number is on there. Don't call my office in Portland. I'll be at the farm with Mom or, if I'm not there, I'll be here visiting Dad. No other place to be."

Now, after digging in her purse and handing me the card from the doctor's clinic, she pushes herself back, away from me, with her other hand and puts both hands on the steering wheel of the truck.

"I'll call tonight and we can make some plans."

"Tom, we just ate at the fanciest restaurant in a 100 miles of here, there's no theater and no bars. There's a front porch swing at the farm or the rockers on the porch here. But, I do hope you'll call and I'd love to do this again. Mom's going to be wondering where I've run off to. So…" Her posture says she's ready to go, and ready for me to get out.

"Take care. I'm going inside and tell my grandfather good-bye." I swing the door out and step down from the truck's running board, give a nod and a little snappy salute. "Talk to you later." After three steps, I have to look back to see if she's looking back. I turn and, yep, she's looking back. I wave. What a little kid I am becoming. Don't wave like your momma's dropping you off at school—wave like Rick did to Ilsa as she boarded the plane. Here's looking at you, kid.

Room 237—Papa Tom's room. Empty. Walking down toward a large activity room I hear his excited voice and the distinctive slap of a domino being laid down hard. "Double-five, that's fifteen!"

There he is, sitting across a card table from the giant sleeping bald man—only now he sits alert, fiercely guarding his ivory bones. Both of them in wheel chairs, Papa Tom with his quilt across his legs, giant bald man in the largest tee shirt I have ever seen and yet it still reveals a good six inches of belly between it and the waist band of his sweat pants. I notice also that his wheel chair must be a foot wider than a regular sized chair. He snaps the blank-five down and slides it up against another blank and loudly barks, "That's twenty!"

Papa Tom smiles and shakes his head. He sees me and motions me over.

"Tommy Boy. This is my good friend, John Henderson. John, this is my grandson, Tom Townsend, Annie's boy."

So, huge sleeping giant is a Mr. John Henderson. "Hello, Mr. Henderson. A pleasure to meet you." I extend my hand—he leaves his dominoes unprotected and swings his giant right arm toward me. It is missing his right hand and his wrist. His remaining arm is nearly as long as mine. It is an extremely eerie feeling to take someone's forearm, sans hand and fingers, and shake it.

"You a player?" he says with a menacing grin. "Your grandpa puts up a good fight, better than most, but he's not much of a challenge."

"Oh, no sir. He taught me how years ago, but I never was very good."

"Well, if he taught you everything he knows about playing dominoes, you probably didn't learn much."

Papa Tom interrupts. "Don't pay any attention to John—he's been in a bad mood ever since he fell asleep eating a fried chicken wing and a coyote chewed his hand off as he slept. He should have let go of the wing but even in his sleep he's a downright mean, selfish old curmudgeon. The coyote choked to death on his watch."

"Served him right!" Mr. Henderson snaps. Papa Tom nods as if to establish his story as true. Mr. Henderson holds his stub up and shakes it in defiance. They exchange glances and a pair of exaggerated winks.

They continue playing their remaining dominoes, John records the count with hash marks on a spiral bound pad, the domino pool is down to three—this game will end soon. I survey the activity room. A giant screen TV is secured to one wall and several couches and recliners circle it. A soap opera is playing, the sound is muted. There are three people seated in the audience—two asleep, one knitting. An upright piano sits in the corner, a piano bench and music stand keeps it company. Three walls are filled with large windows, framed with frilly white laced curtains. In the space between the windows a host of framed cross-stitched Bible verses hang. Numerous card tables fill the room and arm chairs line the walls. A long library table set with coffee service and water pitchers sits behind the couches.

A foursome at one table appears to be playing bridge. Other than these, the room is vacant, still and quiet. Several staff people walk the corridors with purpose, carrying trays of medication and medical charts. I am suddenly aware of the smell of freshly baked cookies. It strikes me that this facility smells like my mom's home more than a hospital. At least not like any care facility I have ever known—no offending smells of bodily fluids, no sour smells, and no overwhelming aromas of disinfectants used to mask unpleasant odors. It looks, smells, and sounds like a home, a real home.

"Tommy, John is going in search of freshly baked chocolate chip cookies. Do you want to visit for a second?" Mr. Henderson scoots his chair backwards down the hall with his feet. I smile and shake my head at his independence.

"Sonny, can I get you a cookie?" He calls out.

"No, thank you, Mr. Henderson." I pull a chair over next to Papa Tom and sit down.

"Could I visit with you in your room… privately?" I whisper.

"Follow me," he says and takes off, spinning the large wheels of his chair, providing his own power. I quickly move, grabbing his chair from behind and as I lean in to push, he releases his grip on the wheels and puts his hands in his lap.

"Next to last door on the right," he says.

Entering his room, I am surprised to find furniture for two occupants—two single beds, two dressers, two overstuffed side chairs, and one adjoining bathroom. There is a dividing curtain on a rail suspended in the ceiling, but it is wide opened and gathered against the wall. There is a large window on the far wall; the sun floods the room with light and warmth. Papa Tom's roommate sits in a chair by the window and seems lost in a thick hardbound novel.

"Jim, this is my grandson." Papa Tom announces.

"Hey, Tommy," Jim says and puts a bookmark in his book, closes it and puts it on a small table. "I've been looking forward to meeting you."

Leaving my grandfather next to the first bed, I walk across the room and shake Jim's hand. "A pleasure to meet you, sir. I don't mean to be rude but I would like to speak with my grandfather privately.

We'll be back in a minute." I turn back to Papa Tom. "Is there a place where we can talk privately?"

"Sure, take me next door—that's John's room. He won't be back until all the cookies are gone."

I push Papa Tom into the next room. There is only one bed in his room and an overly large recliner backed up to the window. Parking him across from the recliner, I sit on its front edge so we can talk face to face, eye to eye.

"What's on your mind, Tommy?"

"This is totally different… this is not for the book, this is just between you and me."

"What can I do for you, Tommy?"

"Well, for the most part, just listen." Emotions course through me that I haven't felt for a long time. They've been building up since I got the call from Mom and now if I don't let them out, the dam's going to burst. I look into his eyes and say, "I'm sorry."

Papa Tom leans forward and starts to speak—I shake my head and shoot up my hand to stop his interruption. "I'm sorry I quit coming during the summers. It seems like every good thing that—all the fun things, all the important things, all the life's lessons I learned in my life—I learned here in Divine, with you."

He folds his hands, closes his eyes and smiles. His eyes sparkle.

"I'm so sorry I started chasing after other things and stopped coming. I met a girl in high school and Dad said if I wanted a car I would have to work during the summer to earn the money for it. I don't know, it seemed at the time the things I wanted to do in Atlanta were a lot more exciting and important than coming out here in the panhandle and watching the grass grow. But, it wasn't the grass that was growing here—it was me. And, you know, I think I quit growing

50

when I stopped coming." I bite down on the inside of my lip. I am not going to start crying. I rub my eyes and hold up my hand again, waving him off from interrupting and stopping my confession. "Did you know how grateful I was—how grateful I am—for all you taught me, all you did for me and with me?"

I had been looking down, letting my feelings rush out and when I open my eyes and look up to see if he is responding to my questions—he is still and quiet, smiling and I think his eyes are beginning to fill with tears as well.

"Mom told me you sold the house and came here almost two years ago. I didn't come then—I should have. I haven't called—didn't even send a card. I didn't realize how sick you were—and then, Mom called the day before yesterday. Tell me, what's going on..."

"I'm dying, Tommy Boy." He interjects and reaches out, taking hold of my arm. "But, shoot, I've been dying all my life—been waiting to enjoy my new life. I'm ready." He smiles the biggest smile I have ever seen—a smile that shows joy, happiness, contentment—that dispels any thoughts of regret, resentment or disappointment.

"I wish I were here to spend another summer with you. I wish we could go do the things we used to do when I..."

"We had some really great times, Tommy Boy. I'm really proud of you. You are where you're supposed to be in your life and you're doing what you're supposed to be doing. Don't waste time worrying about what you wished you had done. Get on with doing what you want to do—the things that need to get done with your life. You've become a successful writer, you're a professor."

"I'm alone. I'm lonely." I tell him these things like I've always known them, but I am just realizing my loneliness, my emptiness for the first time—how I want... more. And then I realize the conversation has gotten back to me again. It's always about me. My grandfather just told me he's dying and I'm telling him I'm lonely. What a damned narcissist I am. "I'm sorry—again—I want to know about you and…"

"Tommy, I've got a pretty full schedule… there is a lot I need to take care of before…" He draws in a deep breath and pulls a small appointment book from his shirt pocket, flipping it open. "Listen, we're scheduled to discuss your book on Thursday morning. Why don't you come back tomorrow about ten—no wait I've got—come at two-thirty in the afternoon and I can give you an hour or so. In the meantime, don't worry about me, I'm in no pain, just don't have much energy, and I've asked God to give me time to take care of certain things before I go. And, you and your book are high on that list. So, go… and come back tomorrow afternoon. I'll still be here—I promise."

"Just one last thing. Do you know a Hannah Harrison or her father, uh, I don't know his first name but he's a patient here?"

"Sure, I know Miss Harrison. I visited yesterday with her and Ray, her dad. She's a real beauty. But, we can talk about her tomorrow."

I nod and start to leave.

"Tommy?"

"Yes, sir."

"You think you could push me back to my room before you go?"

"Of course. I'm sorry, I wasn't thinking."

"Oh, you were thinking all right. You were thinking about Hannah. We'll talk—tomorrow."

CHAPTER SIX
Is there something I should know about Hannah?

My mind wanders as I walk through the parking lot. How could he just dismiss me until tomorrow? He doesn't have time? No, he really doesn't have time. He must be consumed with things he has to do before... I am such an idiot... an egotistical, self-centered, good for nothing idiot! Papa Tom is preparing for the end of his life and I'm asking him about a girl.

I reach my car and want to slam my head against the door glass. I'm not prepared for all of this. I get in, fold my arms around the steering wheel and rest my head on the rim. It's not a good time to be alone. Nearly two thousand miles from here is my apartment, my friends, my job. And, two thousand miles to Atlanta are my family, my home, and Mom. Should I call her? Who do I want to talk to—Mom or Hannah?

Driving back to Divine, I decide to go to my room first and change clothes. I still have my suit pants on and my rugby shirt—oh, God— and my orange Nikes. I never bothered to look in a mirror. What must the people here think about me?

A shower. All my clothes come out of my one travel bag and I arrange them neatly in the top dresser drawer. My shaving kit goes in the bathroom. My Donald Trump's in the closet. I pull out the iron and freshen the crease in my slacks, carefully put them on a hanger, my suit coat over them. I'm prepared for a book signing or a lecture. Or, a redhead from Portland.

I call Mom and spend the next hour with her on the phone. She knows what I know about my grandfather and I tell her about my lunch with Hannah.

"I knew Ray Harrison," she says. "He worked for the Buchanan's. So, Jenny Harrison had a little girl?"

"You knew her parents?"

"Not real well. But, you can't live in Divine long and not know everybody."

Last night my mattress got a real workout—I tossed and turned all night, reliving every moment I could recall of being with Papa Tom during the summers. And while one of the most vivid memories I have is from the graveyard when I was eleven—he promised me then to tell me what has become my obsession, his secret about Morton Podus—I recalled a huge catalog of events and lessons that have shaped my life over the years.

They were more than just good times, they were times that built my character and laid a foundation for the person I have become—or had become. Just being around my grandfather now I can see that the boy he helped create has lost, or maybe just misplaced, a number of the attributes that made my family so proud of me. I see in the mirror what I have become without his being in my life.

The golf pro who was responsible for lowering my handicap from 45 to 12, instructed me on refining my swing, my stance, and how I approached the ball. A year after I quit taking lessons I began relying solely on myself and my judgment—and my game suffered. I need to go back to the pro. I need to get back to the basics, the foundation of what Papa Tom instilled in me when I was young.

And, while my restlessness last night was predominantly related to Papa Tom, there were also a number of thoughts about Hannah that kept me from sleep. Her phone number sits on the night stand next to the phone. I should have called her. I think she expected me to call her last night.

Breakfast. *Jerry's Café* puts out a pretty good breakfast. You can actually get eggs and chicken fried steak or fried pork chops with hash browns and cream gravy. But fried breakfast isn't on my training table. Great coffee, wonderful blueberry pancakes, and to-die-for thick, crispy, peppered bacon. I could go out and work in the fields all day and not want for anything after a breakfast like that—except maybe a nap. Nothing on my agenda until two-thirty when I get another window of opportunity to see Papa Tom. I really should call Hannah and see if she'd like to join me. I look at my watch. Lunch with Hannah? Already I'm thinking lunch and I have pancakes that are still working their way down—ugh.

"Good morning, Hannah. Tom Townsend here. How's your morning?"

"Clear to partly cloudy."

"Huh?"

"Clear to partly cloudy—that's the forecast for today. I really expected to hear from you last night. Did you find something exciting happening in downtown Divine last night?" Her voice was even toned, rapid, but without much expression.

"Uh, no. Talked to my mom for an extended length of time. Watched a little TV, the local news and one of the Pirates of the Caribbean movies on HBO."

"Well, at least you had HBO. Only half a dozen English speaking channels here at the farm and no internet. I, however, spent the evening talking to an Australian shepherd—and I don't mean some strappin' Aussie from the outback who owns a million acre sheep farm."

I don't think she finds me as funny as I do but then I haven't exactly established myself as someone who is keenly aware of how she thinks. I wish I knew what she's thinking—especially about me. Here goes nothing, "I kind of assumed you were more at home here in the Oklahoma outback, or what do you call it, the Panhandle. Unlike me, I thought you would have a full social schedule with family and friends—being as you grew up here and all."

"Well, you thought wrong, Mr. Tommy Townsend. It was just me and the porch swing—and the dog. I thought you were going to call me last night. I sat on the porch, with my phone in my lap, crocheted a throw for the couch, read a few of the Psalms, me and the dog talked about the high cost of fertilizer, and finally, I just cried myself to sleep."

"I can't ever tell when you're joking. You are joking, aren't you?"

"I am joking about crying myself to sleep. Actually, the price of fertilizer is a real issue for the Oklahoma farmers this year."

"Please forgive me for not calling last night. And, please give me an opportunity to get to know you better—at least to be able to know when you're joking. Are you going to see your father today?"

"I'm sitting next to him right now."

"Oh... how's he doing today?"

"He's still pretty much the same. I'm confident he is going to snap out of this and sit up and ask what's for lunch any minute now."

"I'll be right there. Can we talk in his room?"

"Sure. Stop at the *Dairy Queen* and bring me something cold and sweet to drink, will you?"

"See you in a minute. Bye."

There are only two people in Oklahoma I want to talk to and they're just across the hall from each other. This is going to be a great day.

Fountain drink or something with ice cream? Too early in the day for ice cream. Maybe she likes ice cream for breakfast—problem is I don't know what she likes. That's going to change.

I speed away from the *Dairy Queen* with one of each—a thick ice cream drink with crushed Oreo cookies and one large slushy lemonade with strawberries. Something tells me to watch my speed—both my car's and my strange pursuit of someone I just met and barely know. What has gotten into me? I'm like a high school kid with a crush. I know I need to slow down and take it easy.

Wooo-uup, wooo-uup. A look in the rear view mirror confirms my fear—an Oklahoma State Trooper is in hot pursuit—of me.

How far off the shoulder can I get without sticking this rental car in the sand? I lower my window and wait for the officer to arrive.

"License and proof of insurance," the tall, football lineman-sized officer requests.

"Here's my license and, uh, the car is a rental."

"Do you have your rental agreement?"

I hand him my license and rental car folder with all the paperwork. I hope this doesn't take long—neither of my choice of drinks will survive long sitting on the side of the highway in this heat.

"Where you headed in such a hurry?" asks the NFL's number one draft choice.

"The nursing home up the road."

"You a doctor rushing to an emergency?"

"No... uh, no sir, Officer... uh, Martin." I read off his engraved brass name plate on his pocket flap of his crisp pressed uniform. "Going to see my grandfather. I've got perishable items." I point to the two large DQ cups in the cardboard tray on the seat next to me.

"Now, in this heat, that very well might be an emergency." His smile is comforting and leads me to believe I might get off with a warning. Probably the only opportunity he has had to speak to anyone today is me—probably the only person he's seen today that's not related to him. Just my luck.

"Who are the perishable medications for?"

"Uh, for..." And then I get the idea that dropping Papa Tom's name might do me more good than some pretty young woman from out of town. "They're for my grandfather, Tom Howard." Officer Martin cocks his head and smiles. A smile—that a good or a bad sign?

"Which one?" he says.

"Which one what?"

"Which drink is for Tom Howard?"

"Uh, the ice cream with the..."

"Wrong! Tom Howard doesn't like ice cream—says it gives him a headache. I know, 'cause last time I visited with him, he offered me the ice cream cup on his tray—said it gave him a headache. You better come clean..." He looks down at my license. "Don't lie to me, Mr. Townsend. I don't know about the state of Washington, but here in Oklahoma giving false testimony to a state officer is a criminal offense. Why the lie, Mr. Townsend? Who is the ice cream really for? The truth, Mr. Townsend."

I'm busted! I can't believe this is happening. Is he kidding? He's got to be kidding. He's smiling but his hand is resting on his holstered revolver.

"Okay, okay." If he's kidding, I'll play along. If he's not, the truth couldn't hurt. "The ice cream is for a young woman I met yesterday, a Miss Hannah Harrison, and the, well, actually both drinks are for her cause I don't know which she prefers. But, Tom Howard really is my grandfather."

"I know he is, he's told me about you. You the writer, right?"

"Yes, yeah, that's right, I'm the writer."

"You taking the drinks to Ray Harrison's daughter?"

"Yes, uh, yes sir."

"Well, you better get a move-on, before they melt. You want an escort?"

"No, I think I can get there in plenty of time—without speeding. Thank you, Officer Martin, I'll tell my grandfather you let me go."

"Oh, I didn't let you go. I know who you are and where you live—and what you drive. Say hi to Mr. Howard… and watch out for Hannah Harrison." He tipped his broad brimmed hat and motioned me on my way.

I bound up the steps of the nursing center with the two drinks in my hands. As I'm struggling to pull one of the large front doors open, the welcoming committee lady pushes it open, greeting me with her usual smile.

"Good day, Mr. Townsend. One of those for me, I hope."

Why is every person I run into bent on putting me on the defensive? There must be something in the water—everything has to be a joke with these people. "No Ma'am, I'm sorry, these are for a pretty young woman I met here yesterday. She's not as pretty as you are but I just assumed you were already spoken for."

The old woman seems to blush and she reaches up, takes a big pinch of my cheek and pulls on it hard, making my eyes water.

"Now, don't you go flirtin' with me, young man. Tell me, just what pretty young woman did you meet here yesterday?" Finally, she lets go of my cheek.

"She is here visiting her father, Mr. Harrison. Do you know which room he is in?"

Her brows furrow and one corner of her mouth turns up as if she doesn't approve. "Mr. Harrison is directly across the hall from your grand-daddy's room, I believe its room 238."

"Thank you, Miss… I'm sorry; I didn't get your name yesterday."

"You flirting with me and you don't even know my name?" She cocks her head and lowers one eye. She appears to be weighing whether or not to tell me, then she smiles and thrust her hand out without even considering my hands are occupied. "Ann, Mrs. Ann Worsham. But you can call me Miss Ann." She winks. "Mr. Worsham passed a long time ago."

"A pleasure, uh, Miss Ann. Thanks for the information." I turn and quickly walk across the entryway in the direction of Papa Tom's wing.

"You watch out for yourself with Miss Harrison," she calls behind me.

"Oh, I will. I will." Why would she tell me to watch out for Hannah Harrison? I slow as I near Papa Tom's room. I'd rather not get into a conversation with him just this minute. If anyone stops me on my way to see Hannah, I'll explain the ice cream is melting.

Noticing that his door is wide open, I tip-toe past and move to the other side of the hall. The door to Room 238 is closed. I tap lightly once and, balancing one drink on the top of the other, I slowly push it in. Hannah sits across the room, on the far side of her father's bed, holding one of his hands and stroking his arm. She looks up, first places a finger to her lips and then motions for me to come in.

Quietly I walk across the room, placing the drinks on the table at the foot of his bed and then, wiping my cold, wet hands on my trousers. I walk behind her and place my hands on her shoulders as if I had put my hands there many times before. She shudders.

"Your hands are freezing," she whispers.

And then she places a warm hand on mine and rubs it vigorously as if to restore it to life. She leans back and looks up into my eyes and a smile eases across her face.

"Come on, Daddy's sleeping. Grab the drinks and let's go find someplace to visit."

Somehow we manage to slip by Papa Tom and Miss Ann. We make it out to the front porch and to a pair of secluded rockers. We sit and I offer her the drinks.

"What did you bring me?" she asks.

"You said something sweet and cold. This is a frozen strawberry-lemonade—or at least it was when I left the DQ, and this is a vanilla malt with Oreo cookies."

"I'll take the lemonade, if you don't mind. You look like a milk and cookies sort of guy."

I've got to stop being defensive of every remark I hear. Take it in stride and just smile. I think I'm going to be doing that lot when I'm around her.

"Has your dad seen you today," I ask. "Does he know you're here?"

"I think so."

"That's good. How long has he been like this?"

"I came down here—what's today, Wednesday? I got here last Saturday night. Daddy had his stroke at the farm last Wednesday afternoon. He was removing a cultivator from the tractor. Momma thought he was dead when she found him. Had to call a neighbor to help get him into the truck. Then she drove him to the hospital in Beaver. He's been here since Monday. They say there is nothing to be done except watch and wait. Watch and wait for what, a miracle? If he were in Oklahoma City, maybe they could tell more, maybe they could do more. I know enough to know there is not much hope he will ever... He was dead when they got him to the hospital. A young hotshot trauma doc in the E.R. brought him back and all he has been able to do since then is blink. The chief there told me if he had been on duty he would have let my dad go, peacefully. My mom raised so much hell—they have been keeping him alive pretty much for her. Mom won't stop praying, but she won't come be with him. Says she won't sit and watch him die again—said she already did that on the way to the hospital. She wants to see him sitting up, or she doesn't want to see him at all. She sits at home making deals with God. It is easier for me to sit here with him than to be with her. She's losing it."

I can tell Hannah is exhausted just from recalling the past week. I can understand her desperation for a diversion. I'm only glad the diversion appears to be me. But, why does everyone tell me to watch out for her—as if she's evil and dangerous to be around?

"You know, Hannah, my grandfather is just across the hall."

"Your grandfather is wonderful!" She seems genuinely excited.

"You know him?" I ask.

"Do I know him? I've known your grandfather all my life. My family has come through some tough times with the help of Mr. Howard. He has probably been at my folk's supper table more times in the last ten years than I have. And this past week, he has sat with me for countless hours in my dad's room, holding my hand, and praying for Dad." She leans across and takes my hand. "Your grandfather is… he's wonderful." Her head falls and her long firey hair cascades down her neck and nearly into her lap. She cries softly for a moment and then, just like the morning rain in Seattle, she stops abruptly. She sits up straight, takes a tissue from her pocket and wipes away the tears and her face shines bright with the most beautiful green eyes—eyes that seemed to be locked on mine. And like a Seattle afternoon after the rain, she is fresh and clear and radiant. And, she smiles.

For fear of spoiling the moment I make one of the better decisions I have made since arriving in Oklahoma—I decide to remain silent, ready to listen, available to comfort, and dead to self.

Hannah gets up from her chair, turns it around and slides it next to mine. She sits back down and lays her hand across the top of mine. She glances over, I suppose to get my approval, and she leans against the upright of the chair back, next to me, and closes her eyes. I hear a deep sigh and then the slow rhythm of her breathing.

The movements and commotions associated with the serving of lunch disturb her sleep and erase the serene thoughts that have taken up residence in my brain.

"Would you two like to join us for lunch in the dining room?" Miss Ann asks quietly. "We're having King Ranch casserole, green beans, and a salad. And we're having chocolate cake for all the birthday people this month."

I give Hannah a questioning look. She gives a half smile and a full shake of her head as she scrunches up her nose like she got a whiff of a foul odor.

"No thank you, Miss Ann. But maybe I could get a piece of cake later."

Miss Ann turns and walks away, leaving behind a heavy harrumph.

"Let me go check on Daddy and, if you don't mind, we can go out to the house and have lunch with Mama."

While Hannah goes to check on her father, I slip inside the dining hall in search of a cup of coffee, but that is only a ruse to get me close to the birthday cake. Mrs. Martin cuts me off and stands between me and the table with the chocolate cake and a stack of small paper plates.

"How are you today, Mr. Townsend?" she ask as she takes a knife and swipes it along the base of the cake, a ribbon of fudge icing curling on its blade. She looks around the room to make sure she isn't being watched and then slips her finger along the knife's edge and places it quickly into her mouth—and then the crime is complete and unseen. I am the only witness.

"I'm fine and was considering pre-empting lunch with a chocolate fix. Chocolate is my drug of choice."

"Be my guest." She steps aside and clears my path to the cake. "Nursing home chicken casserole not your cup of tea?"

"I've got a date for lunch, thank you. I'm looking forward to talking at lunch and I'd prefer not to talk with my mouth full."

"You and Mrs. Cline have lunch plans, do you?"

"Mrs. Cline? I'm confused—don't remember meeting a Mrs. Cline."

"Hannah Cline. You've been sitting with her on the front veranda."

"You mean Hannah Harrison?"

"Harrison? I didn't know she uses her maiden name. Oh well—anyway, enjoy your cake… and your lunch."

"Can I ask you about her dad?" I chose not to ask her just now about Hannah's last name.

"You can, but I don't know what I will be able to tell you. You need to talk to someone else about his condition. Did you talk to your grandfather about his?"

"Yes, I did, thank you. But, I was wondering how is it that someone in Mr. Harrison's condition is in a nursing home? I would have thought he would have been in an intensive care unit, or at least in a hospital."

"He is in a hospital. Wildflower is not a nursing home. It is a rehabilitation hospital as well an extended care facility, a hospice, and for some a retirement home. I don't know whether you've noticed, but we are a long way out in the sticks—as some folks might call it. And, just because we're a small community, doesn't mean we don't have needs for a wide range of medical care, good medical care."

"I'm sorry. I didn't mean to offend you. I just assumed... well, it must be very expensive to provide this kind of care for such a small community."

"This is oil country, Mr. Townsend—Buchanan Oil country. The Buchanan family owns the lion's share of the land around here, at least most of the land with oil on it. What they don't own outright, they own the mineral rights to. The Buchanan family money built and funds this facility for the sake of the entire community. There is not a medical need around here that goes unattended—regardless of insurance, money or who you are... or aren't. The Buchanan's helicopter rushed Mr. Harrison to the emergency center in Oklahoma City. And, then when he was stabilized, flew him back here so his family and friends could be around him when... well, so he would be among family and friends."

"I guess I don't need to ask about his prognosis." I remark.

"You could ask, but I'm not at liberty to discuss it with you. I would have thought you knew about the Buchanan family."

"Why is that?" I ask.

"Because Randolph Buchanan caused your grandmother's death."

"What! But I thought she died in a car accident—a drunk driver ran into her. Randy, uh, Randy… Randy Buchanan. I remember now."

"Randy—Randolph. One and the same."

"That was 50 years ago. The Buchanan family and my grandfather are close friends now, aren't they?"

"From what I've seen they are almost like family. Mr. Buchanan stops in and checks on your grandfather every opportunity he gets. I don't think he drives by this place that he doesn't stop and spend a few minutes with him."

"That's something. I remember now—Papa Tom teaching me lessons on forgiveness and Randy Buchanan's name coming up." As long as I have her talking, I need to find out more about Mrs. Cline. "Not to change the subject, but Hannah told me she was divorced. Why does…"

"You would have to ask her, Mr. Townsend. Enjoy your cake." And she turns and walks away as Hannah springs into the dining room. She catches my eye and motions for me to come. Cake in hand, I join her and we head for the parking lot.

CHAPTER SEVEN
Everybody deserves a little forgiveness.

As Hannah wields her large truck along the farm-to-market back roads of Oklahoma, I sit and take in the vastness of this land. In Seattle on a clear day you can't get far enough from the snowy top of Mount Rainer to delete it from the landscape; out here there seems to be no distinctive features on the horizon to tell you where you are in relationship to the rest of the world. The sun is now perched at its apex; without a compass you have no clue where you might be headed except for the occasional highway signs indicating 270 North or 270 South—23 West or 23 East.

There are no shadows of telephone poles or fence posts. The fields are ripe with wheat and so thick there appear to be no rows, just an endless sea of golden stalks. The only thing piercing the horizon is a stray windmill or a piece of oil field equipment—a drilling rig or pump jack. From a distance it appears barren—up close it is teaming with vibrant life. My window is down, my right arm absorbing the sun's warm therapeutic rays. In the twenty minutes it takes to reach the Harrison farm, my forearm is hot, dry and already the flesh is pink—an unfamiliar and uncomfortable flesh tone for someone from Seattle.

"This is where I grew up," she says as she turns off the highway and up a nearly perfect straight dirt road, flanked with barbed wire fence, set perpendicular to the highway. There are no curves, twists or turns in this country—everything is straight and true—except for the conflicting remarks about Hannah… Hannah Harrison, or is it Hannah Cline?

As we reach a small rise in the road, a valley reveals itself, as does a large white farm house and numerous outbuildings, livestock pens, and scattered mechanical monsters—tractors, cultivating equipment of various configurations, and something I'm betting is a combine. Three towering, round, tin buildings sit in a small circle with metal tubes and chutes running in different directions. Dirt roads run out from the buildings like spokes from the center of a wheel. One large section of land stands out—it is green and dotted with black cows, nearly every one paired with a white-faced black calf.

When the truck pulls around behind the house, two black and white spotted dogs race out from the shade of the porch and circle us, yelping and crying as if welcoming someone home from a long journey. A cloud of dust rises from the truck's wheels as it settles under the shade of a metal shed. One of the dogs whimpers and rolls on its back at Hannah's feet, the other immediately digs its nose in my crotch—its slobber leaves a dark wet spot on the only pair of good slacks I brought with me.

"Cricket, stop that! Come… Come here, boy," Hannah commands in a deep angry voice I pray I never hear directed at me. She slaps the side of her leg and both dogs cower at her side and follow closely. This must be Hannah's mother meeting us at the door. Exactly what I would expect here in Divine—plain and plump. Hannah is nothing like her mother.

"Mom, this is Tommy Townsend, Mr. Howard's grandson. He's in town visiting from Seattle. Small world, huh?"

"A pleasure to meet you, Mr. Townsend." She quickly turns to her daughter. "How's your father? Any change?" Her eyes seem desperate for any news. For the time being, Hannah appears to ignore my questions. We walk into the house from the back porch. The kitchen is more than a kitchen—it is a great room, surrounded with cabinets and large appliances, a huge dining table, a massive island with a stovetop, and a sink in the middle, and surrounded with bar stools as if the cook performs before an audience.

"I thought I noticed a bit of a smile on his face. But the nurses think it's my imagination," she reports softly. "Have you got enough for Mr. Townsend to have lunch with us?"

"I can certainly whip something up. I didn't know when to expect you so I haven't fixed anything."

"Don't bother. If you don't mind, I'll fix us something. Have you eaten anything, Mom?"

"Nothing for me, thanks. You two go on and eat. I've got some chores." Hannah's mom turns and leaves the room.

"Don't mind her. She has been in another world since Dad's episode. She acts like he's going to walk through that door at any moment. She doesn't want to face the reality of things." Hannah walks to a shelf and picks up a picture of a young man in camo posing with a rifle, standing next to a Hum-Vee. "My younger brother John is stationed somewhere in the Middle East, and my older sister Tiffany lives in San Antonio with three kids and another on the way. She won't be coming home either... until she has to."

I pull up a stool at the kitchen's island as Hannah buries her head inside the refrigerator.

"Ham sandwiches and leftover mac and cheese. That okay with you?"

"Sure."

"White or whole wheat? Iced tea or... water?"

"Whole wheat, with mustard—no mayonnaise. Tea—no sugar."

"Aren't we particular?"

"I just know what I like." She catches me looking at her and smiling. She smiles back.

"I know what I like, too," she says as if filling in the blanks.

I would certainly like to fill in some blanks myself—just not sure if this is the right time. For now I'll just sit back and enjoy the moment. We'll come back to the Mrs. Cline thing and all the little innuendos and little warnings I've been getting from various people around town.

"So, you grew up here? It seems like a wonderful place. Did you appreciate it then?"

Hannah flashes me a look—am I off the reservation again? "I mean, a lot of times we don't appreciate the value of things around us until... well until they're gone, until we move away."

"Would you like a dill pickle with your sandwich?"

"Sure, thanks. Did you leave right after high school? Where did you go to college?"

"You want your bread toasted?"

"No, thank you. Just plain bread... and don't cut the crust off."

"What makes you think I'd do that?"

"Because I think you will do anything to keep from answering my questions," I snap.

She flashes back a look I wish I hadn't provoked. But, it is only a look. She puts her head down and continues working on preparing lunch. Once again, almost too late, I learn when to shut up and just enjoy the moment. I am not sure if she just hates being questioned or is desperate to hide things. What things?

Lunch was enjoyed with small talk—insignificant small talk between two people who were from similar, but different places, coming together for different, yet similar, reasons. We bring comparable stories with comparable pains, one seeking secrets and the other keeping them.

When we return to Wildflower, the afternoon sun pushes the shadows from the trees and flags across the front of the center. The hot sun's invasion of the porch has forced all the guests and residents inside in front of the giant screen TV, onto couches and easy chairs and across cool, quiet beds to languish and pass away the afternoon and wait for dinner.

I accompany Hannah into her father's room. The rhythmic wheezing of the ventilator confirms her father is still present in this world but the darkness of the room implies he is asleep—the stoic countenance of the nurse at his side indicates the sleep carries with it little hope of being anything else. Hannah wheels around immediately and marches back out into the hall. She creeps to Papa Tom's door and peers in. The room is empty.

"Well, he couldn't have gotten far," I say, but then panic when I look at my watch. It's almost four o'clock. Papa Tom told me to come back at 2:30 this afternoon and we could continue our personal talk. It's 4:00 o'clock! "It's 4:00 o'clock," I say—too loud and with too much anger in my voice.

"I'm sorry. Did I make you late?" Hannah asks.

"Huh? No. It's not your fault. It's all mine. I forgot. Papa Tom asked me to see him at 2:30 today. I totally forgot. He's going to kill me."

"I'm sure he won't kill you Tommy."

"It's just that it is so inconsiderate of me to stand him up. His time is very important to him and he made a special point of setting aside some of it for me—today."

"Well, let's go find him. I'll explain it was my fault for keeping you out at the farm."

All I can do is shake my head as we trot down the hall, searching for my grandfather.

Mrs. Martin is at the nurses' station. Her head is buried in a patient's chart when I approach.

"Excuse me, Mrs. Martin—do you know where I can find my grandfather?"

"Yes, he's teaching in our conference center from 4:00 to 5:30 today. He went down there just a few minutes ago. He asked if I had seen you."

"Was he upset? I was supposed to meet with him at 2:30—I got tied up."

"Mr. Townsend, I have seen your grandfather almost every day for the past two years—I have never once seen him upset at anybody. If you go down that hall till you get to the door marked 'Conference Room,' you may be able to see him for a few minutes before the class starts. A few people attending the class haven't arrived yet."

"Wait for me Hannah, I'll be right back." She nods. "And, thank you, Mrs. Martin, I'm sorry to have disturbed you."

"No problem." Mrs. Martin returns to her charts.

As Hannah wanders off somewhere, I run to the conference room. Out of breath, I barge through the conference room door. There must be twenty or more people in the room—some already seated around the longest conference table I have ever seen. Others are milling around drinking coffee, some drinking iced tea. There are men and women in various types of police or state trooper uniforms, two men in black suits—one with a clerical collar, several men and women in white medical coats, and Papa Tom seated at the middle on one side. Everyone looks directly at me and the room seems to go quiet.

"Oh, excuse me. I'm very sorry. If you haven't started yet, I just need to speak with Mr. Howard for a moment." I work my way across the room to my grandfather and suddenly I pass the NFL'S defensive line first round draft choice in State Police uniform and he grabs me by the shoulder.

"Well hello again, Mr. Townsend. You always seem to be in a hurry to get to your grandfather." He grins but I am not sure it is an actual smile. Then he releases his grip.

"Uh, yes, good seeing you again too, sir." I continue around the table. Papa Tom has pushed himself back from the table. His smile is so big and toothy—he almost seems to be genuinely happy to see me.

"I was worried about you, Tommy Boy. Glad you're all right though. As you can see I was about to send out all these officers on a man hunt to find you and the clergy is here to pray for your safety—oh yeah, and the doctors are here to care for you if you had gotten injured." Now he and everyone present in the room have a big laugh—at my expense.

"It's all right, Tommy Boy. I do have a busy schedule but, if you can wait an hour and a half, I'll be through here and we can have dinner together... and have that little talk."

Three more people enter the conference room, one blurts out a hurried apology, "I'm sorry we got held up. Can we get started 'cause I've got a wedding rehearsal at six."

Everyone finds a seat. Papa Tom pulls a walker from behind him, swings it open and pulls himself up and stands to address the group.

I sheepishly smile and slip out the door. When I get into the hall, I notice a poster on a stand by the door. It reads: "Announcing the Death of a Loved One to a Family Member," Instructor – Mr. Tom Howard.

I don't know what ever gave me the impression Papa Tom was slowing down—or that he was losing it. If he can draw a crowd of professional people who take off work to come hear him speak—he apparently is still on his game. And, he's brilliantly funny and quick too. For a moment I actually thought they were all gathered because I was late and he called on them to find me.

Now to find Hannah.

She is right where I expected she would be. I get the feeling Hannah prefers to sit at her father's bedside than spend time with anyone who might possibly speak to her—or about her. I think she also appreciates that he doesn't ask her any questions.

"How are the two of you getting along?" I whisper.

"No need to whisper. You could fire off a cannon and he wouldn't notice."

Her father's room is still dark and quiet, except for the droning breathing machine. The room is uncomfortably inanimate, without light, color, almost motionless.

"Maybe you should turn on some lights, open the blinds, play a radio, or turn on the TV?" I suggest all that because she seems to take on the environment that is surrounding her. When she played with her two dogs and ran in the field behind her house, she seemed to come alive, taking on the warmth of the sun and the freshness and brightness of the outdoors. In the darkness here, now, she appears as lifeless as her father.

"Maybe you're right," she says as she jumps up, pushes the curtains back, and twists the vertical blinds causing the afternoon sun to come flooding in. I join her and flip the three wall switches, igniting a bank of fluorescent tubes, the light over the small sink and mirror, and the single light on the wall above her father's head.

"You know this room needs some flowers," she says as she marches out the door and down the hall. She stops at the nurses' station and grabs a large floral arrangement that until a second ago was apparently unclaimed. The various plastic nuisances that clutter the rolling table sitting next to his bed are swept up and disposed of. Now the grand display of flowers fills the room with life—and hope.

And her eyes fill with tears. And she takes my hand, leans against my arm and looks up at me... and whispers, "Thank you, you make me... you just make things seem... better."

We stand together, like an old married couple and survey the room, the flowers, and her father. With the room completely illuminated, full of light and bright colors, her dad appears to be peacefully sleeping now, and there is an expectancy that he might awaken, sit up, smile and greet his daughter. I can sense that hope has returned to Room 238.

It is too hot to sit on the porch and the great common room offers no privacy this late in the afternoon. Oprah is on the big flat screen and some residents have come to wait for the dinner bell.

"Would you like to go for a drive?" I ask.

"Sure, why not?"

"Let's take my rental—it has unlimited miles."

I leave Wildflower behind in a cloud of dust.

"Where are we headed—in such a hurry?" she inquires.

"I don't know how to get there but I know where I want to go."

"Where might that be?"

"There is—or there was—a school with a playground dedicated to my grandmother somewhere around here."

"I know where it is. When you reach the highway, turn right."

The school is much larger than I remember. It seems much too modern to have been built 40 years ago. "Are you sure this is the right school?"

"They tore down the old school years ago and rebuilt it—with a new playground—but the dedication plaque and the purpose is still the same. When they built this one, the Buchanan family came out and built a new playground—in memory of Mr. Howard's wife. He may not have built it with his own hands, as he did the old one, but Randolph Buchanan turned the first shovel for the newspaper photographers, signed the check and mounted the old plaque on the new playground."

"This is supposed to be about my grandmother, not the Buchanan family and their money." I set my jaw and I can feel myself trying to garner some righteous indignation for myself. "She was murdered in a fiery car crash caused by a drunken Randy Buchanan." It was a dozen years before I was born. How much indignation can I claim for that?

"In all fairness to the Buchanan family—it was an accident—a very unfortunate accident. Mr. Buchanan was eighteen years old and it was the night of his high school graduation. It was the first time, the only time, and the very last time he ever had a drink of alcohol." She spoke as though she was very familiar with all the circumstances.

"How do you know so much about it? It happened long before you were born, too."

"Mr. Buchanan spoke at our senior high graduation. He tells the story of your grandmother's death and accepts the blame in front of every graduation class. He also talks about the work your grandmother

76

did with the Arapaho Indian children. He re-dedicates this playground to her and speaks about the dangers and consequences of drinking— as he did to the seniors a little over a month ago. And, he awards a scholarship—in your grandmother's name—every year to the student who has demonstrated outstanding service to the community."

"I'm surprised you knew all this. I never knew the extent of the Buchanans' involvement and Mr. Buchanan's ongoing commitment."

"My senior year, I received the scholarship." Her eyebrows go up as if to say, So there!

All I can do is smile and put away my unwarranted claim against the Buchanan family.

I turn into the school parking lot—the playground comes into view. It is spectacularly huge for a small town elementary school. It is awash in bold, vibrant colors and huge icons of Indian designs are scattered around the grounds.

"Mom told me about the Indian symbols and how my grandfather used them to make the children from the Arapaho community school feel welcomed here. My grandmother taught at the Indian school and after she died, the school was closed and the children were made to come here."

"They are beautiful, aren't they?" Hannah remarks.

"Yes, they are really something," I say as I jump out of the car and go in search of the marker. There is a vibrant red tower in the center of the various elements and obstacles. Multicolored canvas banners flap in the breeze above it. A giant slide snakes around it, making its way eventually to the soft earth below. There on the side of the platform gleams the bronze plaque. A sculptured likeness of my grandmother is at its top. Below it reads:

Re-dedicated in loving memory of
Susan Lynn Howard,
Loving Wife, Mother, Teacher,
and Friend to All Who Play Here.
1994

And then, a second, smaller plaque—the original one— is affixed in the lower half:

Susan Lynn Howard
Memorial Playground
Erected by Randy Buchanan
July 1963

"Re-dedicated in 1994... I was too busy to come. My book about Morton Podus was just released—I was at a book signing in San Francisco. My Dad, Mom, and Papa Tom were here. But, I was too busy." I turn away and kick the base of the tower. "Damn! It's a wonder my grandfather even speaks to me."

"Tommy, your grandfather has never uttered a bitter or unflattering word about you in front of me."

"No, I'm sure he hasn't. As far as I know, he's never said an unkind word to anyone—about anything. And, I couldn't take time out of my schedule to be here. Even now, I wouldn't have come except I wanted to write another book. What a selfish, egotistical ass I am."

I turn and begin to walk away. Hannah grabs my arm, stopping me, and gives me a hug.

"Tommy, don't beat yourself up. That was fifteen years ago. You need to forgive yourself—your grandfather has. I'm sure you're not the same person now you were then."

I look down at her and state flatly, "That was the person I was two days ago." I break her grip and walk quickly back to the car. Wisely, she lets me go. I sit, my head resting on the steering wheel.

CHAPTER EIGHT

She loves me... She loves me not.

hen we arrive back at Wildflower some of the attendees of Papa Tom's class are already leaving the facility and heading for their cars. Perhaps they finished a little early. Please don't let me be late again. Bounding up the steps and side-stepping a squad of uniformed peace officers, I see him being wheeled toward me. He waves, acknowledging me, and dismisses the young man who powered his chair. I stop directly in front of him and fight to catch my breath.

"I'm sorry I kept you waiting, Tommy Boy. I ran a little long. I either talk too slow, or have too much to say." He grins. "Anyway, I suspect most of them were chomping at the bit to get out of there."

"No problem, sir." I don't tell him I ran ten minutes late getting back. Hannah comes up behind me and grabs my arm, then quickly releases it when she sees Papa Tom. She leans down and gives him a big kiss on his cheek.

"Please forgive us, it was my fault we were late getting back," she blurts out. He looks over at me and smiles.

"All's forgiven, child," he says. "All's forgiven." He takes her hand and brings it up to his lips and gently kisses it. "Will you join Tommy and me for dinner?"

"You all go on. I want to visit with Dad for a while. I know Tommy wants to have some one-on-one time with you. I'll join you two later." She turns to leave and brushes her hand softly across my shoulder as she walks away.

Every time I'm with her, I lose track of time. It's not that I actually lose track of time, it's that I forget there are other things going on, other things worth doing, worth seeing, aside from my preoccupation with her.

"I didn't know you and Hannah knew each other. She's a great gal, don't you think?" Papa Tom says.

"Yes…" I watch as she walks away. "Yes, she is a great gal. We met yesterday for the first time—after you and I first talked."

"Looked like you all were old friends."

"You know, it seems like I've known her all my…Well, you know what I mean." I decide to change the subject. "We just came from visiting Grandma's playground."

"Is that right? I was there a couple weeks ago myself. I lasso someone to take me whenever I can. It's a lot more pleasant to visit Susan there than at the cemetery—especially when it's full of little ones laughing and carrying on." His eyes seem to glisten when he speaks of her.

"Well, shall we?" I point to the dining room. He nods and I take charge and push him down the hall.

"Tell me about your class—that was quite an eclectic group of people." I remove one of the chairs from a dining table in the corner and move it to the side to accommodate his wheel chair. Most are round, eight tops, but there are several small tables for more intimate dining, or I guess more appropriately, private dining. Papa Tom struggles to wheel himself up to the table where the chair had been. I am conflicted whether to take over and help him or give him the satisfaction of doing for himself. I roll him up closer to the table, and when he doesn't object, I remove a chair and park him in its place.

"Several of the state troopers asked me if I could help them find the right words to notify people their loved ones had died in a car accident or some other tragedy. When some of the staff and doctors got wind of the class, they asked to join. Then, some of my clergy friends decided they could use a fresh approach to comforting grieving relatives. Well, the word got around, and it grew from there. The hospital administrator got it accredited and issues Continuing Education credits. Of course Wildflower charges a small tuition, and they pay me a fee which I get to donate to something or someone. The best part is that I get to talk for an hour and a half and, it doesn't hurt my self-esteem that people have to pay to listen."

"What makes you an expert on the subject?" I continue probing. This is what I do best, ask questions.

"Maybe it's because most of my life it seems to have fallen on me to break the news of someone's death. Maybe it's because I've faced so much tragedy during my life. I know I'm comfortable dealing with death—I don't fear it—I know the Lord is sovereign. Although sometimes life doesn't seem fair, the Lord is always just."

"You sure do seem to stay busy around here," I jest.

"Okay, Tommy Boy, enough small talk about me. What is it you want to know?"

"Sir?"

"This is… this meeting is not part of the interview about the secret, is it?" he whispers.

"No, it isn't."

"Well, what can I help you with?"

"Well, sir, as long as we're being so blunt and upfront—and before Hannah comes back—what can you tell me about her?"

"I've been friends with her family for years. Just exactly what is it you want to know?" He leans over and looks me straight in the eye. Then he lowers his voice and continues, "And, Tommy, what makes you think you have the right to know everything I know about her? What makes her secrets your business?"

"Well, I… uh, I know she and I have only known each other a couple of days, but we have a lot in common, we've shared a lot in the last two days, and we've really gotten to know each other…"

"You know each other?" he blurts out uncomfortably loud.

"No, not in a Biblical sense. Jeez…"

"Tommy!" he interrupts me to prevent unwholesome words from escaping.

"Sorry. But, we've shared a lot—our past, our hopes, our fears and concerns about… well, about her father… and me… and about you."

"Nothing draws people closer than sharing personal details—that's for sure. You might be moving things along too quickly? She's not divorced yet."

I almost choke. "She's not divorced yet?" Now, I'm too loud.

"She didn't tell you? I thought you two were close. I thought you and she shared intimate details? I would have thought her marriage or her divorce was a pretty intimate detail."

A young summer intern in a white apron suddenly appears and stands in the small space between us, turns to me, bends down and looks directly in my face and asks in a bright, perky voice, "Chicken and dumplings or Swiss steak and creamed turnips?" I hesitate, failing to immediately respond, so she turns her face and, since she remains bent over, she and Papa Tom are now nose to nose. "What say, Mr.

Howard, you up for Swiss steak tonight—it's so tender you don't even have to chew it. And, even though the mac 'n cheese is a little lumpy, it ain't hard and crackly like last time."

I sit back and put my hands in my lap. Papa Tom moves himself back away from the table and up against the back of his wheel chair. Little Miss Perky stands with her feet wide apart, hands on her hips and says, "Well, boys, what will it be? In a few more minutes it will be whatever's left."

"I'll have the chicken and dumplings, please."

"Same here." Papa Tom says.

"Good. I'll be back in a flash." And she disappears as quickly as she arrived.

Papa Tom and I sit, both our hands folded in front of us, and we stare at the empty placemats. I consider what I've just learned about Hannah's marital status and Papa Tom…? Well, Papa Tom just sits and gives me one of his all-knowing smiles.

We shouldn't have wasted the time—we should have continued on as far as I'm concerned—because before I can get out a rebuttal to Papa Tom, Little Miss Perky waltzes up with our two trays and sits them down gently, silently. Not even the ice in the tall empty glasses shifts. Before us are two trays with heaping bowls of a thick creamy, yellowy mixture of steaming puffy dumplings and large lumps of chicken.

"Be careful. It's hot," she warns. "I'll be back with the drink pitchers."

And, she's gone. Also placed symmetrically on our trays are little bowls of green beans, dinner rolls, salad, and green Jell-O with a spoonful of assorted canned fruit bits suspended in mid-jell. I remember seeing a tray of food similar to this once in a federal prison in Arizona. I was interviewing a prisoner for my second book.

And… she's back—this time with a choice of ice water or iced tea. Our selections made, she pours and moves on. I move to continue the conversation while Papa Tom blows softly across his bubbling caldron of chicken.

"She told me that she was divorced," I complain.

Papa Tom blows across his bowl and stirs the steaming concoction. Is he avoiding me? He appears as uncomfortable answering my queries about Hannah as I am about asking them.

"Tommy Boy, if you really care about Hannah, you should be talking to her about this. If she cares about you, she'll tell you the truth. If you both can't be open and truthful, you need to move on."

"Several people have made off-handed remarks to me concerning Hannah. Some have actually warned me, telling me to watch out for myself."

"Did you mention it to her?"

"Mention what—that I've been told to keep an eye on her?"

Unnoticed, Hannah walks up behind us. "Who told you to keep an eye on me?" she says in a tone I haven't heard from her—until now.

I swing around. She's standing directly behind me, tapping her foot, her arms tightly folded below her chest. I sit exposed and vulnerable.

"Who have you been talking to about me?" she demands.

"Uh, I…" I feel like running. I wanted to know, so maybe now is the time to put it out there. "I was asking someone which room your father was in, and, uh, this woman… well I told her I met you yesterday and that I was bringing you a drink—and I didn't know which room your father was in." One of Hannah's eyebrows arches dramatically. I continue cautiously. "Anyway, she told me to watch out for you. I don't know what that means. I didn't ask her what it meant. I let it go. But yesterday, when the Trooper stopped me for speeding, I told him I was in a hurry to get the drinks to my grandfather and you before they melted." Hannah's eyes narrow and I sense she is ready to explode. "I tried to explain to him who you were and I gave him your father's name and that you were his daughter, and… well when I drove off, he told me to keep an eye on you, too."

"And, what… What else did you ask him about me?"

"Nothing—I promise. Oh yeah…" I stand up and get in her face—as if that will further my cause. "…when I told Mrs. Martin I couldn't have lunch with my grandfather yesterday because I was having lunch with you, she referred to you as *Mrs. Cline*. Who is Mrs. Cline? I thought you said you were divorced?"

The more I talk, the deeper the hole I seem to be digging for myself. Now Hannah's nostrils are flaring and her face becomes beet red—I'm absolutely sure mine is as white as a sheet.

"Seems awfully funny everyone you meet volunteers information about me. Now, here you sit, pumping your grandfather for information about me. You want to know about me—you talk to me—you ask me!"

Now the ball's back in my court. Here's where I get out of this hole. I swell up like an over-inflated balloon and let loose. "Ask you? Ask you? I've been asking you questions ever since I met you and you've been ducking and dodging every question I throw your way. And, evidently when you did volunteer some personal information about you—you lied!"

"I…" she starts and then stops abruptly. She appears on the verge of crying.

I realize this main event, knock-down-drag-out fight is taking place in a packed dining room with Papa Tom, many of the staff, and half of the residents. Only one person is eating and I later learn it's because she doesn't wear her hearing aid to dinner so she can enjoy her meal in peace and quiet. There is no peace and quiet to be had here—not now.

At almost a whisper, a calm whisper, I get in the last—probably not the last—but at least my last words, "You told me you were divorced." I cock my head and raise one eyebrow as if to say, so there!

Somebody sound the bell. The bout has ended. Hannah storms out of the room and out of the parking lot.

After a moment, people begin eating again. A steady stream of small talk returns as does the clinking of silverware. I sit back down, pick up my fork and begin to shovel dumplings into my mouth. They're cold now and my stomach warns me that it won't tolerate food and my ensuing frustration. I push my tray away.

Papa Tom is already down to the fruit in his Jell-O when I finally work up the nerve to look him in the eye—let alone to speak. "Pretty embarrassing display of my immaturity, huh?"

"When feelings and passions take over, good judgment often flees the scene. Both of you kids are in luck, though."

"How's that?"

"You and Hannah don't live around here. This time next week you'll both be half-way across the U.S., surrounded by people that never heard about the tiff you and Hannah had in the middle of the dining room at Wildflower Nursing Center in Divine, Oklahoma. On the other hand, as long as you hang around here, you won't be able to raise your heads in public—the Alva-Courier is probably already setting type on the story so they can get it in Thursday's edition. I can see the headline, 'Rumble at Wildflower.' They have a tendency to overstate in the *Courier*."

"If it doesn't go any further than that, I suppose I'll survive."

"The question is, Tommy Boy, will your relationship with Hannah survive?"

"If she's still married, it's a moot question, isn't it?" I force a smile and wiggle my Jell-O with a spoon and then decide against eating it. I put my spoon down and sit back, putting my hands in my lap. It's quiet. The whole room is quiet. I lower my head. Papa Tom probably thinks I'm praying. I'm not. Perhaps I should be, but part of me is wishing I could get a do-over and part of me wants to know more.

"You want to know her situation and the circumstances concerning her marriage to Woody Cline?"

"Okay. Lay it on me."

"You probably should ask her, Tommy."

"I doubt she'll ever speak to me again."

"Okay, but not here. Let's go to my room—or better yet, let's go to John Henderson's room. He's over there eating and since they've got chicken and dumplings today, he'll be a while. He won't leave till the pot in the kitchen is empty."

"But you've barely touch your food."

"I ate most of my Jell-O. There's too much fat in the dumplings for my taste."

On the way to John's room he begins. "This place is full of gossip, as is the whole town. Divine is a small, tight community. The walls are thin. There are few secrets—except for the one about the Podus family, which I will be telling you soon—maybe I'll get to the end tomorrow. The next room to the right."

"Are you sure Mr. Henderson won't mind?"

"I'm sure. Put me over by the window and you can sit in his comfortable recliner. This might take a while."

I sit and look for a lever to release the back a bit. "This thing is leaning forward. I can't…"

"It's one of those electric recliners that stands you up as well as lays you back. There's a push-button thing in the cushion."

Sure enough, there's a remote with a coiled cord stuffed in between the seat cushion and the arm. I push back on a lever and the seat back begins to move back, the foot begins to rise. "Too much." I push reverse and it settles into a comfortable looking position. I sit down. "That's fine, now what's the story?"

"I feel like Hannah won't mind me telling you now—now that things are out there. Given an opportunity, I am sure she would have preferred to tell you the whole story. Aside from me, her mother and her father, and the Federal Marshall's office, I doubt anyone else in town knows, or cares to know the whole truth, especially when their take on the truth makes for a better story—juicier gossip." He wipes his mouth, takes in a deep breath, and leans forward in his chair. "It is hard to figure when to begin."

"Begin at the beginning. I'm not going anywhere—I've got all evening."

"Well lucky you, but we've only got till John runs out of chicken and dumplings." Papa Tom rubs his forehead. "Anyway, Hannah met this jack-leg, good for nothing excuse of a man while going to med school in Tulsa. That's where she got her PA certificate. She had been away from home for almost six years, the first four years at the University of Oklahoma in Norman. After the first two years there, her scholarship ran out. The lack of rain that summer near defeated her dad's farm. Her older sister had medical problems with one of her three young ones and Jason, her brother, enlisted in the Army just before things started up in Iraq.

"Hannah wanted to become a doctor in the worst way. She worked full time while she went to school and did pretty well on her own—

for a while. She failed to get into a medical school and had to settle for a two-year physician's assistant program. She could have gone to a number of places, people, to get help but she was too proud. She never told anyone, not her parents, her friends, no one. Just one word to me or Randy Buchanan, and she wouldn't have needed to work at all."

"What's all that got to do with this guy Cline?"

"She was alone in Tulsa—across the state from home, no family, friends, and when this joker rode up on a somewhat dingy white horse and paid the least little attention to her—well, she was young, lonely and fresh off the farm so to speak. Woody gave her what she thought she needed. She took him home one weekend to meet her parents and fireworks went off. Ray saw Woody for what he really was—a con artist, shiftless, no-count bum. He had swept Hannah off her feet and all that sweeping filled her eyes with dusty dreams where she couldn't see him for what he really was. Woody spent the weekend surveying the farm, the equipment, and the livestock—and pumped her daddy with questions about how much his crops brought in, how many acres he had cultivated, and how many head of cattle he was running. Even asked him outright if he still had the mineral rights to his property—after counting all of the Buchanan's pump-jacks on the horizon."

"Didn't her dad warn her about him?" I nervously look at the door for fear Hannah might return and catch us still talking about her.

"The more her daddy talked bad about Woody, the more she defended him and drew closer to him. A couple months later they eloped to Las Vegas and got married—she became Mrs. Woodrow Cline. He moved into her apartment, and she soon discovered he had lied about having a job. He appeared to be shuttling cars across the state for a BMW dealer but, as a sideline, moved drugs inside the vehicles from one city to another. When the Feds busted him at her apartment—the drugs were in a suitcase with her I.D. tag on it."

"Holy..."

"Tommy!"

"Sorry..." I am on the edge of my seat, my hands dug into the arms of the chair. "What did the police do with her?"

"Well, they arrested them both. The Oklahoman newspaper ran the story with photographs of both of them on the front page of the state news section. The *Alva-Courier* picked it up and ran it in case anybody within a hundred miles of Divine didn't see it."

"No wonder everybody shuns her. How long ago did this happen?"

"It all took place about two years ago. Everybody around here thinks Mr. Buchanan and his lawyers got Hannah off." Papa Tom leans closer and his voice gets quieter. "Listen, just between you and I and the gate post—and this can't go any further. Hannah found out what Woody was up to about a week before the bust."

"What? Why didn't she get out of there?"

"Hang on—she did. She contacted the DEA and told them what Woody was up to. They followed him around and were able to identify the dealer and his contacts. They arranged to have the bust take place at Hannah's apartment and arrested her as an accomplice. After Woody and his friends got convicted and were sent away, the news media reported Hannah was released and not charged for lack of evidence. Of course everybody around here still thinks she knew what was going on all the time. The bad guys haven't a clue she set them up. Otherwise, she would live in fear of their retribution. Nobody can know—it wouldn't be safe." Papa Tom glanced at the door. Lowered his voice, and continued. "She moved to Oregon and got a job there with a group of doctors. Her family knows the truth. But, they all know better than to talk about what really happened. If word were to get out—well, she must live with the unkindness of some folks around here. That's the reason she doesn't come home much. She came now to be with her dad."

"Why hasn't she gotten a divorce?"

"The federal prosecutor recommended she not file for divorce right away—to keep down any suspicions of her turning him in. Good thing too, because Woody's attorney filed an appeal, and he was released three months ago on bail. He skipped on the bail. Woody's been on the lam since then. Nobody has seen hide nor hair of him. I'm not sure if the law is still looking for him. Now, even if she wanted to, she can't serve him papers for a divorce until he's caught."

"I feel like such a jerk."

"You go on out to the Harrison place tomorrow and have a long talk—just the two of you. It will be all right. Don't pay any attention to what people around here say."

CHAPTER NINE
Trading places.

Papa Tom's schedule forces me to fend for myself this evening. He's got a Wednesday Bible study group and, although I was invited to sit in, I move out onto the porch and watch the sun rest itself against the horizon. Nearly a hundred yards off to the west a lone oak tree sits on a fence row. Its shadow races toward me—in an instant it covers me completely. Swallows swoop across the paling sky and dart about snatching invisible insects in midair. This day is fading but the memories it leaves behind begin to haunt me.

Drug dealers, sleaze bag Woody Cline, DEA raids, Hannah arrested, and me calling her a liar in the middle of the dining hall—I'd say that makes for a full day. If I could only run my cursor over the troubles of this day, highlight them, and hit the delete button.

Was it earlier today when Hannah fixed me lunch—gave me a tour of her family's farm? Was it only a few hours ago that we visited the playground dedicated to my grandmother? She held me softly for a moment there—and then later she held me in contempt, accusing me of talking about her, asking questions. The days out here in the Oklahoma plains must be longer than the days in Seattle. Even as rainy and dreary as they sometimes are, the days seem to flow smoothly like the tide—in and out. Today, here, I feel exhausted, as if I have lived a lifetime since morning—experienced every conceivable emotion, faced every trial life can offer.

My thoughts return to her. The truck stop. She goes there to escape this place and its people, why shouldn't I?

Las Carretas. It looks, sounds and smells like it belongs anywhere but here, at the intersection of two farm to market roads in rural Oklahoma. Bullfight posters with daring matadors side-stepping charging bulls, brightly colored neon tubes outline palm trees and breaking waves, advertising foreign beers and libations with lime and tequila, dot the white stucco walls. Waitresses float among the tables in Mexican peasant dresses with spectacular embroidered flowers. A man could lose himself here.

Funny, but, when I was here for lunch with Hannah, I never noticed any of the trappings. I don't remember who waited on us. I did noticed what Hannah was wearing though—a yellow dress with little orange flowers scattered about. It had thin straps over her beautiful creamy shoulders. She wore white sandals and her toes showed. They were painted bright red. Her hair was twisted in the back and pinned at her neck. She smelled like those lavender flowers—lilac or something. She ordered the beef tacos—I think—and she drank iced tea, unsweetened but, she added a packet of artificial sweetener.

I am only two bites into a red enchilada when the NFL's number one defensive line draft choice, Officer Martin, stops at my table. "Mind if I join you?" he says and, without hesitating, pulls out a chair and plops down across from me.

"You like Mexican food?" he asks.

My mouth is full, so a nod will have to be a sufficient response.

One of the waltzing waitresses stops and hands my uninvited guest a menu. "What would you like to drink, Josh?" she says sweetly.

"Iced tea, please, and I'll have the number three with a beef taco."

"It'll be right out," she says as she grabs his unopened menu and dances away.

"So, to what do I owe the pleasure of your company, Officer Martin?"

"Under the circumstances, I thought you could use some company."

"Under what circumstances?" I snap back.

"I heard you and Hannah parted ways."

"Was that broadcast on your police scanner? And, how did you know I was here?"

"This ain't Seattle. This is Divine—Divine, Oklahoma. Not much goes on around here that goes unnoticed. But, so you know—my wife works at Wildflower. She called me right after she witnessed the altercation between you and Hannah. Plus, your rental is the only blue four-door with Arkansas plates in the area and, finally, you were last seen on highway 270 headed south. Well, *Las Carretas* is the only place to eat for a hundred miles—I was informed you hadn't touched your chicken and dumplings. You can be sure not much goes on in these parts that I don't know about."

"Well, that's a relief—I feel much safer now."

"That's my job—keeping you and the citizens of Beaver County safe."

"Just who are you keeping me safe from?"

"Hannah's a pretty woman. She can be explosive. I know—we went to high school together. I sat behind her for nearly all four years. Don't worry, my wife sat behind me and she's kept a pretty short leash on me ever since."

"What's your point?"

"No need for you to get your feathers ruffled. I wanted to give you a warning—and I don't mean about Hannah. Her husband, Woody Cline jumped bail and has been on the loose, presumably in these parts, for nearly a month."

Why does he keep talking? I snap out of it and start listening intently. "We don't know for sure 'cause he hasn't surfaced since he was released in Oklahoma City. It's not likely he would go back to Tulsa and we don't know that he has any idea she's here—unless they've been in contact. Oklahoma is a big empty place to hide out in. He was armed when he was arrested and he's spent two years in prison, no telling what kind of bad habits he's picked up." He reaches in his shirt pocket, pulls out a piece of paper, unfolds it, and slides it across the table. It's a wanted poster. He stabs Woody Cline's profile with his finger and announces, "That's him. I thought you should at least know what he looks like and what he's capable of in case you run across him."

"I don't think that's very likely."

"Why? You don't plan on seeing Hannah again?" Martin raises a questioning eyebrow.

"Not sure. When she left, she didn't seem too interested in seeing me again and under the circumstance of her being still married to a convicted drug dealer—who is on the run as we speak—well no, I'm not likely to be seeing her any time soon."

The waitress delivers Officer Martin's tea along with his plate of assorted Mexican food items.

"Go on and eat—your food's gettin' cold," Officer Martin says as he wastes no time drenching his taco with hot sauce out of a plastic squirt bottle. Before I can decide whether to eat or get more details on Hannah's estranged husband—he devours the taco and is on to an enchilada. He stops half enchilada, swallows, and with fork mid-air, says, "I was kinda hoping you would be in a position to ask Hannah if she has seen Woody or been in contact with him."

"You know, I don't see that happening." I say that with as much certainty as I can. "I'm really not in the mood to discuss with you my plans of future contact with Miss Harrison... or Mrs. Cline, or... whoever!" Now my voice and my temper are rising. "Listen, Officer Martin..."

"You can call me Josh—everybody does."

"Like I was saying, Officer Martin, when or if I ever see Hannah is none of your business. I don't know this Woody Cline, his whereabouts, or his plans. I'm not certain I know as much as I thought I did about Miss... or Mrs. Hannah. If I do, however, speak with her again, I will be glad to let her know that you are interested in where her husband might be." I locate our dancing waitress and get her attention. "Could I please have a to-go container?"

"Let me at least get your check since I have evidently ruined your meal." Martin offered.

"No, that's..." I stop myself. "You know... Yes, yes you can get my dinner. You have ruined my meal and my evening—my whole day in fact. You can go back and report to your boss that you failed to get me to act as an undercover agent for you. Report to your wife—whatever it is you think you've learned about me and Hannah that she and everyone at Wildflower would be interested in knowing. And, you can report to my grandfather, if you're reporting to him all my comings and goings while I'm in your fair county, that I will be returning to my room at the Antelope Lodge and I will be there for the rest of the evening, enjoying my cold enchilada plate."

The waitress delivers the Styrofoam container and I scrape the contents of my plate into it, swallow down the rest of my drink, and head for the door. The waitress runs after me with the check. I turn and halt her progress, "Give that to Officer Martin," I say. "We're old friends and he asked if he could buy my dinner."

I purposely linger over my breakfast at *The Spot!*. By now I have gotten used to eating cold food and I plan on arriving at Wildflower just in time to begin my scheduled interview with Papa Tom—I'm not ready for any awkward moments meeting Hannah going in or coming out of her father's room. The far corner of the front porch will be a satisfactory vantage point—she would have to go out of her way to confront me there and I am determined not to create a convenient meeting as if by fate.

It's ten minutes till ten and as I pull into a shading parking spot in front of Wildflower and cursorily scan the vehicles in the lot, I am assured her huge white truck is not among them. The kind lady, who gladly eliminates the need for a staff receptionist, has witnessed my arrival, and has set everything in motion. Papa Tom is being wheeled out the front door as I approach the porch. I gesture to the corner rockers and Papa Tom nods approvingly. I sit and, this time, place my recorder in full view. There is no putting anything over on my grandfather. If I had ever thought he might be even the least bit doddering or forgetful, the past two days has completely dispelled that notion.

Mrs. Martin wheels him to our area of the porch. I jump up and help move to a rocker.

"I had dinner with your husband last night." I say to Mrs. Martin.

"Yes, I know. He mentioned it when he got home. I am sorry he caused you so much consternation."

"It wasn't his entire fault. I brought a lot of anger with me. I wasn't having a very good day."

"I think he meant well."

"Yes, I'm sure he did." I turn to my grandfather. "Good morning, Papa Tom. I didn't mean to ignore you."

The niceties dispensed with, Mrs. Martin turns and leaves us to our morning session. Papa Tom's eyes follow her and then return to engage me.

"So, I understand you can't seem to escape the prying eyes and minds of our little community." He smiles and pats the back of my hand which is still resting on my recorder. "You got that thing turned on already?"

"No, sir. I thought we could chat for a little while, first."

"Good. What's on your mind this morning—besides Hannah?"

"If you don't mind, I'm going to try and keep Hannah out of my mind—at least for the time being." I sit back and attempt to appear relaxed and nonchalant. "How are you doing this fine morning?" And, it is a fine morning. The sun has long escaped the horizon's grip on it and puffy clouds have begun to work their way out of the west and brought with them a slight breeze as evidenced by the fluttering of the flags along the parade grounds.

"I am beginning to sense my strength in my limbs has abandoned me, leaving me with arms that appear suddenly heavier. I don't know how much longer I will be able to feed myself. Doc Watson says this is all part of the progression and not to worry until my breathing becomes labored."

"I'm so sorry. Is there any thing I can do to make you more comfortable? Anything I can get you?"

"No, thank you, Tommy. I'm just so glad that you're here. I have really missed visiting with you. Of course, I'll admit our times together used to be a whole lot more exciting than they are now."

"Not to worry, I'm more than thrilled just to be in your presence."

"Speaking of presents, I have something for you." Papa Tom pulls a handkerchief from his shirt pocket and lays it on the wide arm of his rocker. He carefully unfolds it and out tumbles numerous medals, service ribbons and an infantry patch.

"Aside from this scar," He puts a finger to just above his left eye and traces a deep crease in his forehead back behind his right ear. "...and these things, they're all I have left from the war—except for my memories of course. And, along with my memories, I want you to have these." He pulls a small folded sheet of paper from the same pocket. "And here is a list of the ribbons and medals and what they are and where and when I received them." He gathers them up and refolds the cloth around them and hands them to me along with the folded paper. "If we have time later, I'll go over them in more detail—if you're interested."

"If I'm interested? Of course, I'm interested. Thank you. Thank you, very much."

"They have been props in my long winded tales for years. Now, you can learn to tell the stories."

"I will, sir. I most certainly will." There I am, calling him sir again. Calling him sir once made me very uncomfortable. I thought it somehow made our relationship too formal, like we were not best buds anymore—just relatives. I see now that calling him sir is a sign of respect and honor. I carefully place the articles in my small portfolio, being careful to treat them with the admiration and regard they deserve. "When you stopped last time, you were in the forest, the Bois Jacques, with Jake. Bobby Hampton had been missing for a couple of days. The Germans had just ceased firing their artillery and things were still and quiet." I reach down and switch the recorder on.

"Did I tell you how frightened Jake appeared?" I nod. "I think it was the shelling more than the cold, although there was plenty of that, too, but Jake's eyes were wild with fear. We knew their ground troops would begin moving through the forest. It was only a matter of time. I put my rifle on the mound of dirt in front of me and looked intently for the first sign of movement. I could see Jake laying his cheek alongside the receiver of his weapon but I knew with his uncontrollable trembling, he wouldn't be able to aim, let alone pull the trigger. Our men to the right of us started firing. The enemy was moving toward us."

Speaking of the enemy. Before I see her, I hear the familiar sound of her truck's big diesel engine as she climbs up the hill to the center. Papa Tom stops and glances toward the truck as well. My back is to the parking area but I see from the reflection in the window she is coming up the main walk. He raises a hand and offers a smile and a cursory wave. Fortunately it is more of a parade wave and not a come-here variety. I remain frozen in position as her image in the window moves out of my view. I hear the front door open and Papa Tom's gaze returns to me so I assume she has gone inside to visit her dad.

"So," I say to Papa Tom, "the, uh, the enemy was moving toward us."

"No, she went inside." He smiles knowingly.

"No, I meant the Germans were…"

"I know what you meant." He shakes his head slightly. "The Germans were advancing toward us and—well, that is the last thing I remember. The rest of what I'm going to tell you now is pieced together from what others later recounted to me."

"You can't remember what happened next?"

"I was darn near killed." He sits forward and raises his hands slightly, preparing them to aid in his story telling. "A grenade or perhaps a shell burst between me and Jake. The blast or a fragment caught the front of my helmet and ripped it back and over my head. The edge of the helmet caught me just above my eye and peeled off my forehead and a good bit of my scalp. Needless to say I was out. Jake thought I was dead. My hair was laid back exposing the front of my skull and a bloody portion of my scalp draped across the top of my head to the back of my neck.

"Jake figured part of my head was blown off and he didn't wait around to find out for sure. The Krauts were almost on top of our position and our men that had been on our right were now behind us and running like jack rabbits to our left. Jake took off, too. A creature of habit, without Bobby and me there to support him, Jake ran—he literally ran out of bounds. He took off and never looked back. Jake was never a scrapper. He only came along to be with us, Bobby and me. He didn't want to fight the Germans. He never wanted to join the war. He did it to get away from his dad."

"He deserted?"

"Well, that was his plan. Bobby was missing and he thought I was already dead. There just wasn't any fight in him. Fortunately for me, when the Germans overran my position, they also left me for dead, stripping most of my clothes and my personal stuff. I say fortunately, cause later when our guys pushed them back, the medics found me and the doctors said the freezing cold slowed down my heart and the bleeding. I really wasn't hurt all that bad, just a whole lot of blood."

"What happened to Jake?"

"Well, Jake was fortunate too. Before he ran completely out of bounds he came across some of our guys on the left flank and there was Bobby Hampton. Jake was very happy to see him. Bobby had gotten separated from our company and fell in with another outfit. He had been trying to get back to our position. He tried to shake some sense into Jake and when he learned I appeared to be dead; he took Jake and headed back to find me. Bobby wouldn't leave me behind, even if I were dead. They hooked up with a relief squad and returned back into the forest. It was certainly good news for me when they discovered me still alive, but it was bad news for them when someone claimed they saw a soldier from our company cut and run and identified Jake as a coward. That's when Bobby did something Jake couldn't believe. Bobby told them that he had broke and run—and that Jake had run after him to bring him back. Then he added that Jake joined with another squad and forced him, Bobby, to come back and find me.

"Jake ended up getting a Bronze Star, for among other things, valor and rescuing a member of his squad while under fire. It was during that same fire fight that Bobby's knee got shattered. Bobby got court martialed and dishonorably discharged. He was even denied a Purple Heart for his wound. Bobby and I got sent back to the states together— he disgraced with a permanent mark on his record and a bad limp, me with just this permanent mark on my head. We got home in January of '45."

"And Jake?" I ask.

"Word got around about Jake's heroism and eventually some public relations officer in the Army got wind of it and actually sent Jake back to the states to parade him around with his Bronze Star at war bond drives. Jake got back in the states in February and then by June, the Germans surrendered. For the first and only time in his life, Jake's father was proud of his son, the war hero."

"What possessed Bobby to trade places with Jake?"

"That was the kind of person Bobby was. He was a big brother to both Jake and me. Bobby was especially protective of Jake. And, while he missed not having a real father to call his own, he hated the way Jake was treated by his own father. He couldn't stand the way old man

Podus pushed Jake and constantly criticized him for not being number one at everything. Jake could never do enough to win Mr. Podus' love and acceptance. Even when Jake would score a touchdown, Podus told him he couldn't have done it on his own—without those dirt farmers clearing a path for him. He wanted Jake to stand on his own and when he couldn't, Podus would belittle him. Jake always wanted to make his father proud, but he never was quite fast enough, or strong enough. Truth was, Jake never had any self-confidence. He never believed in himself."

"But why would Bobby allow himself to be disgraced like that?"

"I, myself, didn't know what Bobby had done until many years later. Bobby told Jake not to tell me—it was just between him and Jake. He didn't want or need the glory of a being a hero or getting a medal. Bobby knew what he had done for Jake. He said it pleased him to do it. He said God gave him the courage and the strength to do the things he did and that what he did, he did to glorify God—not himself. Bobby Hampton was always my hero, even before I learned about what he did for Jake. I saw the fear in Jake's eyes that day before I was hit. I never questioned him about it later."

"What did you say to Jake when you discovered the truth?"

"What say we take a break? Let's save that for later."

CHAPTER TEN

He's gone.

I leave Papa Tom on the front porch and go in search of something to drink for us both. Being well aware that Hannah is most likely sitting by her father's bedside, I avoid that entire wing.

Looking at the expressions on people's faces, you would think I had grown a horn right out of the top of my head. Every eye seems to follow me—whether a resident, staff or even a visitor—they all have me in their sights as, "That's the guy that was engaged in the shouting match with Hannah, the daughter of Mr. Harrison, the guy in Room 238. She was arrested in the drug bust in Tulsa last year—they're still married don't you know, she and the convicted drug king—he escaped last month—no, not him, her husband—he's the one that's been sweet-talkin' her on the porch and taking her out of town to that Mexican food place at the truck stop. Yeah, him!"

I locate a table with pitchers of tea, lemonade, and water. With a water and a lemonade, I head back to the front porch. Passing the corridor leading to Papa Tom's and Hannah's father's wing, I glance midway down the hall. The door to Mr. Harrison's room is open and light is streaming out. A staff member is exiting the room and heading toward me. She stops at the nurse's station. I should go check and see how Mr. Harrison is doing, but I decide to wait until later, maybe.

Mrs. Worsham begrudgingly opens the front door for me, my hands being full. I smile cordially and thank her, she gives me a "humph."

Papa Tom sits rocking slowly, his eyes fixed on the horizon. "Clouds are starting to build," he says. "The temperature's dropping and the top of that thundercloud is rising. Some rain would sure be nice."

A breeze races across the property like wild horses running loose and the flags flutter and pop to attention as it passes. The wind carries the sweet smell of rain.

"Maybe we should go in," I suggest to Papa Tom.

"If you don't mind, I'd like to see the rain come in. It's been a while since I've felt the rain on my face."

"Okay, but we need to be prepared to go at any moment."

"Oh, we'll get plenty of notice. The beauty of being up on this little hill is that nothing sneaks up on you—as long as you keep your eyes open."

"Have we got time for you to tell me some more about coming home after the war?"

"I suppose. Where was I?"

"Well actually, you were telling me you didn't find out about Jake and Bobby trading places until long after the war."

"That's right. We didn't speak about it much. I thought Jake was being shy, well not shy, but humble about his heroism and all. He never wanted people to make a big deal about it—acted like he hated all the attention. And Bobby, well Bobby never let the conversation get around to the war and if somebody brought it up, he'd leave the room. We all knew the war wasn't a place any of us wanted to re-visit. Lord knows I did that enough in my dreams."

"How did you discover the truth about Jake and Bobby? Who brought it up?" I take a short sip of my drink and a long look at the approaching dark clouds. Papa Tom strokes his chin and looks at the ominous sky.

"The rain will be upon us before I can finish this next part. We better head inside."

Papa Tom suggests we go to his room—his roommate, Jim, was scheduled for physical therapy this morning—and we could enjoy the peace and quiet without prying eyes, ears and noses. Several paces from his room I remember that Hannah sat in the room across the hall and the last time I looked, the door was open. I grit my teeth and steer the wheel chair from the hall directly into Papa Tom's room—no looking to the left, no hesitating, and cutting the corner as tightly as possible. I push him quickly across his room and up to the window. Spinning him around like a pirouetting ballerina, I keep my back to the hall door and sit in a chair which conveniently has its back to the hall.

"Shall we continue?" I say, putting the recorder on a night stand and switching it on. I close my eyes and listen for footsteps that might be coming from across the hall—for a voice, an angelic voice, to break the silence with an Oh, hello or a Wonderful to see you this morning. But, I don't hear the voice and if I did, I seriously doubt it would be singing those lyrics—I doubt she would be singing at all. Papa Tom gives me a quizzical look as if I'm behaving like a child. He knows I am. He knows I'm desperately trying to avoid Hannah. He smiles, taking delight in my awkwardness.

"Why don't you go see how Mr. Harrison is doing this morning?" he suggests. Now he is gloating. He has me where he wants me and his eyebrows raise in expectation of what my response will be.

"Let's just get started, okay?"

"Fine," he says. "How did I discover the truth? Well, Bobby would have never told me. That's the kind of person he was. I had gone back to college in Norman when I got home from the war and gotten my degree in engineering. Bobby enrolled in East Central University in Ada and got a degree in accounting. East Central had just opened and not only was Ada in the middle of nowhere, but no one knew Bobby—or of his war record. He was just another veteran with a pronounced limp. We kept in touch and we all got together occasionally. We never discussed the war. In 1948 Jake's dad opened the coal mine in Divine. Jake told us he thought his father won the mineral rights in a poker game.

"At first, his dad was disappointed when he discovered the land on the lease didn't have any oil or gas deposits—just coal. But, Morton Podus always made the best of what often appeared to be a bad situation. He went out and sold contracts for coal before he ever put a shovel in the ground. Jake convinced his dad to hire me as a mining engineer and Bobby as the company bookkeeper. Jake told him some story about us saving his butt at the Battle of Bastogne. We didn't much care what he had told old man Podus—we were happy to have good paying jobs and we didn't have to break our backs doing them. Your mom was just a baby when we moved to Divine. She would have been three then." Papa Tom seems to smile at the mere mention of Mom. He takes a deep breath and looks up as if to find his place again.

"Bobby Hampton died the fall of '52. It was Election Day, November. Dwight D. Eisenhower ended up defeating Adlai Stevenson. The mine shut down so everybody could go over to Beaver and vote. With the mine closed, Bobby told us he was going hunting early that morning and when the afternoon came and he didn't show up at the courthouse in Beaver like we'd planned, Jake and I went out looking for him. Late that evening we finally found him. The coroner told us his appendix had burst. Bobby had been complaining about something he ate earlier in the week that had given him a terrible stomach ache. He thought it was too many pieces of fried chicken. We could see he had tried to crawl back to his truck before he…" Papa Tom's eyes fill with tears. "Even now I can't bear the thought of him out there, all alone, dying like that. I should have gone with him but he complained I always made too much noise and he'd never get a good shot with me along. He died alone and no one…"

"Help! Oh, my God, someone help!" Hannah runs out of her father's room and heads to the nurse's station. Mrs. Martin meets her half way, the heart monitor alarm had signaled her as well. "It's Daddy," she cries.

They run together back into his room. There is a flashing yellow light in the hall above his door. Two more staff members join them.

I walk to the hall and stop in Papa Tom's doorway and stand. My heart urges me to rush to Hannah's side and put my arm around her. My head tells me to stand patiently and observe, thoughtfully and quiet. My heart is breaking because I will not obey it.

Hannah is standing at the foot of her dad's bed, both hands holding firmly to the rails. Mrs. Martin leans over Mr. Harrison with a stethoscope against his chest and a vigilant eye on the monitors. The thumping of the ventilator continues steady as before with its incessant wheezing. Lights are flashing, numbers are falling, and some seem almost constant. The lines running across the screen undulate like a calm body of water whose waves slowly subside and the rhythm of the ebb and flow calms. Everyone holds their breath.

Mrs. Martin glances toward Hannah. Pursing her lips and slowly shaking her head, she walks to Hannah and takes one of her hands from the bed rail and wraps both her hands around it. She speaks in a low voice, "He's gone, dear." One of the other women in the room comes up behind Hannah and puts her arms around her shoulder and leans against her head. I should be standing there with her.

I turn and look back to my grandfather. I envision him where Hannah's father now rests. Papa Tom sits with his eyes closed, his hands folded, and he appears to be looking to Heaven. His lips move slightly. I am sure he is talking to God.

Mrs. Martin lets go of Hannah and looks at her watch. She picks up a chart hanging from the foot of the bed, jots something, walks around to the other side of the bed and switches off the ventilator and then the monitor. The room falls silent for the first time in days. It seems strange to me that there is no sobbing, only reverent silence. She walks back to Hannah and speaks slowly and peacefully, "Go get your mother. She will want to come now. We will remove the wires and tubes and prepare him for her to visit."

Hannah nods and turns to leave and then turns back and walks to the head of the bed. She leans over and gently kisses her father. On the way out of the room, she looks up and our eyes meet.

"Let me drive you to get your mom?" I say with a sincerity I didn't know existed in me. She tilts her head slightly and stands, hesitating, and then she smiles softly.

"That would be nice," she says. She takes her purse from the floor by the foot of the bed, walks into the hall, and turns toward the front door.

I turn to Papa Tom. "I'm taking Hannah to get her mother. I'll be back shortly." He nods. I catch up with her at the front door, just in time to hold it open.

"Wait!" Ann Worsham screams as she comes running up with an umbrella. I hadn't noticed but it's raining buckets.

"Thank you," I whisper. She smiles and nods—this time there is no smirk or remark from under her breath. The entire population of the center already seems to be aware of the somber event. People's eyes are lowered as are their voices.

Hannah doesn't wait for me at the edge of the porch but walks straight to my car. I run to catch up and offer some protection from the pelting rain. As I open the passenger door for her, the cold wind heralds a mighty clap of thunder.

"I'm sorry," I whisper as I lean down with the umbrella as she slides onto the car seat. She doesn't speak. She sits solemnly in my car.

The noon whistle at the mine blows. It has been a long morning and the remainder of the day promises to be even longer. I start the car and turn the wipers on high speed. It doesn't seem appropriate to talk about the recent altercation or to make small talk about lunch or the weather.

I offer to sit in the car while she goes in to tell her mother the news. I tell her to take as much time as she needs. As she disappears into the house, I remember a book in the glove box I've wanted to finish. Of course, it's in the glove box of my car at home in Seattle. There is, however, an owner's manual for the rented Chevrolet.

The sky begins to darken and the rain falls heavier. The accompanying wind whips the rain almost horizontal to the ground. The storm moves rapidly over the top of me. In slow motion, the horizon begins clearing behind the storm, the clouds move and expose the fields of grain again to the sun in the west—I'm guessing it is the west.

"CRRAAACK!" The black sky to the east is fractured with streaks of lightning and the thunder rumbles quickly on its heels. "PLINK… PLINK…PLINK, PLINK, PLINK, PLINKETY, PLINKETY,

PLINKETY." A torrent of marble-sized hailstones begin bouncing on the car's hood in front of me. In a frightening crescendo, the culminating sounds from various sources assault my ears. The wind howls—the glass and metal surfaces of the car explode with the sounds of steel kettle drums plinking out Jamaican music, intermittent cracks of lightning crash like cymbals while bass timbale drums like thunder thump out a rhythm in the far distance. After maybe five frightening minutes, it all stops. The sunlight sweeps across the farm buildings and the house and then moves off to the right. Only fragments of clouds remain in the sky now. Birds that had taken cover now return again to the sky to find safer shelter. The fence behind the house now holds back a herd of black cows with their white faced calves. The cows, bellowing—the calves, bawling.

"Tom, Tommy!" Hannah shouts from the front porch. She stands waving frantically for me to come in the house. I roll down my window. "Come in!" she screams.

On my second step from the car I stumble into a hole recently filled with water and a mixture of hail. I begin rolling forward, my hands outstretch to break my fall—my feet desperately sprint to try and catch up. When my hands touch the ground, the sloppy earth slides away and the hail and collected rain make way for my entire body as it crashes hard and careens up to the front gate.

As I struggle to get to my feet, gripping the gate, I feel Hannah's hands grab me by my shirt collar and she struggles to lift me. She tucks her shoulder under my chest. Like a beginning roller skater I shuffle my feet, fighting to keep them under me. In a panic I reach for anything— and find Hannah's neck. We collapse together in a heap—a wet, muddy, icy mass of tangled limbs and... I hear laughter. It's coming from the front porch—from Hannah's mother. And, there's more laughter and giggling. It's coming from Hannah. And now, it's coming from me. I roll onto my back and try to extricate myself from her. She is on her hands and knees, straddled across me, her face directly over me, and her wet, muddy hair brushes across the bridge of my nose.

And then, she kisses me. Not warm and tenderly for mud and near frozen slush run up into my nose, causing me to choke. Still, it is a most delightful kiss.

"I believe your mother is watching." We both turn our heads to look and sure enough she is standing on the porch with her hands on her hips, grinning like a Cheshire cat and shaking her head in disbelief. I get to my feet and help Hannah up, being very careful this time to maintain a stable footing.

The rain has stopped but it continues dripping from the trees and the gutters still send a rush of water down the spouts and out into the yard. The small pockets of hail that remain on the grass glisten like piles of diamonds. They are melting rapidly—the warm earth will completely devour them before long.

Reaching the porch I kick off my electric orange Nikes. They are caked with mud as are the knees and backside of my good slacks—and the entire front of my shirt.

"You two wait right there—you're not coming in my house like that. I'll bring you some dry clothes." The screen door slams shut and she disappears.

I try to make eye contact with Hannah but she is looking down at our muddy feet. Water is dripping from our hands, our hair, and our clothes—creating a brown, muddy puddle on the porch. We both stand still and without speaking until her mother returns with an armful of clothes and towels. She comes out onto the porch and places her load onto the porch swing. A large pair of work boots dangles from one hand.

"I hope these will fit you," she says looking at me and setting the boots down beneath the swing.

"Thank you very much, Ma'am. They look like they'll do just fine. Do you have a garbage bag I can put my wet clothes in?"

"Yes, I'll get one." She turns and goes back in.

I grab a towel and hand it to Hannah. She looks up, smiles, and takes the towel. Her eyes are now locked on mine but she still doesn't speak. She has effectively moved the ball into my court.

"Yes, we do need to talk but I don't think just now is the time and if it's all right with you, I think we should try doing it in private." I look down at her and give her a look—and I pray she understands it—the look that says, are you okay with what just happened?

"I'm okay with that," she responds to my unspoken question. I am feeling very good about our ability to communicate now—with or without words.

"Turn your back," she says as she begins peeling off her soggy clothes and dropping them on the porch in a muddy pile. She reaches across and grabs a towel. "Back in a flash." She giggles and then I hear the screen door slam.

I pull my shirt over my head and stuff it into the large black plastic bag. My shoes go in and then I sit down on the swing, remove my socks. After scanning the porch and the windows, checking for any onlookers, I slip down my muddy slacks and stash them along with my wet socks on top of my shirt. With the towel I get what mud I can out of my hair and off my hands. There are a pair of—I'm guessing—the late Mr. Harrison's overalls, and a red plaid short-sleeved shirt. A pair of thick white socks tied in a knot remains on the swing next to me.

All I need now is a straw hat. The towel comes in handy to remove the wet muddy spots on the porch swing. As I sit down, I put it into motion. It squeaks as it moves back and forth—I outstretch my arm across its back and look out across the yard to the trees and beyond to rolling hills and the horizon and survey and consider—for only the briefest of moments—the serene life that Mr. Harrison must have led.

The screen door creaks as Hannah swings it open. "Howdy neighbor!" she bellows as she takes in my new rural look. She places her hands on her hips, leans back, smiles a huge toothy smile, and shakes her head.

"Like the new me?" I say.

"I liked the old you," she responds.

"Are you and your mom ready to go? I can move the car up on the grass a little so you won't have to walk through the mud."

"Yes, that would be nice. She will be down in a minute. Why don't you go ahead and put it up to that side of the porch, the grass is thicker there."

I nod, pick up my bag of clothes, tip toe to the car and open the trunk. Hannah stands on the porch with one arm around a column on the front porch and watches me—I suppose as I'm watching her now. She's wearing a long dark blue dress. Her hair, still wet, is in a ponytail and it hangs in a thin dark, glistening strip over the front of one shoulder. Her skin is only slightly darker than the white clapboard across the front of the house. Is it any wonder that I can't think of anything else but her?

I move the car closer to the porch steps and wait patiently. Mrs. Harrison comes down and gets into the back seat with an umbrella and a large bag. Hannah climbs in the front, removes the towel wrapped around her head and begins brushing out her hair.

By the time we arrive at Wildflower, her hair is completely dry and pulled into a pony tail. I drive up to the front walk as close to the building as I can because it is still raining softly.

"I'll be along in a minute after I park the car. Don't wait for me." Something draws me to stay behind and give them space and time to be with her father, alone. When I get inside it becomes obvious everyone is in the dining room.

I walk in and find it full of people, sitting around the tables, but there are no trays of food or drinks on the tables. Papa Tom is at the far end of the room, standing in his walker, addressing the residents and staff alike.

"…a time to embrace, and a time to refrain from embracing; A time to get, and a time to lose; a time to keep, and a time to cast away; A time to rend, and a time to sew; a time to keep silence, and a time to speak…" He looks up and across the room and I notice he sees me. He smiles. Is he happy to see me or is he astonished at my costume? Or both?

He lowers his head and continues. There is no movement, no fidgeting in the room, no coughing, and then I notice Papa Tom is not reading—he is reciting—from memory.

"He hath made everything beautiful in his time. He hath set the world in their heart, so that no man can find out the work that God maketh from the beginning to the end. I know that there is no good in them, but for a man to rejoice, and to do good in his life." He pauses, picks up a glass and takes a long swallow. Renewed, he continues a little louder with a little more emphasis than before, "Rejoice my friends. Rejoice with me. Ray Harrison did well with his life. As for you, are you ready to be offered? The time of departure is at hand. Have you fought a good fight, finished your course, and kept the faith? There is laid up for you a crown of righteousness, which the Lord, the righteous judge, shall give you at that final day." He bows his head and raises both hands above those seated, "Father, we know Ray is now seated with you at your banquet table. Bless us now as we sit here at the table before us and enjoy the bounty that you have and continue to provide us. Amen."

The staff breaks like a well-trained team from the huddle and moves quickly to their positions to bring in the luncheon meal. You would expect there would be a sadness lying heavy on the residents but the room erupts with lively good-hearted chatter. There seems to be a celebration in their voice rather than a dirge. I move quickly to Papa Tom's side—the sooner I am seated and my uncommon attire shrinks from view—the less I will have to endure the embarrassment of this outfit. I pull up a chair next to him and take his hand.

"That was some sermon, preacher. I've never been at a happy funeral before."

"Tommy Boy, when a godly man leaves to go home to his Maker, especially when he has made such good use of his life on earth and has brought so much joy to others and faithfully glorified his Heavenly Father—it is cause for celebration, not tears." He looks me up and down. He always seems to be smiling. He nods his head in apparent approval of my outfit.

"I like your new duds," he says.

"It's a long story. Well, maybe not a long story but it's a funny story."

"Well, let me hear it. I'm always interested in hearing a funny story."

CHAPTER ELEVEN
Finally—the secret revealed.

I push Papa Tom down the hall to the reception area. Most people remain in the dining area, visiting and commenting on Papa Tom's impromptu memorial service. Many search for and find my grandfather to compliment him on how inspiring his message was. I discover gatherings such as these have become commonplace since Papa Tom became a resident of Wildflower. Seems he determined to not only prepare a message for those whose passing is imminent but makes a concerted effort to schedule quality time with them during their final days. He comforts them as well as their families. He never permits the dying to depart without assuring them of their final destination or at least giving them the opportunity to choose. I understand since he came here not one has opted for the alternate destinationl. I also discover that Wildflower is a primary hospice for those in the county who have no appropriate place to live out their remaining time. As suspected, this service is provided by the Buchanan Foundation to those who do not have insurance or their families do not have the resources.

After a short while, his audience disperses and returns to their prescribed duties, or in the case of the residents, their daily routines.

It amazes me how upbeat everyone is and how undisturbed they are about the recent death of one of their own. I am reminded of a certain television special on the wildlife of Central Africa featuring the taking of antelopes by lions. Once the death hunt ended, the antelopes immediately returned to grazing and continuing their lives—their young frolicking and their tails swishing back and forth as though no sadness, no ending of life is present. I know, in the case of the antelopes, they do not dwell on the memory of the tragedy, but these people are well aware of the memory of the day—but choose to dwell on the promise of a new, everlasting life. I know that because long ago Papa Tom taught it to me.

We move to a quiet alcove. Once alone, I share my tumble in the chilling mire of hail and mud. Papa Tom embarrasses me with his boisterous chuckling.

"It didn't seem that funny when it was happening. Although, Hannah's mother was bent over laughing at the site of us rolling in the mud." I look around nervously, trying to avoid drawing attention to myself and my new duds. "I have become a real topic of interest around here—what with my display of bad manners in here yesterday and now my Farmer Brown costume."

"Your costume? Those bright orange tennis shoes of yours made you look like a Ringling Brother's clown. Those T-shirts with the crayon-colored stripes might be appropriate for school kids. What you're wearing now is typical dress around here—you look like somebody who actually works for a living, somebody who builds things, grows something… Costume? Humph." He shakes his head.

"Well, if you don't like the way I dress, just say so." I snap.

"I just did. Didn't I?" He snaps back. And then, he does what I truly love about him—he smiles. He smiles with his whole face. His eyes,

119

his mouth, his cheeks form a smile that is truly genuine, forgiving, and most of all, says I still love you—no matter what you do or how stupid and immature you act. God, I love this man!

Hannah walks up behind him, leans down and grabs him around his head as though Papa Tom was a huge teddy bear.

"Hello, my dear. How are you doing? And, how's your mom?" he adds.

"Mom's fine. She's been expecting this for some time. She told me God prepared her for today—told her to be strong—He was bringing peace to Dad and to her as well. I only wish I was doing as well. I wasn't ready. I prayed every day that Daddy would get better, sit up, look me in the eye, and smile."

"Your prayers are answered. He is better—he's at peace, and he's smiling. Is there anything—anything at all—that Tommy and I can do for you?" Papa Tom always seems to know what to say—and when to say it.

"No, thank you. Mom and I are going to the funeral home in Beaver and make the necessary arrangements."

"Would you like me to drive you?" I offer.

"No, our truck is here. We're going to run back to the house and get Dad's good suit and I think Mom and I need some time alone to just sit and talk. And, I've got to make some phone calls. I'll get back to you later this evening." She smiles, touches my hand tenderly and turns to leave. "Oh, and Mom said you can keep the clothes. She said you look real handsome in them."

"Tell her thank you for me. I'll wait to hear from you."

"Bye," she says. And something amazing happens as she leaves—as she walks back to the entrance of the dining room, all those who can, stand up and take her hand or give her a warm embrace and whisper their condolences. Yesterday, they barely acknowledged her presence.

"Death brings out the best in some people," Papa Tom remarks when he sees the look of astonishment on my face. "Especially this crowd. Everybody wants to have a clear conscience when they face their maker." He strains to roll himself back from the table.

"Where're you headed?" I say.

"I've got a domino game. Wanna play?"

"No, but I'll be happy to sit and watch... and maybe learn something."

"You just might. But no quarter-backing from the bench."

"I'll be quiet—at least about the game."

"Okay then. Let's go to John Henderson's room. Grab a piece of cake from the cart, will you? It improves my chances if he's busy eating while we're playing."

"Why's that?"

"Cause he's only got the one hand. If he's busy stuffin' his face, he can't be slappin' down count."

As we roll into John's room, he looks up from his electric recliner—a card table sets in front of him. "Shuffle them bones," Papa Tom barks jokingly. With his one huge hand, John deftly swirls a table top full of face-down dominoes. He stops and then dives down into the mass of faceless plastic, plucking one, flipping it, and slapping it down hard on the table. It's a three-one. "Pfff," he drones.

Papa Tom rolls up to the table, waves his hand over the table and, as if using magical powers, descends on a random domino and rolls it over, displaying a six-one. The exposed dominos are turned back over and John continues swirling the tiles, the hard plastic pieces clicking like a roller skate speeding across a cracked sidewalk.

121

Papa Tom draws seven tiles almost before John can remove his hand. John's huge hand descends back on the table and scoops up his lot of dominoes, drawing them close, and flipping them on edge to face him.

Papa Tom leads out with a double-five. "Ten," he claims and marks his score on a cribbage board. This game is scheduled every week and John had been sitting patiently, prepared for the moment Papa Tom would arrive. Everything is scheduled—the time for the sun to rise, the morning meds dispensed, and the meals—prepared—served—and consumed. And, dominoes in John's room on this day, at this time. Woe to him that alters the schedule.

There is less talk than I might have expected. There is the repeated slapping of tiles on the card table and the calling out of count—when it is scored. There are the occasional hoorays of achievement, sighs of exasperation, and an odd fist pounded in regret. But, there is no talk of the weather, random chat about politics, or anything that might pass for pleasant conversation. Any need I might have for communication is inconsequential. I find myself nodding off, interrupted only by the plopping of plastic tiles.

John wins the final game with a thunderous pounding of his final domino while Papa Tom has acquired most of the bones in the bone yard. John's victory is overwhelming, as usual. He is somewhat less than a gracious winner but no matter to my grandfather.

"All right, Tommy Boy, let's take a look outside and see if we can find a dry, hospitable place on the porch to spend the rest of the afternoon."

"I'm game, but first I need to use the facilities. Do you...?" Papa Tom lifts the blanket over his legs and exposes a catheter bag hung from the side rail of his chair.

"Oh, I didn't know…" I say discreetly. "That wasn't there yesterday, was it?"

"No, it's a new acquisition. I thought I'd try it out and see how I like it. Saves a lot of time, you know. Of course, it slows down my tennis game a tad."

I get him to the front door, and make a quick pit stop. When I return, I open the front door and peer out. The storm has disappeared. The sky is now dotted with a few puffy clouds but the dark ones are removed to the far horizon and the light breeze returns warm. Either the chairs have been wiped dry or what rain there was has already evaporated.

"Let's go," I say and I swing the door wide and stick the front of his chair out to prevent it from closing.

"Tommy," he says, "There is a button on the door jamb you can push that automatically opens the door."

"Oh, I see. Why hasn't anyone pointed that out to me before?"

"Because most people would rather take the opportunity to hold the door open for you. There is a wonderful attitude of helping people around here. People like to be needed—they like to think what they do is important, appreciated. After all, if you use the button to open the door, who are you going to thank afterwards?"

"You've got a point."

We head down to our usual spot and I park him next to his usual rocker. I go to his side to help him up and he says, "Not this time, Tommy. I think it's best if I just stay in my chair."

Realizing my recorder and notepad are in my car, I excuse myself to retrieve them. He stops me. "Let me just talk and you just listen this time. I don't think you'll have any trouble remembering what I have to tell you."

I submit to his wishes and sit in the rocker facing him, fold my hands in my lap, and lean toward him.

"Bobby's appendix burst on Election Day, 1952. A month later, in December, Ike headed for Korea even before he took the oath of office. He oversaw an exchange of POWs. The Korean war was finally drawing to a close. The local VFW Post put together a party and dinner honoring local boys who had served in WWI, WWII and Korea. There weren't but about 15 of us in all, representing various services and war efforts. By far the most decorated individual we had was Jake Podus, and we didn't really have him—he lived in Oklahoma City. But, since his daddy's coal mine was the largest employer in town, Jake was sent a special invitation to attend. He was a great speaker—had all that experience with the War Bond drives and all. The *Alva-Courier* sent a reporter and a photographer.

"It was quite a spectacle, the high school band made an appearance and the ROTC Honor Guard from the Beaver High School sent an honor guard to present the colors. Jake hadn't been able to attend Bobby's funeral so this was the first time he and I had an opportunity to get together since Bobby died. I brought a photo of Bobby. All three of us were standing in front of a tank just outside of Bastogne. One of the honorees there served in the infantry in France and knew about Bobby's court martial. He raised nine kinds of hell about his name even being spoken at the awards banquet. He spit on the picture and called Bobby a coward—said if he had been there, he would have personally kicked his butt all the way back to Germany. When we told him Bobby had died the month before, he grunted, 'Good riddance.' It was a sickening outburst. Bobby was the closest thing I'd ever had to a real brother. But Jake, Jake lost it. He gave away at least forty pounds to this guy. It took three men to pull Jake off of him, and keep him from killing him right there in front of the high school band and half the town."

"From everything you've told me about Jake, he didn't seem like a guy that would go off like that."

"That's when I found out the truth of what really happened that day during the war." Papa Tom looked around to see if we were alone on the porch. "I've never told this to another living soul, Tommy. When the three guys escorted Jake out of the VFW Hall, I went out to talk to him and try to calm him down. I found him sitting on the curb, bawling like a baby. Jake said he was the one that fellow ought to be cursing, not Bobby. When I asked him what he was talking about, Jake broke away from me, jumped up, and took off running down the street."

Papa Tom stops and looks into my face. He seems to be contemplating something, considering something—maybe whether he wants to continue. I am beginning to understand the gravity of what he is telling me and the burden it must have been on him to keep this secret for so many years.

"We can stop here," I say. "Maybe it would be better if we continue later. Are you struggling with whether you should tell me the rest of the story? Would you rather we never discuss it again."

"Tommy Boy, this... this is what I promised you years ago— promised I would tell you someday. Well, that someday is today— it's now." Papa Tom's eyes seemed to be looking for a place to focus. He draws a breath and I wait for him to blurt something out. He fidgets a little and then he exhales loudly. He seems to be spent. He swallows. Fidgets. Exhales again.

"Can I get you something? A drink?" I lean closer and take his hand. He holds up a finger and closes his eyes as if summoning the courage to jump...

"I ran after Jake and caught up to him just as he scaled the chain link fence surrounding the Divine water tower. He looked into my eyes from the other side of the fence. And then, he raced to the tower. I yelled for him to stop but he hopped up onto a support brace at one of the main legs. He grabbed a guide wire and walked up the diagonal brace to the next leg. The lower ten feet of the ladder was folded up and locked to prevent unauthorized people from climbing up to the top, but Jake was now high enough on the cross beam to reach the ladder. Once on the ladder he moved hand over hand up to the catwalk around the tank. I pleaded with him to stop. He never slowed, never turned, or acknowledged that he even heard me. Once at the top, he walked along the catwalk until he got to the side facing Main Street. He stood for a minute, feet apart, looking first off to the edge of town and then he looked down. The whole time I had been yelling at him. I'm not sure if he could hear me. After a moment he sat down and dangled his feet over the side of the narrow walkway, his head rested on the middle hand rail."

"Was anyone else around?" I asked. He shook his head.

"No, at that time no one else in town knew Jake was on the tower. I thought about running for help but I was afraid if I left, he might do something crazy. So, I jumped the fence and following Jake's path, I got to the ladder and slowly made my way up to the top. He seemed startled when I walked around the catwalk to where he was sitting. I remembered seeing that look in his eyes before—in the forest outside Bastogne. He was disconnected with the reality of where he was. I knew he was prepared to take the ball out of bounds rather than carry it downfield. I didn't know what to say. I wasn't sure what had gone on between him and the veteran he attacked inside the VFW. I took another step toward him—he jumped to his feet, warned me to stop, and not to come any further. I sat down—about five or six feet from him. He was breathing very hard, as was I. It was a hard climb and we had both run the three to four hundred yards from the VFW. He wasn't just breathing hard, he was sobbing. I asked him what I could do for him.

"He told me what had really happened the day—after I got wounded. After the grenade exploded, he looked up, my helmet was gone, and so was the top of my head or so it appeared. He thought I was dead. He cut and ran—deserted, left his buddies dying and unprotected with the enemy bearing down on us. He threw away his rifle and raced like a frightened rabbit for as long and as far as he could. He was headed for the English Channel and, if need be, he would become the first American to swim it. He ran headlong into Bobby. He told me how Bobby forced him to come back and look for me even though he assured Bobby I was dead. Bobby told him he wasn't going home without me. Jake revealed how Bobby convinced a sergeant it was him who had deserted his comrades on the field of battle and that it was Jake who hunted him down and brought him back. When Bobby was being called a coward and deserter at the ceremony—he lost it. After living a lie for all those years he broke.

Jake was devastated by Bobby's death—that he didn't make the funeral, then all the attention they lavished on him at the VFW ceremony, and, finally, all the years he had lived as a hero while Bobby had been branded a coward. 'All for what?' he screamed, 'so my dad could parade me around as a hero. You tell them,' he told me. 'You tell them that Bobby was the hero and I was a fraud.' Then Jake stood up and lifted one leg over the rail. 'Don't come any closer,' he said as I reached for him. I tried to tell him no one would believe my story, that if he wanted to make Bobby out to be a hero, he would have to go down and tell the truth, himself."

"How did that work out?" I said.

"Well as far as keeping Jake from going over the edge right then, it worked out pretty well. Jake began screaming at the top of his lungs to get somebody, anybody, to hear him. Before long he had acquired quite a crowd. His dad, Morton Podus, was among them. Now that he had an audience, he proceeded to spill his guts and cleanse his soul. But, after Jake screamed his story to half the VFW crowd and his father, he determined to literally spill his guts at the base of the water tower."

"He jumped," I gasp.

"Almost. Like I said, I recognized that gotta-run-outta-bounds look and I tackled him. He fell back, hitting his head against the water tower and, well, it kind of gave him a slight concussion. It took three firemen to lower him down from up there. Several days in a hospital with restraints and then two months of therapy, and Jake appeared as good as new."

"What happened to him?"

Jake didn't realize that way up there on the water tower people below couldn't make out what he was yelling about. Everyone thought it was battle fatigue and that he just snapped. Later, I got credit for saving his life. And, that is why people thought 'under the circumstances, Morton Podus owes Tom Howard for saving his son's life.' After he quit working for his father, Jake moved to Chicago and opened a pizza joint. The pizza joint became a pizza chain and *Hampton's New York Style Pizza* became a household name."

"You and Jake kept in touch?"

"No, not so much. I read about him in a business magazine once. I did read he died several years ago. A lawyer from Chicago contacted me and said Jake had left me some money in his will."

"Really!"

"Before you get all excited, I've already given the money away. He established a football scholarship fund at the University of Oklahoma in Bobby's name. I would have thought since you interviewed old man Podus for a book that he would have told you a little something about his son."

"No, I asked him about his family. Mr. Podus said he was an orphan from New York and that he never had any children. After you saved his son's life, you would have thought he would have been more diligent in rescuing you from the mine collapse."

"Like I told you before, Tommy—I never figured Mr. Podus owed me anything. Of course, back then folks around here thought he owed me for keeping Jake from jumping. But, I saved Jake's life because it needed saving—I didn't do it for old man Podus."

Papa Tom appears spent after completing his tale. He asks I return him to his room, telling me I would be on my own for dinner tonight. I leave him by the side of his bed in his wheel chair. He waves me on as though he is shooing away a stray animal.

"Not to worry, Tommy Boy. They will be bringing my supper shortly. You run along."

CHAPTER TWELVE
I'm put in Time Out.

On the way to my room, I grab a burger to go. With the evening news as my dinner companion, I wolf down dinner from a DQ bag and call Mom.

Picking my words carefully, I bring her up to date. "He looks and sounds fine but I've noticed some dramatic changes. He has a catheter now. He's not walking—even with a walker. He stays in his wheelchair all the time, whenever he's not in bed."

"I know, dear. We knew it would progress to this eventually. Have you talked to him about it?"

"No, there has been a lot going on and I just noticed most of the stuff today. Wait! What do you mean you know?"

"You don't need to be afraid to discuss it with him, dear. He calls me nearly every day. In fact, since you've been there, he calls me every night to tell me how you're doing and what you're up to. By the way, how are you and the Harrison girl getting along?"

"Mom! Is there anything you don't know?"

"I hope not, Tommy. Moms have a need to know everything about their children. You haven't called me once to let me know how you're doing."

"Fine—really. The Harrison girl, Hannah, is…has, uh…"

"That's what I was afraid of. Your grandpa says you are quite smitten with her—and evidently the feeling is mutual."

"Well, that depends on what time of day it is. We've had our ups and downs. Everything has been moving really fast. Shoot, I've only known her… what's today?"

"Don't you think you better slow things down a little?"

"The days here aren't like the days in Seattle. I'm accustomed to high speed internet, high volume traffic, fast food, and fast… well, you name it. Here, everything seems to be happening in slow motion."

"How's your book coming? You are working on it, aren't you?"

"That's the only thing moving right along. I planned on being here two weeks and Papa Tom and I are all but finished. I've already got it—the whole story, the big secret. And, it's going to make a great story. I've just got to research a few facts and get a little more history on some people, but I now know all the gory details."

"So, are you going back home soon?"

"Don't know. It depends on… well there are a few things to still work out here."

"Like what?"

"Well, if you must know." I make a bad choice to continue. "There is a little question about Hannah's husband, or ex-husband. I don't know…uh… well, I'm not sure which it is, actually."

"What?"

"And, I don't know when the funeral is going to be."

"My father's funeral?" Mom gasps.

So much for picking my words carefully. "No, Hannah's father. He passed away today."

"I'm so sorry to hear that, Tommy."

"Did I tell you Hannah lives and works in Portland? That's just a little ways from Seattle."

"I know where Portland is." She seems exasperated with me.

"She will be going back after the funeral."

"Tommy, listen to me. You need to stop and clear your head about this girl. Right now your grandfather and your book are your priorities. Your grandfather's disease is progressing faster than we anticipated. Your dad and I will make plans to come out there soon. I want you to stay until we get there. No sense you going all the way back to Seattle and then having to come back for a funeral."

"How can you talk so nonchalantly about his dying?"

"We've known this was going to happen for some time, Tommy. Your grandfather has been preparing me."

"Well, you should have let me know sooner."

"I'm sorry, Tommy. I should have…

"Listen, Mom. Let's talk some more tomorrow. I'm expecting a call. Tomorrow morning, if Papa Tom's busy schedule will permit, I need to sit down with him and have a talk about his condition. Have you talked with him today?"

"No, he usually calls me around 10:30, my time."

"Well, tell him you talked to me tonight and that I'm concerned about his condition and that he should tell me tomorrow when he sees me. That way, I won't have to bring it up."

"Tommy, you never were good about dealing with the tough stuff."

"I need this from you. Please help me get past this. Help me deal with him and his condition. I can deal with Hannah, her dad's funeral, and her husband but, not with grandpa's dying. A little help on your part would be nice."

"Fine. But, when your father and I come down there, it will be to prepare for a funeral—not a wedding. Wait a minute... did you say her husband? Never mind. We are not coming for a wedding. Do you understand?"

I undress and hang up my new wardrobe. With half of my favorite things to wear still in a trash bag on Hannah's porch, my clothing choices are limited. I take a quick shower, leaving the bathroom door open in case she calls. Still wet, I lay on the bed in front of the TV. I wait for her call…and sleep.

My phone rings and I nearly fall off the bed reaching for it. "Hello?"

"Hi, Tommy."

"How are you? Back from the funeral home?"

"Yes, we're home now. I can't talk long. I still have phone calls to make and I should spend some time with Mom. She doesn't want to be alone in the house. I think she has been hoping Dad would walk in any minute. Now that she's seen him… Well, I think reality has sunk in."

"I certainly understand. But, I want you to know that I'm here if you need anything—anything at all."

"Thank you."

"I do have a book I need to work on."

"Good, because I need to take the day tomorrow to be with Mom, get the house child-proofed for my sister's kids, go through some papers and, well, just sit and hold Mom's hand and be here for her."

"Okay. The day after tomorrow?" I say.

"Let's get away—just you and me—alone, okay?" She nods.

"Sounds wonderful. What time does your day start?"

"It starts with the chickens."

"Huh?"

133

"Here on the farm—the day starts when the roosters start crowing—about five-fifteen, five-thirty."

"I'll be there! What can I bring?"

"You don't need to bring anything. In fact, I will pick you up at six at the Lodge. Have a good night, Tommy. I look forward to spending the day, the whole day, with you."

"Me, too. Good night, Hannah." I put my phone on the night stand and reach for the TV remote. Tomorrow I write.

Before I land on a suitable channel the phone rings again.

"Tommy, this is your grandfather."

"Yes sir?"

"Our church service begins at nine. Breakfast at eight. Sunrise at six-fifty-three. See you then, Tommy Boy. It promises to be a beautiful day." And then, he hangs-up.

CHAPTER THIRTEEN
Up with the roosters.

Yesterday I arrived late for breakfast with Papa Tom. He was thrilled to see me and made no mention of my late arrival. He said he thought it was time he told me his prognosis—according to Dr. Watson, reminding me that God also knew his prognosis and although he considered Dr. Jim a great physician, no man knows the time or the hour; all the days ordained for him are written in God's book.

The church service at Wildflower was very uplifting. Why wouldn't it be? My grandfather gave a very inspirational message. Then, the choir comprised of several staff members and a handful of residents sang a special hymn. All but one sang on key and in harmony, but no one seemed to notice or care.

I needed that day of rest to ground me—and awaken the Spirit in me. I wasn't even sure if He was still there.

At three o'clock, Monday morning, I sit straight up in bed. It's four o'clock in the morning in Oklahoma, but it's two o'clock in Seattle. My body and mind are in Seattle and they both want to go back to sleep. I'm only a week away from experiencing the sun rise off Puget

Sound and every mid-morning facing a light rain—Starbucks—the Seattle Times—smoked salmon on an onion bagel with cream cheese—flipping between KOMO and CNN. I still get goose bumps when I see Dad's rugged face and frosty white hair at the news desk in Atlanta. I email him immediately and write how wise he looks—so much more intelligent and trustworthy than that old Walter Cronkite ever was.

I can't dally. I use a dirty sock to try and create the semblance of a shine on her daddy's work boots. The motel iron and ironing board allow me to put a crease in the sleeves of his plaid work shirt but I don't even try to put an edge to the legs of his overalls. My Sonics' ball cap seems a little out of place here but at least it will keep the sun off my forehead. All I need now is a red bandana. I really need to do some laundry.

A quiet tapping comes from my front door. Opening it I discover a ray of sunshine. The real sun hasn't even thought of making an appearance yet but here is Hannah looking radiant in her faded blue bib overalls, a bright yellow T-shirt and a blue denim work shirt over that—its sleeves rolled up. Her pants legs are cuffed halfway up her calves. I never noticed how short she is. I suppose it is the first time she hasn't worn heels.

"Are you ready?" she says in an excited but quiet voice, I suppose not wanting to wake anyone.

"Absolutely! I was born ready." I grab my keys and cap and put my hand on the small of her back, guiding her to her truck. Around to the driver's side and I open her door—as if I have done it every day of my life.

"Why, thank you, kind sir," she says as she climbs up on the running board and steps into the cab.

I quickly walk around to the other side and bounce into the seat. "What's the plan?"

"Have you got a picture of yourself?" she says.

"On me?"

"Yes, on you."

"Just my license."

"Well, let me have it."

"Is this a ploy to assure I don't skip out on you today?"

"No." She takes my picture and pulls down the visor in front of her. She slips it under a clip. Then, she pulls my visor down, and clipped to the back of it is a picture of her. She must have been about eighteen or nineteen when it was taken. "There you go. By the end of today, I want you to know everything there is to know about that girl, and I want to know everything there is to know about…" she scrunches up her nose and scrutinizes my license, "Tommy Lee Townsend? What is that? That a name of a cartoon character, or maybe somebody in a Mark Twain story or Tennessee Williams play?"

"Only my mother calls me that. You, on the other hand, haven't earned the right to call me that. You can call me Tommy, if you like."

"I like."

She backs out of the Antelope Lodge and onto Main Street. Few lights are on in town, one flashing yellow traffic light down the block, and a single red blinking light on a tower perched on top of the water tower. *That's the water tower.*

"Where are we headed?" I ask with as much excitement as I can muster for—let's see—five-twenty-two in the morning.

"I want this to be a special day we'll both remember for a long, long time. And, I want to start if off right. There's a place, not far from here, where we can see the sun come up long before anyone else in town."

"Is there a Starbucks on the way?"

She reaches over to the center console, grabs the arm rest and swings it up. "Pull out the thermos and those two cups."

"What a wonderful way to start the day." God, I wish I could see the smile on my face right now. I look up next to Hannah's picture on my visor and there it is—a mirror with an image of me—with a big grin.

When we get to the flashing yellow light, she turns left down an alley. She pulls into a small parking lot and stops the truck. Hannah leans across the center console, pops open the glove compartment, reaches inside, and pulls out a strange tool I'm unfamiliar with. It looks like a large pair of pliers, but on one side is a hammer head, on the other something that looks like a climber's pick. "What in the world is that?" I ask.

"It's a multipurpose tool, used primarily for building or repairing fences."

"Are we going to mend a fence today?"

"Well, in a way, I hope. But, first we are going to take one down. Come on, follow me."

"What about the coffee?"

"Unfasten the strap on the thermos, then run it through the handles on the two coffee cups, then re-buckle the strap and throw it over your shoulder." I cock my head and give her a questioning look.

"Just do it and come on," she says as she hurries around to my side of the truck, shoving the fence tool into the cloth loop on her overalls. "Be quiet and follow me. Don't let anyone see you."

"It's five-thirty in the morning, who's going to see us?"

"You'd be surprised." She runs like a mouse darting behind furniture. She crouches and takes four or five quick steps and then leans against a wall. She almost appears to be sniffing the air. She looks around and scampers through a small pathway between two buildings that empty out onto Main Street. She stops and looks up and down the street. It's dark. Quiet. She gives me the sign a squad leader gives to his troops to move out, and we move out, now trotting across Main Street and into another narrow path between two store fronts. She turns and puts her finger to her lips to prevent me from asking any dumb questions I suppose—like *where're we going?* My eyes widen and I give her my best where are we going look accompanied by an elaborate shoulder shrug and I throw up both hands as if surrendering. My team always won at charades. Hannah gives me another follow me signal and we run across a vacant lot lined with empty barrels and several rusty, tireless trucks.

We reach a chain link fence. It must be at least eight feet high and there are three strands of barbed wire on top of that, leaning out at an angle as a definite deterrent to anyone who might consider climbing it. She kneels down at a corner post and takes her strange-looking tool from the loop at her waist. She looks around and with a couple of quick moves—she and her tool have created a gap in the fence. She slips easily through and then turns and extends a hand to me.

"I can get through on my own," I say with absolute certainty.

"Not with the thermos and those dangling cups strapped around your shoulder." She motions me to hand the coffee service over.

What could possibly be behind this fence that is so special? "I thought we were headed to see a spectacular sunrise?" I ask.

She stands, feet apart. One hand holding the thermos and dangling, clanking coffee cups—her other hand points directly up to the sky. I look up. There it is, looming directly above us, the Divine water tower. From here it looks like the biggest and tallest structure I have ever seen, rivaling the Seattle Space Needle.

"Come on," she whispers and we creep like terrorists to the foot of one of the legs. "Follow me, and I don't think I need to tell you this, but, be careful." She attacks the steel braces and girders like she is scaling the Matterhorn and I follow in blind obedience. Finally we reach the ladder and from here on it's hand over hand—a lot of hand over hand.

It's still dark and the dark hides the danger. There is a faint impression of a horizon, a place where land and sky get acquainted. Fortunately I run out of ladder rungs before I run out of breath and we step out onto the walkway around the waist of this giant steel sphere. There is a sturdy handrail and the walkway is just wide enough for one person to walk around the tank, keeping one hand on the rail and the other on the steel wall. I am standing next to the "V" in Divine. The single red painted letter is nearly twice my height. I follow her around to just past the "D" and we sit down, dangling our legs above the town, my hands tightly gripping the hand rail and my back up against the security of the tank, waiting on the sun to make its grand appearance.

She unslings the thermos, sets the coffee mugs between us and pours. Faint whiffs of steam rise from the mugs and the bitter aroma of black coffee swirls up and then an imperceptible breeze catches it and sends it off. She grasps her mug with both hands and leans her body into me, sipping her coffee and giving a nod to what must be the eastern sky and then she whispers, "It will come up there. It will signal a new day, a new beginning. The new will come—the old has passed away."

I think of her dad and wonder if that is what she meant. She recognizes my quizzical look, "Not just my dad, silly. Our old past— past lives, past mistakes, past history—that's all gone. We're starting new with the new day that's coming." Again, she nods to the horizon. I think now I understand what she means.

Looking to the horizon, I see a ribbon of gold and pink streaming across the top edge of the land. The ribbon of sunlight grows wider and wider—and brighter.

"Wait for it… wait for it." She takes one hand from her cup and, searching, she finds my free hand. She takes it, interlacing our fingers and she squeezes it hard—I can feel a pulse throbbing. Is it mine or hers?

"There it is!" she squeals. The sun peaks over the edge of the dark earth.

I look at her and she is looking into my eyes. Fumbling to find a place to put down my coffee, I begin, "Hi, Tommy Lee Townsend, I'm Hannah Elizabeth Harrison Cline. I am so very glad to meet you and… I look forward today to getting to know you."

"Me too," I say—especially that Cline part.

"Feel that? Feel the warmth of the air? Feel it heating up? Now, close your eyes."

Reluctantly I close my eyes and try to relax. Not easy when you're sitting on a narrow walkway on the highest point for miles. Not easy when you've just broken into a municipal facility—and there was a "No Trespassing" and a "Keep Out" sign affixed to the fence we pushed aside. And the NFL's number one draft pick is still out there— somewhere— keeping an eye on me.

My eyes are still closed and I feel a warm breath envelope my face. Then, she kisses me. It is not the sun's warmth on my face, but hers. I draw in a long breath, and open my eyes to see if this is real. It is. She is. The kiss is.

141

I put my arm around her and pull her closer—not wanting to risk this kiss coming to an early end. What a way to start the day.

When the kiss comes to its conclusion, the sun is fully present and becomes our witness. Long shadows are forming and defining the structures, separating trees from sky, sidewalks from buildings. Hints of color appear in the landscape that only minutes before was washed with gray hues of various degrees.

Hannah starts, "This is how I want our relationship to begin. This is the exact place I want it to begin. I want everything to be out in the light of day. No secrets, no unspoken words, thoughts, or fears." She looks up at me. "I think I..." She hesitates. "I think I like you a lot, Tommy Townsend." She looks sternly, straight into my eyes and asks, "Is that all right with you?"

"Absolutely. Who do you want to start?" There are reservations in my mind but not in my heart.

"I'll start," Hannah says. "I guess I've got the most to come clean about." She picks up her coffee, blows across the top—which is ridiculous because the mugs have a snap-on top with a small sipping hole. I know and she knows it is just a stall tactic, a nervous habit. She pulls her legs back from the edge and crosses them beneath her. Leaning back against the cold metal of the tank, she folds her arms across her knees. Her body language screams defensive posture and I want to point it out to her, but I decide that's probably not a good idea. I try to remain patient. I want to yell at her, *Come clean!* But, I smile, sitting uncomfortably still, and wait for her to begin.

"I grew up here in Divine. You already know I have one younger brother and one older sister. Until I was eighteen, the only other state I had even been to was Kansas. The farthest I ever traveled was to Oklahoma City and I only went there three times. Except for four or

142

five church camps and a couple of sleep-overs, I never slept in any bed except mine. I was fifteen the first time I kissed a boy. I was eighteen the first time I kissed a boy with my eyes closed. And I don't think I opened my eyes again until I had been married for almost a year—I was twenty-five then. In case you haven't noticed, Divine is a very small town. There are more places to pray on Sundays than there are places to eat. There are no movie theaters, and before I left for college, I had never watched a TV that had more than seven channels. The closest place to renting a movie is forty miles and we didn't own a player anyway. I didn't get a driver's license until I was twenty-two. I still have never owned my own car. I'm smart—really smart. I read a lot—I've never read one of your books, though. Sorry about that. The Buchanan family gave me a scholarship to the University of Oklahoma—full scholarship, housing and everything." She pauses and takes in a deep breath of courage.

She continues. "I always wanted to be a doctor, a pediatrician. The doctors I work for in Portland are a pediatric group. The year before I started medical school, we had a really bad drought here and my daddy lost his entire crop. He had to sell off most of the cattle to make the payments on the farm equipment and feed the few cattle we kept. I found out that the Buchanans, through your grandfather, helped my dad out that year, along with a lot of other farmers around here. Too proud to go back to them to ask for help with medical school, I took a job at night. I got behind with my medical studies and I was cut from the program. I transferred to a medical school in Tulsa to get my P.A.'s license. That's where I met Woody. I take it you've heard about Woody?"

"Sorry to say, a number of people around here have tried to warn me about you and Mr. Cline. I would have preferred hearing it from you."

"I know. We seemed to get off to such a fast start and before I knew it—well, we were just too far down that road it seemed. Now, I want to go back and start over. I want to cover all that ground with you, leaving no stone unturned... or un-*thrown*. No more lies."

I start to speak and she stops me cold with her hand going up to my mouth. She shakes her head. I yield the floor.

"Please let me finish while I've got the nerve. I never dated much—outside of school dances and church socials. Tommy..." She moves her hand from my lips and cups it around the back of my neck, stroking my ear with her thumb. "You're one of only a handful, a very small handful, of boys...uh, men, I have ever kissed." She lowers her eyes and seems almost embarrassed. "I met Woody at a sandwich shop next to the campus in Tulsa. I had never had any boy flirt with me before or pay attention to me. The first time we spoke, he said he had been watching me on campus. I just assumed he was a student. I was working at a telemarketing company at night handling customer complaints for a catalog store. I also worked the early drop-off shift at a daycare center in the mornings from 6:00 until 8:30 AM. The rest of the time I was in class. I didn't have any friends—didn't have time to hang out with any classmates. Woody was the first person I sat down and enjoyed a meal with since I moved there. It just seemed whenever I had a free moment, he was there. He always made me laugh. At first he asked me lots of questions about myself and my family. I felt secure with him. I thought I was crazy in love with him. And, I thought he loved me. But, Woody never loved me. He isn't capable of love. He used me." Hannah begins to fight back tears.

"I'm sorry. It wasn't...

"It wasn't what? It wasn't my fault? I'm not blind, Tommy. I'm not stupid. I needed to be needed. It wasn't that Woody had something special I needed. I had so much love to give. I just wanted to give it to someone. Mom had my dad. They had each other. My older sister never wanted a younger sister. She had her friends, and then she had her boyfriends, then her husband, now her kids. My little brother needed me—until he was potty trained. He's a soldier now, he doesn't need me. My father doesn't need me anymore." There's no fighting back tears now. They're here. I reach for her but she pulls back and wraps herself tighter in her own arms, wiping her eyes with her sleeve.

"I'm sorry, Tommy. Let me finish. Please."

"Go ahead." I back away and start to cross my arms and then, I reconsider the inappropriate display of defensive body language. I guess I did learn something in those psychology classes.

"I needed to be needed. I realize that now. Of course, a year of counseling and therapy helped open my eyes. I thought I could change Woody. I knew he was a bad boy. But I thought I could fix him. I took him home to meet my parents—not so they would approve of him but so they could see he was someone who needed me and that I could meet those needs.

"Daddy hated Woody straight off. It took Mom a couple of weeks to get where she really disliked him. So, then I married him to really screw things up. Woody thought he was marrying into a rich, wealthy family. He thought my father was a cattle baron, a rich oil tycoon. By the time he discovered the truth, it was too late. We had eloped to Las Vegas. And, we had done it all on my credit card. It turned out Woody hadn't even graduated from high school. He didn't have a steady job. The only thing he had was a drug habit. He needed drugs more than he needed me. And, what he most needed me for—money—I didn't have."

I start to speak again, but I'm not sure what to say. If she has the guts to open up her whole life to me, I better be patient enough and hear her out.

"Did you want to say something?" she asks.

"I didn't mean to interrupt. Please go on." I put my hand on her knee and lean toward her. I hope my body language is saying all the right things.

"Woody used me—big time." She grits her teeth and disappointment and anger paints her face. "He was a mule for a big dealer, moving drugs across the state and down through Texas to Mexico. I found large bundles of drugs hidden in our apartment. He even had drugs stashed in my travel bags. I went to the police one Sunday morning. I told him I was going to church because I knew he wouldn't want to go along. They brought in people from the DEA in Oklahoma City and they set up surveillance of our apartment and followed Woody around for a couple of weeks. I was scared of Woody and the people he hung around with. When they were ready to make a raid on our apartment and Woody's partners, they arranged to take me in as well and then later let me off claiming they didn't have enough evidence to arrest me. They wanted to protect me from any retribution Woody and his buddies would have if they found out I had turned them in."

"Weren't you scared?"

"Well, of course. But I was more afraid that Woody wouldn't let me go. He had gotten very abusive—he threatened me and my family when I told him once I was going to leave him and go back home."

"Did he hurt you?"

"He never left any lasting marks. Mostly he just intimidated me and threatened to hurt me. His eyes would get really crazy when he was high. He would get sadistically mean and evil."

"What happened after the arrest?"

"We weren't able to talk much. We were separated when we were taken to jail—so I didn't have to see him. But the DEA said to just go back to work and finish school. And not have any contact with him. Nobody said what I was to do about getting divorced. And, when I finally found someone to ask, they said I should wait until he got sentenced. Well, the dealer had some really high priced lawyers and they kept postponing hearings and stuff and I just kept my head down and finished my degree. I was ashamed to even talk to my parents and then a friend sent me a copy of a local newspaper article that told of a Divine girl that got arrested in a big drug bust in Tulsa. I couldn't go home. Somehow your grandfather and Mr. Buchanan found me a group of pediatricians to work for in Portland."

She pauses, leans over, and looks down at the earth far below.

Seconds pass as does a flight of doves. She continues, "For the longest time my parents wouldn't even speak to me but Mr. Buchanan met with a DEA agent in Oklahoma City and took him out to visit my parents and tell them the truth about the whole ordeal. Of course it was still my fault for being involved with Woody in the first place. Mr. Buchanan wanted them to know their daughter not only wasn't involved in any criminal behavior, but actually was instrumental in setting up the bust, so to speak. They just aren't allowed to let anyone know. Even now the whole town looks at me as though I'm a criminal."

"That's quite a story."

"You don't believe it?"

"No, I, uh…"

"You think I'm lying?"

"No, please Hannah, let's not go there again. I do believe it. I'm sorry, but my grandfather already told me most of it."

"Well, why didn't you say so?"

"I wanted you to tell me. I wanted you to tell me about Woody. I thought you were hiding it from me. That's why we're here today, now, doing this—having this talk. Please don't feel like you have to be defensive around me. I'll admit I got a little uptight when I heard you referred to as Mrs. Cline, when I assumed you were Miss Harrison. I think we're pretty much on the same page now, aren't we?"

"I suppose—but I used to be Miss Harrison—come see." Hannah jumped up and took my hand, helping me up as well. She ran—I can't see running as a good thing on this narrow walkway so high up above the town, but we get around to the "N" in Devine, and now that the sun has shed its light on things, I watch her point to one of the many names written next to the large painted letter—*Hannah Harrison.*

"It was considered a rite of passage around here—when you start high school, you sneak off with some classmates, break-in, climb up the water tower, and write your name on the tank to prove to those who follow that you were, indeed, here."

"Do you think my mom's name is up here?"

"I doubt it, Tommy. They've probably re-painted the tank once or twice since your mom was in high school. Every time they repaint the tower, the *Alva-Courier* gets the list of names written on the tower and posts it in the paper. It is one of their most popular issues—we all get a copy and save it in our scrapbooks. Of course, we all get a reprimand from our parents, the County Sheriff, our pastors, teachers and anyone else who thinks they have the right to scold us. We also get praise from our friends. So, I've told my life story. Anything you need to come clean about?"

"You don't have a marker in your purse so I could leave my name up here, do you?"

"No, but I do have some lip stick."

Now Tommy Townsend is immortal.

CHAPTER FOURTEEN
I come clean.

We carefully trek around the tower. Selecting another view of the small town, we stop and sit with our legs again dangling below the narrow walkway. I re-fix my grip on the rail and inhale.

"Let's see, is there anything I want to come clean about?" Funny, but I don't remember ever facing this question, either from any law enforcement official or any sort of social partner. There were certainly times as a child when I was involved in some action or interaction where I made a decision, a choice, or a response that I'm not especially proud of today—but will I ever face a tribunal of some sort for my actions then? "I guess I would have to say I've pretty much always been squeaky clean." I get the look I was expecting—the one that says, *"Oh, really?"*

"No, seriously. I don't have a rap sheet either with the law or from my parents. I pretty much was a model child—still am according to Mom. And, my role models? The problem with my dad and especially my grandfather is their shoes were and still are impossible for me to fill, but lately they're getting more comfortable for me to walk around in."

"I can believe that." She nods and gives me an agreeing smile. She holds up the coffee thermos. "Care for another cup?"

"Yes, please." I extend my cup. She refills both mine and hers. "Getting back to filling shoes—I didn't mean that it was an impossible task for you, just that your grandfather sets a pretty high bar."

"Papa Tom has been a heroic icon for me since I could walk. His notoriety coupled with my dad's exploitation of his personal trials and philanthropic and selfless endeavors has put my life on a path that has always been an uphill climb. For my grandfather I had a male version of Mother Theresa and my dad, a network TV talking head. People occasionally ask me if that Townsend guy on CNN is my father. To keep up with the family tradition I will have to win a Nobel Peace Prize or a Pulitzer in order to have my photograph put on the same wall with these guys. Any pressure for me to perform? Naw—not much."

I take a breath and can't help but notice the transformation taking place on the landscape below. The rising sun is breathing new life into Divine as well as Hannah's and my relationship. From up here I can see lights coming on in buildings and surrounding homes. Cars begin moving up and down Main Street. Birds are beginning to fill the sky—smatterings of white wing doves are moving in formation from their nightly roosts to find grain and wild seeds among the fence rows. And, the few roosters that are in town are letting themselves be heard.

I've never seen Divine from this vantage point. From this height you see the sidewalks but not the cracks. You see the life in people but not their pain. I have spent a good deal of my life watching people from a distance. They are easier to deal with when they seem to have fewer problems, and are certainly less demanding of your time. When you don't commit to sharing your life on a personal level—actually having to respond, becoming engaged—it seems less complicated.

How long have I been silent? Looking to Hannah and seeing her blank stare, I guess she is waiting for me to continue.

"So where was I? My goals: to be famous, certainly. But, I suppose Jeffrey Dahmer was famous. Last week I would have told you I was on track to achieving everything I ever hoped to become. I always wanted to be a teacher—always wanted to be published. The truth is, I would rather sign books at a book signing than actually sit down and write one. But, you can't have your cake without spending time in the kitchen."

"Was it you who said that?"

"It is now."

"What about a family, Tommy. Do you want a wife? Kids? And, what has changed in the last week that you now question if your life is on track?"

"I suppose my confrontation with mortality has changed. Before last week, death wasn't a part of my vocabulary. Lately, I have been bombarded with the reality of death—my grandfather, stories about his best friends, now your father's... I'm sorry..."

"It's okay. My mother prepared me over the phone before I flew down here. I sat by his bed for several days praying he would wake up and everything would be all right. I think I knew it wouldn't. But then, you opened the blinds, turned on the lights in his room, and you turned on the hope in my heart. But, you know, it wasn't that I saw him sitting up and smiling. It was that I saw him going home—going home to something far better. I am glad I got to be here with him, if even to just hold his hand. I'd like to think he knew I was there in the room. I want to think he knew I had finally come home." Her tears come again. And, with them, the opportunity for me to hold her again.

I hold her, sharing her warmth, and realizing a sensation that is totally new to me—comforting someone else, sharing emotions, giving something in a relationship rather than only taking.

After a few minutes, her breathing becomes quiet and regular. No longer does she seem to be sobbing but, instead, she seems to be at peace, almost as if she's dreaming. I begin stroking the hair that lies in quiet waves along her cheek. She looks up at me—her eyes, dark and lazy.

"Why is it you have never married, Tommy? You really aren't that bad looking, you know. And, a gal could do a whole lot worse than having a husband who writes for a living."

"I think you should understand right now, because I don't want you to be misled, but I'm not making a living writing. I've only had a few books published. Without a movie deal, most writers don't really make that much money. I could support a wife—and perhaps a small child or two on what I make as an associate professor—provided she is very low maintenance and doesn't eat too much."

"And a dog?"

"What?"

"You can support a wife, two kids… and a dog?"

"Depends—does the dog eat much?"

"Speaking of eating—we should have carried up a picnic basket. I'm ready for breakfast. I don't suppose we could get something delivered?"

"*The Spot!* is open. See, over there, the building with the four cars out front. You got a coin?" she says.

"A coin?"

"Yes, I'll flip you to see who goes."

"Do you think we could go get breakfast and then come back?"

"We'd probably get caught trying to sneak back up here in the daylight. Besides, watching the sunrise was my big production number for the first act. Let's break for breakfast and then I'll raise the curtain on the second act." She smiles as she pours the rest of her coffee over the side. "Look out below," she pretends to scream as she looks over the edge.

"Not much traffic for almost eight o'clock in the morning," I say as we look out between buildings before we sprint across Main Street to *The Spot!*.

"There never is a lot of traffic—not like Portland or Seattle."

We scamper across the street and into the café. The bell on the front door jingles and all the customers, five, stop mid-chew, and the staff, two, freeze in place—everyone, all seven, making note of our arrival.

Hannah turns to me and whispers in my ear, "Next week's *Alva-Courier* will report our dining at *The Spot!* this morning, following a mid-night frolic on the Divine water tower." She laughs. I laugh—but not so much. I'm not sure if she's joking.

We sit in a far booth close to the kitchen. All the tables with a front window view are taken.

Hannah notices that I notice. "They will sit there all morning, drinking coffee, and tracking the comings and goings of all the people that walk or drive by. If just one of them noticed us climbing down the tower, they all know it by now."

The waitress brings us two glasses of water and greets Hannah, "Hello, Hannah. So sorry to hear about your dad. How's your mom doing?"

"Thank you, Claudia. Mom's doing well."

"How's your brother, Albert?"

"I left the news about Dad with the Red Cross in Afghanistan. He called late last night and is making arrangements to get home for the funeral." The waitress's eyes brighten up.

"When is the funeral?" she asks—much too excitedly to be appropriate for such a question.

"Don't know for sure yet. We haven't scheduled it—probably wait until we find out when my brother can get here. My sister and her family will be here Monday."

"Oh… right," the waitress responds. "Coffee?"

"Yes, please. Two." Hannah says.

"Wait, Miss, can I have a menu?" My request sounds more like a plea due to the urging of my empty stomach.

"Look down!" she says in a tone I find a little disconcerting. And, when I do look down, I find a laminated placemat that doubles as a menu.

"Oh… okay. Thank you… I guess." My final words tail off. Doesn't matter though—she didn't wait around to hear them. "Friendly little place," I say with a smile to Hannah.

"It's the company you keep."

"So, when does the curtain for the second act go up?"

"Right after breakfast. You better see what you want—she'll be right back with our coffee and if you haven't made a decision by then—well, she ain't likely to wait around with a cute little smile while you make up your mind."

I quickly survey the one column of breakfast choices and make the selection that includes the most items. That was a long climb and then a fast run through the alley and across the street. I normally have to go to the gym to get that kind of workout in the morning.

"Is she coming to the funeral?" I ask.

"Probably, but only because my brother is going to be there. She's been sweet on him since high school but he left and joined the Army without even saying good-bye to her. You'd think she would get a clue. Speaking of clues… I still don't have a clue about your past love life."

155

"Well, that's just it. It's a past love life—there hasn't been anything going on for some time. There was one, in Seattle, but after a while the fire just kind of blew out. I think maybe I let it go out by not tending it."

"What do you mean?"

"Well, I thought we were doing just fine, but I looked up one morning and the fire had pretty much gone out. Maybe we both quit tending it. One day I think I woke up and didn't even look around for her. By the time I noticed that I hadn't noticed where she was… well, she was gone… for good. Haven't seen her since."

"You can let that happen?"

Before I could answer or even begin to think of an answer, Little Miss Sunshine waitress was back with the coffees. We were both ready with our orders so she wouldn't have to linger.

"Now…" Hannah continues when the waitress leaves with our order, "You can let that happen? You can commit to a relationship and then let it go unattended, even give up on it, and just move on?"

"I guess I just wasn't in to her that much." I realize I hit a sour note and I glance around to see if there are other people in the place with the same disgruntled look on their face. Nope. I guess no one else heard— or cares. But, obviously Hannah cares.

"You just weren't in to her that much? Maybe you were just in to yourself too much!"

That last part was a little too loud and I look around to see if now anyone has noticed. Evidently not.

"Oh, they noticed," she says.

"What?"

"They heard what I said. They act like they're not listening, but they're straining to hear everything we say."

"Well," I continue in a low whisper, "Let's just wait and talk after we leave. Besides I'm not too crazy about where this conversation is going."

"Oh, you mean you're just not in to this… what… this conversation? This relationship?"

Again, she is too loud. "I get it, Hannah." I try to keep my voice low and my temperament calm. "Let's just go…" I pull out a twenty and lay it on the table, careful not to throw it down or to grit my teeth and set my jaw. I slide out of the booth and when as I stand up I reach for her hand. She doesn't respond. I turn and walk to the door. Praying that she is following close behind, I push the door open and walk out. The door doesn't slam so I'm pretty sure she is only a step or two behind me as I cross the street, slip between the buildings and walk to where she parked the truck. I can hear her steps in the gravel behind me. If I hear her suddenly speed up, I'll turn and prepare to deflect a blow to my head. I don't think she's carrying a gun—but I am afraid she still has that dangerous looking fence tool.

"Are you still hungry?" she asks.

"Yes. Let's go to the truck stop where we can eat in peace and if you still want to raise your voice, people won't hear you over the mariachi music."

"I don't care if they do hear me!"

"Yes, you do. You do care, Hannah. And, I care—I care about you."

We stand—the hood of the truck between us. She is about to cry again. She points the remote on her key ring at the windshield and the door locks pop up. "Get in," she commands.

Less than a mile from town, she slows, pulls off the road, and makes a U-turn. "If you don't mind let's not drive all the way out to the truck stop. Let's go check on my mom—I'll make you some pancakes and sausage. Besides, the second act of this drama takes place behind my folk's house."

"I don't mind—sounds great."

Several more miles go by and we still haven't spoken.

"Listen," she says, "Maybe we shouldn't talk while at the house."

"You think you might shout at me in front of your mother?" She flashes me a look I am becoming too familiar with.

"Maybe we shouldn't talk while I'm driving either."

"That sounds great, too." I sit with my arms folded and look straight ahead. She sits with her hands at ten and two and looks straight ahead. You would think we had been married for years the way we fight like an old married couple. Boy, am I glad I didn't say that out loud. Maybe I should be extra careful what I say out loud from now on. You think?

CHAPTER FIFTEEN
Curtain going up on the 2ⁿᵈ Act

Sure enough we don't talk to each other while she makes breakfast, while we drink yet another pot of coffee, and while I eat a huge stack of pancakes and several sausages. Hannah eats only one pancake and speaks only to her mother. She talks so incessantly that I don't think her mother even notices no words are exchanged between the two of us.

After swallowing the last bite of pancakes and the last patty of sausage, I jump up, clear the breakfast table, and wash the dishes—dry them and put them away. Hannah still has not stopped talking—inquiring about the expected time of her sister's arrival, when the pastor is coming to discuss the service, whether or not her mom had any further news from her brother.

Hannah's mom thanks me profusely for cleaning up and makes a point of singing my praises to her daughter—who only smiles sarcastically. I wink back. Hannah kisses her mom good-bye and tells her not to prepare anything for lunch—we'll be back and take her to *Las Carretas*. Hannah turns to me, tilts her head in an impish manner and says, "Let's go!" in a biting tone.

Without looking over her shoulder to check if I am in tow, she marches out the back door, letting the screen slam behind her, and heads for the truck. I linger behind and take the opportunity to thank Mrs. Harrison for her kind hospitality and remind her again how much I appreciate the loan of her husband's clothes.

"Oh, you are certainly welcome," she says. "You keep them and please, take this—it's going to get hot today. You don't want to burn that fair skin of yours." She hands me a straw cowboy hat—I'm guessing also her husband's. Then she walks to me, wraps her arms around my neck and kisses me on my cheek. "I like you, Mr. Townsend. You're a good man."

"Thank you. I guess you know I'm quite fond of your daughter."

"I suspected as much when I saw you two rolling around in the mud yesterday."

"I apologize for my behavior."

"Weren't nothing to apologize for. Kids will be kids, I guess."

"I guess." I smile, put on my newly acquired hat, and head out the back door. Guess I have kept Hannah waiting just long enough. There she sits, racing the engine, fumes pouring out of the truck's exhaust as well as her ears. Hot damn! She's really got a fire in her belly now.

Stepping up into the truck's cab I feel like a fireman running into a burning building. Saving Hannah and getting myself out alive are my only two priorities but it is looking as if I need to focus on just one—but which one of us do I save? I am as guilty as she is when it comes to fueling our little spats. I have an idea but almost as quickly as it comes the possibility and probability it is a bad idea presents itself. I am going on gut instinct here—instead of fastening my seat belt, I throw it off, open my door, and jump out of the truck. As I run around the front of the truck, headed for Hannah's door, I hear the door locks engage. What's your plan now, genius?

160

I stand like Johnny Depp on the deck of a pirate ship, fighting against the sea and a mass of marauding… well whoever pirates fought against… my feet set wide apart, my hands on my hips, and my teeth clinched tightly like a swashbuckling fool. With my eyes narrowed and fixed beneath one extremely raised eyebrow, I growl, "Open the door." No response. She is matching me, eyebrow for eyebrow. "Open the door… please."

She hesitates. Did my eyebrow go up higher? I thought maybe it did, I really tried.

"Thunk!" The door locks pop up.

I swing her door wide, reach in, grab her off the truck's seat, and throw her over my shoulder. Oh, I hope her mother's not watching this—the Sheriff could be here any minute—times a wastin'.

I head for the barn as quickly as my wimpy runner's legs will carry both me and my plunder… who is kicking the wind out of me with her hiking boots and now she takes both hands and grabs the strap on the back of my overalls, pulling with all of her strength. The crotch of the baggy blue denims slides painfully up between my legs—I gasp and nearly gag. My legs come up behind me, I'm on tip toes and her weight shifts forward. Shiver me timbers! I and my captive are down. I'm face down, in the dirt, and she is on top—with a knee in the back of my head.

"And he's down!" She screams with glee. "Ten yards short of the goal line."

I'm gasping for air, she's raising her fists in the air and usurps the moment of my glory—my time to shine, or what was supposed to be my time.

I struggle to roll over so I can breathe again. Hannah gets up and brushes off the knees of her pants and looks down at the fallen quarterback… pirate? I don't know anymore. She puts her hands on her knees and leans down to my barnyard dirt encrusted face and quips loudly, "Unnecessary roughness—fifteen yard penalty. First down, Hannah's ball."

So much for my plan to rescue her. I think I'm the one who needs a helping hand. And, there it is. Her hand is extended to me, hopefully to help. It's open, not a fist, and thankfully, there's nothing in it, like a rock, a gun…or a fence tool.

Instead of her helping me to my feet, I encourage her to take a seat next to me on the ground. We sit, legs folded Indian style, facing each other, so close we are actually able to form a very small circle, holding each other's hands—the only thing missing is our singing a chorus of kumbaya.

I start. "There's a hurdle we need to get over."

"Oh, and what is that?"

"In all seriousness—no joking, no sarcasm. I think we both are broken…"

"Did you hurt yourself when you fell down and went boom?

"Stop it, Hannah. I'm not talking about physically hurt—I mean psychologically impaired. To some extent, and we knowingly or unknowingly are putting up barriers to keep from being hurt. Listen, I know I'm damaged goods when it comes to being a part of a loving, understanding, giving, caring relationship—all those self-help, psychobabble descriptive words. You're absolutely right in that I've never been able to sustain a healthy relationship. For one reason or another I've failed—failed miserably. I don't want to fail now. I have always used my sarcasm to keep things from getting too serious. It must be some self-preservation mechanism that kicks in."

"Well, kick it out, Tommy."

"If it were that easy I would have already done it. I'm just asking you to work with me here. Since I came back to Divine, I've changed—changed not into somebody totally different, but back into somebody I used to be—somebody better—better than what I've been over the past ten, fifteen years. I know you would like this person. This person wants to come out and play. This person wants to come out and stay. But, the Tommy that came here last week is not comfortable with all these new feelings. That Tommy doesn't want to be vulnerable. That Tommy is comfortable sharing or taking care of anything or anybody—except himself. Hannah, I hate that person. I hate that I keep upsetting you. Please be patient with me."

"I'm afraid of getting hurt, too. But, I am so drawn to you, Tommy. At the same time, I'm afraid of where we're headed. Oh, I like where we're headed, don't get me wrong, but it's scary."

We sit, holding hands, holding our breath. I think we both are afraid to let go. On one hand, neither of us wants to walk away, and, on the other hand, both of us want to turn and run the other way as fast and hard as we can—before it's too late. It is already too late for me. When this whole thing here in Divine is over, I can't just go back to Seattle—not alone. This is stupid. How can this be happening? A week ago I never knew anyone like her existed. If her daddy hadn't been in the room across from Papa Tom, all this would have never happened. We would have never met. I might have left for Seattle today. A week ago I almost considered not even coming.

"I know you want to slow things down," she says. "Can we do that? Can we just be friends and just take care of the business at hand? I've got a funeral and a homecoming of my siblings—and my job in Portland. You've got your book and you've got your grandfather with his health issues. We've both got enough on our plates without trying to build a relationship now."

"And, don't forget you've got your husband."

"Oh my God. I almost forgot. No, really, I almost forgot about Woody."

"I wish I could."

"Stop it, Tommy! One thing at a time."

"You're right. That wasn't fair."

"Oh, it is fair. But, let's just deal with one problem at a time."

"Fair enough. By the way, what was the second act all about?"

"Pretty much the same script we've been speaking here I suppose, only a different venue, a different stage."

"Oh yeah, where at?"

"Just about a mile past that fence line." She points off to the north.

"What's there?"

"Just a large oak overlooking a field of ripe maize. Just a place of quiet solitude where we could have had this same conversation. A place where all the well-meaning people in town or at Wildflower wouldn't have been eavesdropping. A place where I could have had you to myself—all to myself—without my mom spying on us."

Hannah cocks her head and gives a quick little nod over her shoulder. Mrs. Harrison is standing inside the back screen door, same smile as last time.

When her mom realizes we see her watching from the back porch, she shouts, "Are you two playing nice?"

"Yes, Mom, we're playing nice."

"Would you like to go on out to the field with the large oak tree?" I ask.

"You know, if you don't mind I think I should stay around here and help mom get the house ready for my sister Christy, and her brood. We'll need to child-proof the house for the two youngest ones." Hannah shifts onto her knees and puts her arms around my neck. She appears to be considering whether she is going to kiss me or not—then, mind made up, she kisses me. It's a long, familiar, lingering kiss. And then, it's over and she stands. I realize too late it wasn't long enough for me. I raise my hands to her and wiggle my fingers, beckoning her, and pretending to be a child who wants more.

"You are such a brat, Tommy Townsend."

"I know. I just can't seem to get enough of you." I roll over and struggle to get to my feet. "When does your sister get here?"

"She and Steve are driving up tomorrow. It's an all-day drive if they drive straight through."

"You do what you think is best. I should really spend as much time as I can with my grandfather."

"Yes, you should," she says and she wraps her arms around my neck and gives me another kiss. "Is that what you wanted?" My broad smile should be a sufficient answer and we continue standing with her arms around my neck, looking into each other's eyes. "Are your mom and dad planning on coming anytime soon?"

"I think mom wants to come as soon as she can. My father has a really busy schedule—I don't think he'll come until he absolutely has to."

"That's too bad. Is he not close to your dad?"

"You would think Papa Tom is his real dad, not just his father-in-law. I never met my father's dad—or his mom for that matter. They both died years before I was born. My father was never as close to his dad as he is to Papa Tom. You know, the really funny thing is that my father knew more about Papa Tom *before* he even met him than he ever knew about his own father."

"How is that?"

"Long story—I'll tell you some time—sometime soon. How about running me back to town so I can get my car?"

"Don't you still want to have lunch with Mom and me?" She gives me another little peck, I suppose as an incentive.

"I think I'll take a rain check. I hadn't thought about Papa Tom much this morning. Now he seems to be weighing heavy on my mind. I really think I should go."

She releases her hold on my neck but grabs my arm as we walk to the truck.

The truck is still idling! The driver's door still wide open.

"Did you leave the truck running?" I ask in an accusing manner.

"Did you give me a chance to turn it off when you kidnapped me and carried me off?"

"We've got to quit acting like kids."

"Never. You make me feel like a kid again."

Papa Tom's door is ajar. I ease it open enough to determine that he is inside. He is on his side, facing away from the door, his legs slightly bent. He lies on top of his bedspread; his shoes and his wheel chair wait for him on the far side of his bed. His roommate's bed is empty. I tip toe around the bed. His deep breathing lets me know he is resting comfortably, his eyes confirm he is asleep. But, even at rest he looks exhausted. He looks as though he has aged considerably just in the week I have been here.

I sit down on Jim's bed and watch the old man sleep and try to recall the vibrant tough guy who would lift me high above his head and toss me to the middle of the pond—the pond where he taught me to swim, to fish, and to skip stones. I remember the gentle giant who cut a treble hook from the soft space between my thumb and index finger. I rub the scar that still testifies after all these years. I look at his weathered face, so worn and creased by time and the harsh sun—the scar which once snaked clear across his forehead now seems to only gently trace a furrowed brow. His arm falls from beneath his pillow and dangles a leathery opened hand from the edge of his bed. That hand has guided me, tickled me, and protected me for half my life. How could I have neglected it, neglected him all this time? *God, don't take him from me now. Let me have him a little while longer—not for my sake, but for his. Let my grandfather see that the investment he made in me has not been in vain. Whatever value I have as a human being, he has instilled in me. Whatever I have accomplished, he gave me the strength, the drive, the desire. If I have fallen short, it is because of my own pride and selfishness.*

"He's not dead, yet," an authoritative voice whispers.

"What?" I jerk, open my eyes, and look up. A huge man in a white coat fills the doorway.

"I said your grandfather's not dead yet," he repeats.

"Who are you? Was I praying out loud?"

"So, you were praying. I was right."

Papa Tom stirs, rolls over and looks up, first at me and then toward the door.

"Doctor Jim! How are you today, sir?" Papa Tom wipes his eyes, reaches to the night stand to secure his glasses, and puts them on. "Have you met my grandson, Tommy?"

"We were just about to when I'm afraid I disturbed your sleep and his prayers."

"He was praying?" Papa Tom says. "O, happy days!"

"I was just sitting here waiting for you to wake up."

"He looked like he was praying to me. You know it's not the first time I've walked into this room and caught somebody praying for you, Tom. Could be why you're still with us." The doctor smiled at me and then winked at my grandfather. He comes around the end of the bed and extends his hand. "I'm Dr. James Watson. I just stopped by to see if your grandfather had died yet so we can have this bed for somebody who could really use it."

"Excuse me?" I almost choke.

"Don't mind him, Tommy Boy, he's joking you." He turns to the doctor and says, "Tell him you're just joshin' him, Dr. Jim. He's from Seattle. You know how uptight those people are—always complaining about the rain and drinking too much coffee. Always depressed, never laughing."

"Well, let's take a look and see if I'm joking or not. Do you feel up to sitting up on the side of your bed for me?"

"Anything you say, Doc."

I jump off the roommate's bed and help Papa Tom sit up. He seems weaker today.

Taking his shoulder I help him twist, dropping his legs off the side of his bed. His catheter is tangled around his leg. For the first time I see just how atrophied his leg muscles are. The doctor comes around and opens my grandfather's shirt and places his stethoscope up against his chest.

"Would you like me to leave?" I look first at the doctor and then at my grandfather.

"Give us a minute, would you?" the doctor says.

"Okay. I'll just be outside." I leave, quietly closing the door. Across the hall the door to Mr. Harrison's room sits wide open. The curtains are pulled back and the blinds are set to let in all the available light from outside. The bed is freshly made and a blanket is neatly folded across its foot. All the peripheral equipment is gone. The room is empty and quiet. *How long before my grandfather's room looks like this?*

I decide to take a walk around the parade grounds.

CHAPTER SIXTEEN
Dr. Jim fills me in.

The rain earlier in the week has transformed the flower beds around the parade grounds. The brilliant colors of the blooms are deeper and the stalks are straighter, and all the flowers appropriately stand at attention. Even the blue in the sky seems darker. The lush green vegetation reminds me of Seattle—before it seemed faded and parched. I miss the thickness of the air after a rain. Things appear cleaner at home than here in the Panhandle. Everything is usually dusty. But, not today. Today, everything looks newly painted, everything smells fresh—and clean.

I follow a hawk as it rides the wind, catching a rising thermal and climbing effortlessly higher and higher. When I look back down, Dr. Watson is walking down the front steps coming toward me.

"Beautiful day isn't it?" he says.

"Yeah, reminds me of home."

"You're from up Northwest, aren't you?"

"Seattle."

"Your grandfather asked me to let you know how he's doing."

"Okay. How is he doing?"

"Well, it's a good thing you came when you did. Your grandfather has acute myelogenous leukemia."

"What can you do for it?"

"We've already done it—we found it five years ago. He had aggressive chemotherapy then and it went into remission. It returned about two months ago."

"Nobody said anything about five years ago. I didn't know."

"He didn't tell anybody then. He told your parents and all of his friends here that he was going to Galveston to visit an old Army buddy who was dying with cancer. He spent almost two months at M.D. Anderson in Houston. When he returned he told everybody his friend had passed. We thought your grandfather had beaten it. Then, at the beginning of this year, his symptoms returned."

"So, what kind of treatment is he getting now?" I know there aren't any good answers but I have to ask—I've got to hope—why didn't anyone say anything earlier?

"Mr. Townsend, your grandfather doesn't want any more treatments—no more chemo."

"How long does…?"

"A couple of weeks—maybe. Maybe a month—but sooner if he gets an infection. His body won't be able to fight off an infection and antibiotics will be ineffective due to the leukemia."

"Can't you do anything?"

"It's time, son. He's had a rich, full life. Every day he has now he pours into the lives of others."

"Can't you extend that time?"

"He wants his life in God's hands—not mine."

"How much pain is he in?" Why am I asking this? For my benefit—to ease my conscious? Papa Tom put off dying, until I could get here—

until he could fulfill his promise to me—tell me his secret. And, now I know. Now, he's through living. This is entirely my fault. He's in pain because of me. "Is he suffering?"

"No. He told me he is thoroughly enjoying every breath he takes. I have him on a pretty strong pain management regimen. He has never wasted a moment of his life, never regretted anything he has done or hasn't done. Can you say that?"

"Hardly. I have yet to do anything I am proud of—I mean, truly proud of."

"Oh, I doubt that. Don't beat yourself up. You're young. Your grandfather is proud of you. And—you can start today—start today doing the things that are really important. You've got the rest of your life. Don't waste any of it. Your grandfather sure hasn't."

"Did my grandfather tell you to tell me all this?"

"Well, pretty much. And, if he didn't put it in those exact words, we've talked enough over the years for me to know pretty much how he feels about things—and you. He especially doesn't want you to feel guilty about not spending time with him these past years. As wise a man as your grandfather is, you could have never learned everything you needed to know from him. But, he is glad he was able to have this time with you. He has kept me busy keeping him strong these past weeks. I'm glad you came when you did."

"How will I know when... when he's...?"

"It won't be painful—and it won't take long. But, if you have anything you want to tell him, don't put it off."

"Does my mother know...?

"Yes, your parents know. Your mom is planning on coming soon. Here's my card, please feel free to call me if you have any questions. My office is in Woodward. I see patients here at Wildflower on Saturdays.

But, I can be here within the hour. I've said my goodbyes to your grandfather just in case, and the nurses can always Skype me, as can you, if I'm needed. I'm glad I got to finally meet you, Tommy. I read your book on Morton Podus—good book, bad character. I'm looking forward to your book about your grandfather. What's the title going to be?"

"Haven't decided yet. He told me a secret. But, he hasn't told me the ending. Thank you, Dr. Watson. Thank you for everything."

"My pleasure, take care of yourself."

He shakes my hand and with his left hand he grabs my shoulder, pats it, and leaves me with a warm smile. My eyes follow him to the front door and I struggle internally with all I've just learned. I think that porch rocker and I need a few minutes together.

It is nearly noon when I leave the rocker and return to Papa Tom's room. Ahead of me, one of the staff carries a food tray into his room.

"Is my grandfather eating lunch in his room today?" I ask.

"Yes, I'm afraid so. The doctor wants him to stay in bed for the rest of the day."

When the attendant goes around the other side of his bed with the tray, I notice several new pieces of equipment in his room. At the head of his bed is an I.V. pole with a large bag of fluids, a long slender tube winds around, tethered to the stand, and terminates at the back of his left hand. A small oxygen tube encircles his ears and comes together at his nose. A clip on the index finger of his right hand is sending signals to a monitor towering above his head on the near side of his bed. It beeps with regularity. You don't listen to the beeps. You listen for the next beep. Anxiously you anticipate its signal. You fear hearing silence. When I left his room earlier, the only thing next to his bed was a night stand with a box of tissues.

"What's all this?" I anxiously ask.

"Doctor's orders," says the attendant as he sets the tray down on a rolling table and inspects the I.V. drip. "Doc Watson was concerned that Mister Howard wasn't getting enough nourishment from the dining room. So we're giving him a quick fix of vitamins and liquid nourishment. The doctor didn't like his color much either, so we're giving him a little oxygen to put some rosy color back in his cheeks. Don't let all this stuff worry you—your grandfather flits around here seeing to it that everybody else does what they're supposed to be doing. He gets plum worn out and forgets to take care of himself. He'll be up to strength later on this afternoon. He just needs to rest now."

I move to his left side and take his hand, being careful not to disturb the I.V. site. His hair, what little he still has is twisted around the oxygen tubes. His complexion is anything but rosy—it is gray. He looks up at me and struggles to smile.

"I'm sorry you got to see me like this," he whispers. "I've been feeling an episode coming on since yesterday. Normally I can nip it in the bud, but I just got behind the curve on this one."

"What's he talking about?" I ask.

"He doesn't like all the contraptions and Doc Watson lets him tell us when he needs a boost of oxygen and a pick-me-up in a bag. He won't go out of his room with an I.V. pole or oxygen tank. He doesn't want anyone seeing them. He's even been hiding his catheter under a blanket and telling people he done sprained his ankle—that's why he gets pushed around in a wheel chair. Says he'll be up and dancing again in no time."

Papa Tom squeezes my hand and pulls me closer to him. He beckons me with his finger to lean down and he whispers, "Don't pay him too much mind. I'll be up and at 'em by morning. You'll see. This happens all the time."

"You just rest," I tell him and I start to pull away but he grabs my hand and pulls me back.

"Did you and Doctor Jim have a good talk?" I nod. "Did he tell you everything?"

"Yes, he told me everything." I look down, unable to face him or reality. "Evidently you need to rest now. I'll come back tomorrow."

He won't let go of my hand. "How are you and Hannah getting along?"

"Just fine. Did you know Mom is coming soon?"

"Yep, I asked her to come." He coughs repeatedly and points to a water glass on his tray. The attendant reaches across and takes the glass and then pulls a straw from a pouch on his belt. He bends the straw and positions it so Papa Tom doesn't have to sit up. He sucks nearly half the glass dry, smiles and mouths a thank you. He takes a number of large, deep breaths with his mouth open.

"Now stop that, Mister Howard, don't you be breathing through your mouth, breathe that good oxygenated air in through your nose."

Papa Tom takes several deep, rapid breaths through his nose and glares at the attendant. "Like that?" he says.

"Exactly like that."

"Tommy... before you go, could you leave me your recording device? I'd kind of like to go over what you've recorded and see if I left anything out."

I run out to the car and get my recorder and return with it. When I enter the room, he is already back asleep. I leave it next to his food tray and slip out. I wish I could find Doc Watson again. I could call him on his cell—but what would I ask him? I'm afraid I already know the answer—I just don't want to know. I walk out the front door and head to my car. Glancing at the porch rocker, I consider crawling into it, curling up in a fetal position, and wishing my mother were here.

I run back into his room with the recorder and put it on his night stand.

"See you later, Papa."

"Thanks, Tommy Boy. Thanks for everything. Take care of yourself. I'll be looking for you."

I've experienced entirely too much today—witnessed the sunrise, before anyone else in the county, been pummeled and thrown to the ground by a girl half my size, and I've been told that my grandfather has been fighting to stay alive until I got here. And, now that he's seen me and told me his secret—well, now he's apparently ready to go home.

All that… and, the day is only half over.

It's an uneventful drive to the Harrison farm. I find it hard to believe this part of America is productive. That is to say, there is little or no traffic coming or going. And, what little traffic there is appears to be displaced individuals trying only to get from one unimportant and uninteresting place to another. Virtually no commercial traffic— no semi-trailer trucks delivering groceries or car parts or building materials. No Fed-Ex or brown UPS trucks scurrying from one stop to another and no airplanes on final approach, no taxis, no mass transit. What does this part of the world do to validate itself? If it all dried up and blew away, would anybody notice, would anybody care?

In Seattle, if a plane is delayed fifteen minutes at the airport or I-5 is backed up, it becomes late-breaking news, a quarter of a million people text that they're going to be late and oil futures sky-rocket. I stop to get a newspaper at the convenience store on the way out of town—to see if Mr. Harrison's obituary is in it. There's no local paper and the paper that might carry his obit is the *Alva-Courier*. It comes out on Thursdays—three days from now! Why bother? I wonder, does the local paper have a website—a Facebook page—does the local funeral home Tweet?

Just outside the Harrison farm, I pass two large harvesting machines on the side of the road. Good thing they were pulled off the road, otherwise I don't think I could have gotten around them on this narrow highway. They look like humongous green metal insects prepared to devour whatever is ripening in the fields. Whatever it is, the tops are heavy with grain of some sort and they seem to struggle to remain upright. Now, with Mr. Harrison gone, who will see to it that his fields are harvested?

After turning off the main road, I wind up toward their house. Good—the truck is here—she must be here with her mother and not off running errands. I pull up next to the truck and, before I can shut off the engine, Hannah comes running out of the house, bounding down the steps two at a time, and meets me as I open the car door. She is breathless and displays an expression on her face I've not seen before—fear.

"What's the matter? Are you okay? Is your mom okay?"

Gulping air, she blurts out, "I need to talk to you—but not in front of my mother." She runs around to the passenger side and gets in. "Drive." I give a questioning look. "Just drive down the road—until you get out of sight of the house. Just drive, pull over when I tell you." She flops back against the seat and buries her head in her hands.

I drive.

CHAPTER SEVENTEEN
Woody

When I get to the road she lifts her head and scans up and down the highway.

"Go right," she commands. She surveys up and down the highway.

"What are you looking for?"

"I want to make sure no one is following us."

"Why would anyone be following us? What's going on?"

"I didn't want to upset Mom, but… Woody just called me—on the house phone. He knows I'm here."

"What does he want?" I ask.

"What does he want? What does he want?" The second time she implied my question was incredulous.

"Okay, then. Why did he call?"

"Why did he call?" she screamed.

"Okay, okay. I'll shut up—you just tell me about the call."

"You know he jumped bail, right? There's a warrant out for his arrest."

"Yes."

"You know he's a wanted felon?"

"Uh huh." I give her one of those TV sitcom looks that is usually accompanied with an and… and then some charade signals requesting more information. She just gives me an Are you crazy? look. Her nostrils flare and now I appear to have totally exasperated her. I shut up.

"He found me. Don't you understand? I haven't had contact with him in over a year."

"Didn't he come out to the farm with you once?"

"Yes. But he called the clinic in Portland first… and they told him I was home visiting my father in the hospital. How did he know where I work? He knows where I live and … and now he knows where I am and he's here… somewhere around Divine. He says he wants me to meet him."

"Where?"

"He said he put instructions in the mailbox at my parent's home. He might be watching the house. He might have seen me drive off with you."

"Why didn't you have me stop and check the mailbox?"

"Yes, I should have checked. Quick, let's go back and check the mailbox. I shouldn't have left Mom alone. Let's go! Let's go! Please."

I turn the car around and head back to the front gate. The car slides to a stop at the mail box and I reach in and grab a single folded sheet of paper. She might consider my reading it an invasion of her privacy so I offer it immediately to her.

"No, no. You read it. I'm too nervous," she says.

First, I look around to see if we're being watched—no vehicles on the highway except for the two green monsters parked off the road. I unfold the note—scribbled in large letters is:

COME ALONE TO THE DUCK POND…
NOW!

"He must have put this in the mailbox before he called you and drove to the…" I look back at the paper to be sure I read it correctly. "The duck pond? Do you know what he's talking about?"

"Yes, it's in a remote area on the other side of town, below the cemetery. You can't see it from the road."

"What do you want to do?" I ask.

"What do I want to do? I don't want to do anything. Have you got your cell phone? I left mine at the house." I nod and retrieve my phone. "Call the Sheriff—call Josh Martin!" she screams.

"Well, what's the number?"

"I don't know. Call 9-1-1."

"That won't work on my cell phone—we'll end up talking to Seattle. What's the area code here?"

"5-8-0."

I punch in 1-580-411 and press TALK.

"Information—what city please?"

"Can you please give me the local Sheriff's department?"

"Is this an emergency?"

"An emergency? uh…" Hannah's head is nodding frantically. "Yes, it's an emergency," I blurt out.

"One minute, I'll connect you." The phone rings.

"Beaver County Sheriff's department."

"Is Officer Martin there?"

"Is this an emergency, sir?"

"Yes, yes it is."

"What's the nature of your emergency, sir?"

I close my eyes and shake my head, thinking this is ludicrous. "There is an escaped felon at the cemetery in Divine."

"Do you know who the felon is?

"Woody, uh, Woody Cline."

"Is he armed?"

"I don't know."

"Is he alone?

"I don't know, I…

"Can you see him?"

"Uh, no. I'm not at the cemetery."

"Sir, how do you know Mr. Cline is at the cemetery?"

"The note said to meet him at the cemetery… No, not the cemetery, the duck pond… below the cemetery."

"The note said you were to meet him at the duck pond…?"

"No, not me, Hannah."

"Who's Hannah?"

Finally I am too frustrated to continue. Here, you talk to them." I hand my phone to Hannah."

"Can you please connect me to Josh Martin, this is Hannah Harrison?"

"Where are you now, Miss Harrison?"

"I am five miles west of Divine on Highway 64."

"Please stay on the line. I will connect you to Officer Martin."

After a brief moment. "This is Officer Martin, go ahead."

"Josh. Thank God. This is Hannah Harrison. Where are you?"

"I'm just north of Beaver. What's the problem?

"Woody is at the Divine Cemetery. He called me and he wants me to meet him at the duck pond. Don't you have a warrant or something for him?"

"I sure do. Is he armed?"

"I have no idea. He called me at my parent's house and left a note in the mailbox for me to meet him at the duck pond."

"Is he alone?"

"I have no idea."

"Where are you now?"

"I'm with Mr. Townsend in front of my parent's place."

"Go to my office and wait for me. That will be the safest place for you. I'll call you when we capture him."

"Okay. Thank you, Josh." Hannah ends the call and returns my cell phone. "He says to go to his office and wait for him."

"I heard…"

"Well, let's go to his office, then."

"Wouldn't you like to go back and get your mother—first? I don't think we should leave her alone—just in case Woody eludes the Sheriff. You know, if he realizes you sent the police instead of coming yourself, he might be a little upset."

"Of course… You're right. Let's get Mom. It's just that I didn't want to worry her about any of this until… well, until it is over."

I back up the car, pull back in through the gate, and head down the drive to the house. Hannah waves to her mother who is sitting on the porch swing as though she is expecting us.

Something isn't right. Hannah's mom is vigorously shaking her head. Hannah jumps out of the car and runs toward the house. I follow and as I round the front of the car, I notice a man in a white T-shirt and blue jeans walk out the front door onto the porch. When I look over to Mrs. Harrison, I see her mouth is bound with a scarf and her hands are tied to the slats in the swing.

"What have you done, Woody?" Hannah runs toward her mother.

"Stop right there," he growls, pointing a gun at Hannah and looking straight at me. "You, you come on up here on the porch," he barks directly at me—waving a pistol back and forth from Hannah to me and then back again. "Hannah, sit down next to your mother. You won't scream anymore now—will you Mrs. Harrison?" Her eyes are wide and red from crying.

"He hasn't hurt you, has he, Mom?" She shakes her head as Hannah removes the gag and starts to untie her hands.

"Leave her hands tied, Hannah. I don't want her running off. Who is this guy? Your new fella? Anyway, the three of us are going for a walk."

Hannah looks back at me and then at Woody. She is speechless.

"Come on you two. Let's go around back." Hannah sits frozen on the swing. "Get up, Hannah. And you…" Pointing at me with the gun again. Every time he waves the pistol my way, it appears larger. "Both of you—to the barn."

Hannah comes to me and grabs hold of my arm. She is trembling. I lead her down the steps and around to the back of the house.

"Hold up a second," Woody says as he checks the cords securing Hannah's mother to the swing. Evidently satisfied she won't get loose—he follows us down the steps. "Get on with it."

"What do you want, Woody?"

"Well, I wasn't sure how you would feel about me showing up, here, unannounced and all. You know, we haven't talked in quite a while—you never did come see me in jail. My attorney tried to contact you, but couldn't find you. He thought you might want to come to my appeal—you being my faithful wife and all." He shoves the pistol into my back. "Keep moving, and stop eye-balling me."

I turn my eyes back to the front and pull Hannah along with me toward the barn.

Woody continues. "I heard you skipped town when they turned you loose—never even looked back. You just disappeared. You didn't go into some witness protection program, did you? Going to testify against me or something? You make a deal with the prosecutor?"

Hannah didn't answer. She didn't even turn around—she just kept walking toward the barn—clinging to me—Woody, right behind us. His gun didn't look like the kind you need to pull the hammer back on but, just in case, I keep listening for a 'click.' God, is he going to shoot us? I close my eyes and the muscles in my neck and shoulders tighten.

Hannah stops and snaps around like a crack drill team doing an about-face. I may not have recognized the expression of fear on her face when she ran out with news of Woody's phone call, but this look—this fierce look of determination she now shoots at Woody—this look I have seen.

"Listen, Woody. Just what is it you want? What do you expect from me? You're a criminal, a drug pusher, a user, a fugitive, a thug—I didn't want you before and I sure don't want to have anything to do with you, now." I recognize that stance—her hands on her hips, her jaw clenched, and eyebrows arched.

"Why, sugar, I thought we'd get back together. I need to get out of this state and get settled somewhere—somewhere where my face isn't on the bulletin board at every police station between Tulsa and New Mexico. I think we should take a ride up to Oregon—maybe get us a little cabin in the woods. What do you think?"

"I think you're crazy. Just what makes you think I'd go to Oregon with you, or anywhere else?"

"Well, I thought maybe you might still want me. You know, it was you who came onto me when we first met."

"That was before I found out what a scum-bucket, drug dealing, worthless bum you are."

"Does that mean you don't want to go to Oregon with me?"

"That's what it means."

"So, your boyfriend, here, he wouldn't let you go to the duck pond? That why you didn't run to see me after all this time?"

"You jerk! I didn't have any intentions of running to you. I sent the Sheriff to the duck pond. When he doesn't find you there, he'll come here."

Sometimes I think Hannah just talks too much. Woody's face is red and he appears to be about to explode. I wish she wouldn't rile him up like that. She has a way of driving people right to the edge with that tongue of hers.

"So, I guess that's a no, huh? I guess we don't have much time then. This guy of yours seems to be standing between you and me, Hannah. I can fix that."

Woody turns to me and I see the gun follow as well. With the gun pointed away from Hannah, I dive for the gun, grabbing Woody's arm, and scream at Hannah, "Run! Run!"

When the gun went off, I felt like I had been hit by a bowling ball. I'm not sure which was louder, the gun shot, or my screaming in pain. I don't remember hearing the gun go off. But, I will never forget the sound of my screaming. When a bullet tears through flesh, it ignites the senses and neurons, or whatever it is that sends signals to the brain, firing off a white searing heat throughout your body.

I let go of Woody's arm and he swings at me, the gun crashing against my head. Things go blindingly white for a moment and then black... and then red as the blood streams into my eye. I drop to my knees.

Any thoughts I had about protecting Hannah and defending her honor vanish as I crumple face down on the ground. Now everything is black, but I can still hear Woody yelling at Hannah and Hannah screaming hysterically.

"Boyfriend isn't standing in the way anymore, is he? Shut up and get into the house. I need all the cash, valuables and guns we can find."

Woody stops, jerking Hannah backwards. He bends down and fishes in my front pocket for the car keys, then rolls me over and pulls my wallet from my hip pocket, and grabs my cell phone. I can't see but I hear them moving away, Hannah protesting in vain. I hear the screen door slam and I struggle to get to my feet. No chance. I think I'm going to pass out. Mrs. Harrison is screaming uncontrollably, still lashed to the porch swing. I try to make it to the porch, but before I get to the corner of the house, I hear the front door swing open. I dive and roll under a large honeysuckle on the side of the house.

"Now, are you going to behave, or do I have to put one in your momma too?"

"I'll do whatever you want, please don't hurt my mother."

I hear the two of them run down the steps and get into my car. The car starts and then the tires spin as it fishtails out away from the house and toward the highway. Mrs. Harrison continues to scream. I'm getting woozy… and the… the pain doesn't…then everything goes black and silent.

The fog in my mind is lifting. A strange man in a white uniform is leaning over me. Another stands above me with one of Papa Tom's bag of fluids and a tube running down into… my hand.

"Mister Townsend, Mister Townsend—can you hear me? It's Sheriff Martin. Where's Hannah?"

Why is he shouting at me?

"Do you know where Hannah is? Was Woody here? Did he shoot you? Was he alone?"

"What... Where am I...? Hannah? He's got Hannah!" I shout. I try to sit up and the moment my head rises so does the level of my pain. "Ohh..."

"I'll give you something for the pain. Just lie back, be still. I've stopped the bleeding but you've lost a lot of blood." The man in white cinches a strap across my waist and with the flick of a lever, the contraption I'm laying on springs upward.

"Mr. Townsend, where is Hannah?" Sheriff Martin repeats.

I try to focus on... Boy is he huge. Then I remember... "Hannah! He has Hannah!" I scream.

Martin leans down, putting his face directly above mine. He spoke slowly and clearly. "Does Woody have Hannah?"

"Yes, yes. He shot me! Hannah's mother? Is she..."

"She's fine—but hysterical. She's no help. You need to tell us where they are."

I strain to look around. Two police cars and an ambulance are parked in the front drive with lights flashing. Two officers come out of the house and off the porch, guns drawn. "There's no one in the house," one of them reports.

"Check in the barn. Listen, Mr. Townsend, did they leave in a car?" Sheriff Martin barks.

"To a cabin in Oregon..."

"Where?" Martin shouts in my face again.

"Woody wants Hannah to go to Oregon with him—to hide out in the mountains."

"Mr. Townsend, you're not making any sense. Think. Did they drive away from here?"

I try to look around again. "My car? He took my keys. Is Hannah okay?"

Sheriff Martin turns and opens the mike attached to the shoulder of his uniform. He sounds like a sportscaster giving a live radio broadcast at a football game, "Suspect Woody Cline has a hostage, Miss Harrison, and they are traveling in a late model 4-door blue sedan registered to a rental company. The suspect is armed and dangerous and has already shot one person. The suspect should still be within 20 to 30 miles of Divine on 64 West. Be extremely cautious when approaching. Alert all law enforcement agencies and personnel within a hundred mile radius. The suspect is a white male, 34, brown hair, brown eyes, approximately six feet, 220 pounds. The hostage is a white female, 30, blonde hair, approximately five foot, seven inches, 125 pounds."

They slide me into the back of the ambulance—one of the technicians gets in with me and hangs the bag of fluids above my head. I look down at my chest. My shirt has been cut down the front and only the sleeves remain. A huge bandage is taped across my left shoulder. I realize I can barely see out of my left eye—a large piece of gauze runs from my nose across my forehead to my left ear. The driver slides a small window open from the front seat, "Let's go to Beaver?"

"Yep, that'll be the best bet," my guy says.

"How long was I out?" I ask.

"Sheriff Martin thinks you were shot about fifteen to twenty minutes ago."

"How did you get here so quickly?"

"When Sheriff Martin got to the cemetery and no one was there, he tried calling your cell. When you didn't answer he dispatched us here, just in case, and told us to stay parked outside on the highway until he or one of the other officers got here. He told us no sirens—he almost beat us here. Lucky for you—another five minutes and you might have bled out."

"How is Mrs. Harrison?"

"Physically she's fine. Mentally, she's a basket case—hysterical. We gave her a sedative and an officer stayed behind with her."

"I hope they catch up to him soon."

"Don't worry, there are only two roads out here and it's a long ways to anywhere. You can bet the Sheriff's got men coming the other way on each of them."

"Can you listen to the police radio in here?" I ask.

"Sure can."

"You think you could turn off the siren, slow down and let me listen to what's going on? That woman he's holding hostage—she's kind of special to me."

"I guess so, I got the bleeding stopped and your vitals are good. You're going to have a real shiner on that eye. What did he hit you with?"

"Huh?" I reach up and gingerly touch my head. "Ohh... that must have been when he hit me with the pistol. I don't remember anything after that." He reaches to the window partition, opens it and yells, "Turn off the siren and slow it down. Radio into Beaver E.R. and tell them we may be a little while... and turn on the police channel back here so we can monitor the chase."

"Do what—why?" responded the driver.

"Just do it! If there's a shoot-out, we'll just have to turn around and go back anyway."

"Is he stable?"

"He's fine. The bullet went clean through. The gash on his head has stopped bleeding. He's just worried about his lady. If we don't do it, he said he's going to jump out and run back." My guy smiles and gives me a wink.

"Okay, but, if he dies on our watch, it's going to be your butt," the driver yells back.

The siren stops and the ambulance slows. The squawk from the police radio comes over the speaker in the back.

"All responders… This is Sheriff Martin. Listen, I came from the east and the suspect's probable route is west on Highway 64. Set up a road block on the junction of 64 and Highway 270. I'm pretty sure that unless he's pulled off the road into some farm, they'll be coming your way within a few minutes."

The radio squawks and another voice comes on, "Roger that, Martin. We're almost there now. There are two other vehicles on their way. We'll have the escape route locked down. Over."

"I'm in pursuit. Hold your ground. Sheriff Martin, out."

"How far is that from here?" I ask the EMS guy.

"Right now, about fifteen miles, but then we're slowly getting further and further away."

"Well, can't you stop? Let's turn around, please! I'll be okay."

After a second, my guy agrees, "Jeff, let's turn around and head toward the road block—just in case."

"You're the boss—until we both get fired." The ambulance slows and then makes a giant U-turn, I can hear the gravel when we go off onto the shoulder, and when the ambulance straightens out again we begin picking up speed.

"Thank you, thank you, thank you."

"Stay calm, sir. Your heart rate is climbing."

After a few minutes, whatever was in that syringe to kill the pain was doing a bang-up job. And, the stuff from the swinging bag above my head was now coursing through my veins. I am ready for anything. Let me at him—I'll tear him apart with my bare hands. When all this

190

is over, maybe I can get Doc Watson to give me a prescription for the courage in that bag there.

The radio blares, "The suspect's car is approaching our road block at 64 and 270. He's stopped. Now he's turning around. Josh, he's headed back your way. We're in pursuit."

"Roger that. He's got a hostage. Give him a little wiggle room. I don't want to force him into making a desperate decision of any kind."

"The suspect is clocking 85 to 90."

"Don't close on them, maintain your distance," Martin ordered.

A few minutes go by without any word over the radio and then it squawks again, "Suspect's car approaching. He's coming fast... he just blew by me... who's at the Harrison farm? Gary, are you still with Mrs. Harrison?"

"Yes, sir. I'm still here at the Harrison place."

"Listen, there are two combines parked alongside the highway half a mile east of you. Get out there now—do whatever you need to do to get them and your vehicle across the highway. That's the only place we are going to be able to block this guy."

"I'm on my way."

"Oh, God!" Our ambulance driver shouts. "Here comes trouble."

My guy stands and looks out the front. "Quick! Get off the road."

The ambulance quickly slows down and it seems like everything that's not tied down slides by me heading toward the front. The ambulance leans to the right and the cart I'm strapped to slams up against the cabinets.

"Ummph." Good thing I can't feel that. Before we can turn around, the Sheriff's car speeds by—siren blaring.

"Well, come on guys. Turn around. Let's get going." Not only am I brave now but apparently I have developed into an authority figure.

The ambulance swings around and we, too, are now in hot pursuit.

"Gary, how are you coming on getting those combines in place?" Martin's voice blares over the radio.

"We're in luck. The combine drivers are here. In just a minute we'll have the highway completely blocked from fence to fence."

"Clear out all civilians. I don't want anybody getting hurt. Deploy your spike strips across the highway about a hundred yards in front of your road block." Martin ordered.

"I'm already dragging them out."

"Hunker down, I'm right behind him—we're about five minutes from you. He's traveling awfully fast. I don't want Hannah getting hurt."

"I don't either," I whisper.

Looking down between my feet, from the windows in the back doors I see a stream of law enforcement vehicles coming up behind us. The cars speed past us, their sirens screaming, lights flashing.

"Everything in place?" Martin's voice squawks over the radio.

"We're ready here."

"I'm going to back off and give him a chance to think things over. I don't want him trying to run this thing. Gary, I want you standing out front with your hand up. No guns! Do you understand?"

"Uh, yes sir, but…"

"Get your bull horn out and if he'll listen, assure him the guy he shot is okay. He hasn't killed anybody—yet. Keep your gun in your holster. Assure him this doesn't have to end badly. Let's slow this thing down and try not to get anybody killed."

"I understand, sir… I can see him coming now."

There is no more talking on the radio—just silence. "What's happening? Can you see anything?"

"They're too far ahead of us. We'll be there in a minute," my guy assures me.

"Come on, come on," I beg.

The ambulance driver turns off the siren and slows down.

"What's happening? Why are we stopping?" Can you see Hannah?"

"We gotta wait here," the driver says.

"Tell me what's going on." I struggle against the restraints but it's useless.

"Be still—you're going to start bleeding again."

"What's going on?"

"Well, everyone is stopped. All the cops are standing outside their vehicles and the guy in front is talking on a loud speaker."

"What's he saying?"

"We aren't close enough to hear."

"Get closer."

"I'm not moving. Just be quiet," the driver orders.

"Wait... the girl is getting out of the car and the guy is getting out right behind her. He's holding a gun to her head."

"Oh, God, no." I want to get up and look but a part of me—a huge part of me—wants to crawl under the covers.

The ambulance driver begins giving us in the back a play-by-play. "The deputy with the microphone is saying something... the guy is pointing the gun at the deputy now... oh, oh, the girl broke away from him and she's running... he's going to shoot her..."

"BAM! BAM...! BAM...!"

"Oh my God—did he shoot her?" I yell.

"Uh, no. The Sheriff shot him... he's down. We better go. Grab the tool box. Let's go."

The ambulance driver throws open his door and takes off running. My guy grabs a red plastic tool box and dives out the back—doors opened, leaving me alone and strapped in.

"Hey, guys. Let me out of here." Who am I kidding? They're not coming back for me. "At least tell Hannah I'm in here!" I scream at the top of my lungs.

I sit alone, undisturbed, unattended, unnoticed for what seems like an eternity. The ambulance is too far away for me to hear anything—or for anybody to hear me.

"Tommy. Tommy." I hear Hannah call out as she approaches the back of the ambulance. At least my guy left the back doors open.

"Hannah!"

Hannah burst into the back of the ambulance and throws herself across me, smothering me with kisses—her tears falling on my face.

"Are you all right?" she cries out.

"Are you all right?" I struggle to free my arms. I want desperately to hold her.

"Yes, yes. But you…?"

"I'm fine. Well, not fine maybe—but I'll live. The bullet went straight through, in and out they say—didn't hit anything vital. They stopped the bleeding. But you, what happened out there? When I heard the shots, I thought…"

"Josh Martin shot Woody. I think he's dead. But, you're okay?" she asks again. Her eyes are full of tears and when she smiles the tears gather at the corner of her mouth and fall on my chest.

CHAPTER EIGHTEEN
Recovering

And just when I was getting comfortable with Divine—I awake in a hospital room in Beaver, Oklahoma. I know it's Beaver because that's what's painted on the water tower outside my window. Compared to Wild Flower Nursing Center, this facility is as different as night and day. The walls are stark white, sans pictures and nothing if not antiseptic—lots of stainless steel, chrome and soft gray laminates and porcelain. It smells, looks, and feels clean—and cold, unfeeling, and uncomfortable. Maybe it's just me. Maybe it's just that it's unfamiliar, I'm alone, and not a face in sight that I can put a name to. Sometime on the way to the hospital everything went black. Where's Hannah?

A clear bag now hangs above my head, its fluids drip into my arm. An adjacent monitor tracks my heart beats, my breathing, and my... what is that bottom undulating line that appears to be tracing the flow of slow moving waves? Must be my level of pain. I don't think I'm feeling any—and if I am, I don't seem to care.

I'm beginning to remember why I'm here—how I got here. Kind of foggy about how I got here.

"Well, hello Mister Townsend," says a friendly if unknown voice. It emanates from a dark, young woman who appears out of nowhere at the foot of my bed. Her stark white uniform contrasts against her olive skin and long, thick black hair. I try to sit up. She quickly moves around to the side of my bed and puts her hand against my good shoulder and pushes me back against the bed.

"Just lie back. I'm your nurse, Sandra Wolfchief. Do you remember what happened to you?"

"Yes, I remember what happened—for the most part—I think. I just don't remember arriving here at the hospital."

"I understand you were unconscious when the EMS boys brought you into the E.R. Your color is coming back. You were pretty white when you arrived on the floor but it looks like your color is beginning to come back."

"Don't look for it to come back enough to match yours. I live in Seattle—I don't see the sun nearly as much as you do out here. But, I'm pretty sure with a name like Wolfchief you come by it naturally."

"You think?" she smiles.

It is her smile and those eyes that cause me to snap out of the fog I'm in. Then I remember... Hannah? "There was a person with me in the ambulance..."

"Yes, there was," she says matter-of-factly, "When she was assured you were going to be all right, she left—said she had to check on someone else, her mother I believe. She said to tell you she would be back as soon as she could."

"She's my... I mean, she was nearly... But, she is all right... Right?"

"Yes, she's fine. And, I can tell she cares a great deal about you... she is pretty special to you, too. Am I right?"

196

"Yes. Yes, she is." I relax, lay my head back down on the pillow and close my eyes. She is very special to me. When I thought she might have been shot I realized just how special.

When my eyes are closed and I allow myself to lie quietly, the nurse slips out of the room.

I sleep.

"Mr. Townsend?"

There is a hand on my shoulder—my good shoulder. I open my eyes. It's Doc Watson.

"I hear you got yourself shot," he says dryly.

"Are you my doctor now... here?"

"I was in the hospital. They asked me to take a look at your x-rays. You're a lucky man, Mr. Townsend. The bullet just nicked your left lung and missed any major arteries. And, evidently you got a pretty good blow to the head. We x-rayed that too. Your head is alright. The doctor who treated you in E.R. said you were a quart low." He looked at my bloody overalls which lay folded neatly on a chair in the corner of the room. "We're going to top off your fluids. You won't be doing any farm work for a few days."

"How soon before I'll be up?"

"Let's talk about it tomorrow. You may not be so interested in jumping out of bed in the morning after the pain meds wear off. You lost a significant amount of blood. We'll see how well your body does on producing some more. The food here is pretty good. Eat whatever and as much as you want. You're a lucky man, Tommy Townsend."

"How's my grandfather?"

"He's holding his own. Don't lie around here too long, though." With that, Doc Watson closes my chart and shoves it and my x-rays under his arm and walks toward the door. "See you in the morning." Before I can respond, he's gone.

"You want me to raise the bed up so you can eat?" the attendant asks.

I look over at the remote hanging from my bed rail. "No, thanks, I think I can figure this out." I grab it with my right hand and press the appropriate arrow. The motor whines and my upper body moves up with the bed. I wince a little from the pain.

"If you want more grub, just press the 'call' button. The doc says you are to have as much food as you want." He smiles and leaves.

I locate the television's power button on the multi-use remote and bring it to life. I soon discover there is no such thing as local news coverage in this part of country. There is no CNN—if I want to catch a glimpse of Dad, I'm out of luck. Seems if you want to know something around here, you just ask someone. From what I overhear outside my door, someone getting shot around here is major news. Two people getting shot on the same day is really big news.

I remove the dome from the plate on my tray. There are more mashed potatoes on this plate than I can eat in a week and the last time I saw a piece of meat this big, it was passed around the table for four people to share. I've never seen a single serving of orange Jell-O this big.

CHAPTER NINETEEN
Even getting shot doesn't get your name in the paper.

Am I dreaming? Am I dead? I hear a voice and see a light far away. I hope I'm dreaming and I hope I am about to wake up in my apartment in Seattle.

"Mister Townsend? Mister Townsend? I need to check your vitals."

My eyes open and the light triggers a pain in my head. As sharp as the pain is behind my left eye, my memory of the night and the previous day is blurred. Someone, a nurse I suspect by her dress and the sterile looking surroundings, stands over me and shoves a probe in my ear.

"Ninety-eight point nine." She hits a few keys on a rolling laptop. "Someone will be by to draw some blood shortly." She plops a plastic urinal on the tray next to my bed. "If you need to go, use this. We don't want you trying to get up just yet. Besides, you're connected to that bag of fluids up there."

With one eye closed to reduce the pain from all the light in the room, I reach for the remote and hold down the up arrow to make myself sit up. I soon realize I couldn't have made the maneuver on my own. My head is throbbing, my left shoulder is stiff and the one eye that seems to be working isn't able to focus.

"What time is it? And what day is it?"

"It's five-fifteen, Sunday morning. Do you know where you are?"

"Yeah, the hospital in…"

"Beaver."

"Yes, Beaver."

"Do you know why you're here?"

"I think I was shot."

"It's your head that has us worried. The bullet missed the vital stuff. But, according to the x-rays that bump on your head has left you with a mild concussion. That's why the twenty questions." The nurse peers under the bandage on my head. "Ouch… that's quite a laceration you've got over that eye. Can you open your left eye?"

I struggle tentatively to open it, but soon realize it's more comfortable to keep it closed.

"Come on, try to keep it open and focus on me."

I try again. It hurts and the twin images of her struggle to come together. They slowly form just one middle-aged but handsome woman with one long braid of silver and brown hair lying lazily over her shoulder—obscuring her badge. I strain to make out her name.

"Mrs. Olinger," she says.

"Excuse me?"

"My name is Nancy Olinger. I'm your nurse this morning. Now, you want to tell me your name and what you're doing here?"

I think about it and after a few seconds my mind begins to kick into gear.

"My name is Thomas Townsend. I'm from Seattle. I'm visiting my grandfather in Divine. I was shot yesterday by Woody Cline… that enough or do you want my social security number?"

"Well, I guess you won't be needing a psych evaluation. I'll be back later. Push the nurse call button if you need anything." And with that, she and her rolling laptop depart.

For the next three hours I apparently slept until breakfast arrived along with a strong desire to empty my bladder. Reaching for the plastic urinal on the nightstand, I upset the water picture, causing it to tumble onto my plate of scrambled eggs and off onto the floor.

"I'm sorry for the mess." I look over at the young man who is now scrambling to save what he can of my breakfast.

"Not to worry, I'll clean up the mess and see to it that you get another plate of food."

"I really am sorry. Can you reach that thing?" I point and he gets the picture. Retrieving the plastic jug, he pulls the curtain between the bed and the door, affording me a comfortable amount of privacy. While I rearrange myself he rolls the table of food away and proceeds to clean up my mess. And, I proceed to attend to my needs.

"I'll be back shortly," he says and then hear him speaking to someone else, "Oh, hi. You can see him in a minute. Right now, he's, uh… he's taking care of business."

"Oh? Is he on the phone?" It's a voice I have become familiar with.

"No, not that kind of business," the young man says.

"Hannah? Is that you? I'll be with you in a minute." If I didn't have a shy bladder before, I have one now. "This may take a few minutes, make yourself comfortable."

"Take your time. I brought a book to read."

"What are you reading?"

"Actually I'm reading your book about Mr. Podus. I stopped by to see your grandfather last night and while I was there I picked up your book in the center's reception area. I wanted to assure Mr. Howard you were all right. I didn't want him to worry. You know how some people can blow things out of proportion."

"I've heard that can be a problem around there." All this conversation isn't helping my situation much. "Listen, I really want to see you but could you just leave and come back in a few minutes?"

"Well... all right. But don't you go anywhere."

"I won't, I promise." Hearing her walk out the door makes things all better. Now, where can I put this thing?

Too many minutes pass before Hannah returns.

"Are you ready to see me now?" she says as she enters the room.

"Yep, I ready. Please come in. Come over here and let me see that you're okay."

She draws the curtain back against the wall. Her eyes are wide and begin to tear-up. "Oh, Tommy. I'm okay but you're... you're a mess." She shakes her head and gives me a pathetic look as she rushes to me and pretends she is going to give me a big hug.

"Careful... careful. I'm still a little sore. You know I stopped a bullet for you."

"I heard the bullet went straight through you. What were you thinking?"

"I was protecting you."

"Protecting me? Last time I saw you, you were lying on the grass in a heap. You know when that bullet went through you; it could have hit somebody else, one of the dogs or something." She smiles—big. A tear runs down her cheek and catches in the corner of her mouth.

"Did he hurt you?"

"No."

"Your mom okay?"

"She's calmed down. She asked about you. Thinks you're a brave man, Tommy Townsend. She thought you put up a real fight. I told her you did, too."

"You can kiss me now, if you're real careful." I hold out my good arm and beckon her to come in close and I close my one good eye. For a moment, when she kissed me, all the pain disappeared.

"Did they... what about Woody?"

"Oh, he's dead," she says in a matter-of-fact sort of way. "If you ever had any thought that I might have any feelings for him... the answer is no. You, on the other hand..."

Nurse Olinger enters with her rolling computer. The thermometer comes out and I am prevented from continuing the conversation for a few minutes. Hannah moves across the room and garners a chair, sliding it around and up to the head of bed. She plays with the hair on my head that isn't covered by the bandage. The nurse takes my urine bottle and notes the amount of contents, empties it in the bathroom, rinses it and hangs it on the rail of bed. She makes a few more entries on her computer. When she leaves, my replacement breakfast is brought in, placed on my table and rolled up to my lap.

"Hungry?" the young man asks.

"Yes. Any coffee?"

"Yes, enjoy." The young man leaves. I turn to Hannah and pushed the remote to elevate the head of the head.

"Do you need any help?" she asks.

"No, I think I can manage." Between gulps of coffee and bites of food, my eyes return to hers and we quietly enjoy each other's company. For now, there are no words needed. I am content that she is safe and beside me. I am confident she feels the same.

An hour went by. Even though I had finished eating, we still had not spoken. When they came to retrieve my food tray, the silence broke.

"You said you visited Papa Tom last night. How was he?"

"I hadn't seen him like that before. His didn't look like himself. He had an I.V. and was on oxygen."

"I know. They had started all that stuff yesterday. He told me it was only temporary, that he had gotten run down and was regaining his strength."

"I tried not to upset him, but I wanted him to know you were okay, even though you had been shot. I tried to minimize things as much as possible. I wanted him to have a firsthand account of what happened and not some exaggerated tale after it had been passed down from person to person."

"How did he take it?"

"Actually, pretty good. You know how he is about trusting God for things. He was praying for you when I was walking out of the room."

"If I don't get out of here today, would you please go by and check on him?"

"I'll be glad to. Why don't you call him?" Have you called your parents?"

"I need to do that, don't I? Where's my phone?"

"Oh, that's right. Last time I saw it, Woody was pitchin' it across the yard. I'll look for it when I get home. Want to use mine?"

"Yes, that will be... never mind. I haven't known their numbers for years. They're in my contacts on my phone."

"Not to worry, I'll go home and get it. I'll come back with lunch. Want something from *Las Carretas*?"

I shake my head. Breakfast is not sitting all that well. As Hannah prepares to leave, Sheriff Martin fills the door to my room.

"How's our wounded writer?" he says much too loudly.

"He looks worse than Woody, and Woody's dead."

Even if I thought that funny, it would hurt too much to laugh.

"You're cold, Hannah," Martin says, shaking his head.

"I'm sorry but I can't thank you enough for what you did yesterday. I'm so glad that part of my life is over. I want to forget any of the past several years ever happened."

"Before you forget it all, I need to get a statement from you and Mr. Townsend about everything that took place yesterday. Do you mind?"

"Please, Sheriff, pull up a chair. I want it part of the record how I attacked a crazed killer with a gun in an attempt to save Miss Harrison, well it is Miss Harrison now isn't it?"

"Yes, I suppose it is," he agreed.

"Absolutely! I won't need that divorce now. Thanks again, Josh, for saving me the time and trouble of divorcing that piece of scum."

"You are a cold woman," I say in agreement. She scoffs at me while nodding to the Sheriff.

"Let's get on with it, Josh. Where do you want us to start?"

"Well, Hannah, why don't you start at the beginning?"

Hannah recounted from where she got the phone call from Woody at her mom's house. I pretty much agreed with everything she said until she got to the part where Woody came out of the house waving the gun.

"We left Mom still bound to the swing and Woody walked us back toward the barn. I assumed he was going to shoot Tommy, so I tried to keep between him and Tommy."

"What? Woody had a grip on your arm and was pointing the gun at you, telling me to keep walking to the…"

"That part doesn't really matter," Martin interrupts.

"Yes it does. Let me finish," Hannah continues. "Tommy waited until Woody waved the pistol away from me, you know, so I wouldn't get shot. And then, with the gun pointed at himself, Tommy sprung like an animal on top of Woody and fought to wrestle the gun away." Hannah looks at me admiringly, and proceeds. "The gun went off and Tommy fell back, clutching his chest and falling to one knee." Her voice became even more dramatic. "Tommy jumped up in a valiant effort to overpower Woody again and screamed, 'Run Hannah, run.' That's when Woody clobbered him in the head with the gun's barrel and Tommy dropped face down in the dirt. I ran for my life, fearing Tommy was dead or dying. But, Woody yelled at me to stop or he would do to Mom what he did to Tommy." She looked at me and smiled again. "That pretty much what happened, Tommy?"

"I wouldn't know much about that last part. I was pretty much out of it by then. But, if you say so, I kind of like that part about me springing on Woody like an animal. Did you get all that, Sheriff?"

"Well she makes you out as some kind of hero."

"Hey, I'm the one with the bullet and the bandages. And, while we're setting the record straight, you make sure the press stops by and gets the full story, especially about the part where Hannah worked with the DEA to set up the bust in the first place."

"Not too fast, Tommy. There are still a number people alive and behind bars that don't know that part. As far as they know, Woody got caught and killed in a shoot-out with the Sheriff of Beaver County, Oklahoma. I think I could be persuaded to pose for that picture." Josh smiles at Hannah. She returns the smile.

"I really don't care what the people of Divine think. Everyone I care about knows the truth…now." Hannah squeezes my hand and winks at the Sheriff. "As far as the rest, Woody took me and Tommy's car and made a run for it. I think you pretty much know how that ended, don't you, Josh?"

"Yes, Ma'am. I do."

The inquisition completed, Hannah left in search of my phone and the Sheriff, with notes in hand, left to complete his report. With a smile on my face and a song in my heart… and a knot on my head and a hole in my chest, I dream while I wait for lunch and my phone.

I see the lunch trays in the hall, but Hannah has failed to return. I thought being a stranger in Divine was uncomfortable. Being an out-of-towner—no, make that an out-of-stater—you would think I came from another country… or another planet. Doc Watson is the only face I recognize and he hasn't been seen since earlier this morning. Nurse Olinger evidently has other fish to fry. If they would get this I.V. out of my hand, the bag was sucked dry hours ago. And, I have to use this plastic thing again.

I struggle to get the bed rail down, push away the table with this morning's unfinished breakfast and cold coffee, and swing my legs over the edge. Too late I realize I should have raised the back of the bed first, but better late than never. Great! Now I'm sitting up on the right side of my bed and the urinal is on the night stand, the wrong side.

I lie on my back across the bed and stretch to reach the urinal. Why is everything always just out of reach? I make a valiant effort like a shortstop diving for a low line drive over second. I pray I don't make an error on the play. Again, too late I consider pressing the nurse's button—now near my knees and again on the opposite side of the bed. Eureka! I reach my saving vessel and strain my underdeveloped abs to perform a sit-up, one hand extended over my head, the prize in the other.

Out of breath and my stomach muscles feeling the burn of my morning workout, I return upright. The alternative to a catheter in my free hand, over-full bladder busting from the strenuous workout, and now—wouldn't you know it, the curtain way behind me. I fashion a tent from my sheet and begin to let things flow when…

"Mr. Townsend?"

Now someone comes ro my aid?

"Mr. Townsend, is that you under there?" It's Nurse Olinger. Shy bladder syndrome returns. Off comes the sheet. I would put the urinal down but there is no flat surface in reach. The hospital gown is stuffed under my useless arm. The cold air begins waging battle with my nakedness and whatever muscle I have that is keeping back the flow from my bladder.

"Can I help?" she asks.

"Too late, things have started which no one can stop." The urinal begins filling and requires the attention of my one free hand. The other hand is un-available for any kind of assistance. My shyness, my modesty, but not my embarrassment, have left the room. I forget that medical professionals have seen it all. Nurse Olinger patiently waits behind me and at the appropriate time steps forward and retrieves the half-full vessel. I recover, re-cover, and rearrange myself in a proper manner to present themselves.

"I'll remove your I.V. and you can resume a more comfortable lifestyle." She returns from the bathroom and after removing her latex gloves, logs the expelled fluid volume on her rolling computer. She dons another pair of gloves and removes the needle from my arm along with the tape and an inch of hair which was reluctant to depart my company.

"Ouch!"

"Anything I can get you? Your lunch will be here in a minute. How are you feeling?"

"Better now that my bladder is empty, and that useless tube is gone, along with my pride."

"You're a very lucky man, Mr. Townsend," she says while she peers at my wounds—first my chest from the front, and then the back. "I'll need to re-dress these." She inspects my head. "Yes, we need to put another dressing on this, too. It's healing nicely. But first, why don't you take a shower, just be careful not to get any of the bandaged areas wet. We can sponge bathe you from the waist up. Be careful getting up at first. We don't want you falling and banging your head again. There are towels and a wash cloth next to the shower. There's an emergency cord you can pull if you require any assistance. If you think you're going to need help, I can get someone in here to bathe you." She smiles. I don't.

"Is Doctor Watson going to come by today?"

"He was here earlier, but he got called away to Divine. He'll probably be back this afternoon. You'll live until he gets back. I'm pretty sure of that."

"I just want to know when I can leave the hospital."

"Probably this evening... if he returns and releases you."

CHAPTER TWENTY
He left me a message.

I can now relate to John Henderson's struggle with the loss of a hand. Fortunately my right hand is free to do as it wishes. One hand washes the other, but not itself. One hand pulls a zipper up... or down, but not without the cooperation of the other holding the other end in position. I would give anything for my loafers, these Nike's won't tie themselves, and overalls—forget it. Time to call for assistance.

A tall young man in blue hospital scrubs bounds through my door.

"Ben Payton at your service. What can I do for you, Mr. Townsend?"

"I require a little assistance but you look over qualified to be helping me get myself together. I'm not sure how to explain it, but I need help cleaning things I can't clean and zipping things I can't zip."

"I'll be glad to help with whatever you need. I normally work in the E.R., but I was at the nurse's station flirting with one of the staff when I heard your call for help. I wanted to see the guy that got shot in a fight with an escaped killer. I've never treated a patient that got shot by someone other than himself."

"Huh?"

"A guy came in her last fall with a self-inflicted gunshot wound to his foot—the jerk rested his rifle barrel on the toe of his boot while he lit a cigarette. His buddy, seeing a buck running out of the brush chasing after a doe, tapped him on the shoulder. When the rifle went off, so did the guy's toe. The buck disappeared into the next county."

"Are you kidding me?" I said.

"No. The buck is probably still running. And, I know for a fact the guy's toe is still missing, too. He was in here last month with a badly infected blister from wearing a poorly fitted boot."

"What?" I must be dreaming. I can't believe what I'm hearing. This is crazy, even for the Oklahoma panhandle.

"I'm just pulling your leg." The young man's serious face turns into a huge smile showing all of his teeth. "We're kind of understaffed and I'm just filling in and helping where I can. Besides, I really did want to meet you. I'm related to most of the patients that come through here. I wanted to meet someone I hadn't met before. So, how you doing, Mr. Tom Townsend? Like I said, I'm Ben Payton." He holds out his hand. "Nice to meet you." We shake.

"Nice to meet you, Ben. Now, I need a little help… another hand if you will."

"Well, I'll be glad to get the rest of you clean and tie your hospital gown behind you. But, I've seen your chart and until Dr. Watson dismisses you, you won't be needing pants zipped or shoes tied. I'll be glad to get a pair of hospital slippers and we can take a walk around the halls to see how you're navigating. It's about time you had a bowel movement, don't you think?"

This is insane. I have no phone, no phone numbers, and none of my things, my computer, my recorder, and nothing to read.

After a few laps of the halls outside my room at Beaver County Hospital, my system returns to its usual routine and I begin to wish I had curbed my appetite yesterday, this morning and during today's lunch. I am spit and polished with the help of my new friend, Ben Payton. And, I have rehearsed my speech to Doc Watson extolling the virtues of my early dismissal from the hospital. I am concerned Hannah hasn't come back, but not enough to obsess over it.

My prayers are answered. Doctor Watson brightens my doorway. And, he brightens my day for he carries with him my recorder. His expression, though, is anything but uplifting.

"Well, I'm certainly happy to see you, but why the long face?" I ask.

He stops at the foot of my bed, places my recorder down on the table there, and takes in an uncomfortably loud and long breath. "Your grandfather's gone home."

He doesn't say anything else. I suppose there isn't really anything else to say. The words, gone home, echo in my head. I'm at a loss for words, or thoughts. I search for a response, an emotion, but I'm unable to find one.

"It was peaceful. He didn't suffer. He was prepared. Hell, he was more than prepared. He had his bags packed, said all his goodbyes, and let the cat out."

"Said all his goodbyes? He didn't tell me goodbye!" The reality takes hold of my body and I feel numb and cold—hurt and angry, and sad. The biggest, deepest, darkest despair I can imagine falls over me.

"He did tell you goodbye, Tommy. He evidently recorded a message to you on your recorder and left a note on top of it for it to be delivered to you. He knew God had finally come to take him home but he must have kept God waiting until he could finish this. A little before noon yesterday he summoned the nurse to take the recorder and the note and leave it for you at the reception desk. When they returned with his lunch tray, he was already gone. They paged me and I drove over there as quickly as I could." He waits for me to respond but I guess he realizes I'm still incapable. "I called your mother. Not only did I tell her about your grandfather but I had to tell her about you."

"Oh, no! How is she doing?"

"She was prepared for the news about her dad, but she was really shaken about you. I assured her you were not in any danger. I told her I would see you shortly and put you on the phone to her when I got here. She said she would fly out in the morning—said your dad would come as soon as the funeral arrangements were made. Are you prepared to talk to her now?"

"Yes, please. I don't know her number—it's in my phone. I don't have my cell phone. Can I borrow yours?"

"Certainly. I've got her number here, just hit redial." He hands me his phone and, after one ring, she answers.

"Doctor Watson?"

"No, Mom. It's me."

"Oh, Tommy…"

I am emotionally drained. I ache all over, not from the knot on my head or the wound in my chest—from the emptiness in my heart. Doc Watson stayed with me for as long as he could after I got off the phone with Mom. He even let me call Hannah while I still had his phone. Her sister had arrived at the farm with her kids. They had news from her brother that he would be flown out on a hardship pass and their father's funeral would be in three days. She wanted to come see me tonight but I insisted she stay with her family—at least for now.

Tonight I remember Papa Tom. I read, re-read, and read again the handwritten note he left with my recorder:

Tommy,

Thanks for the use of your recorder. I have left a personal message for you and your mother. Don't feel sad that you weren't there when I went home. This is easier for me too. You remember the last thing I said to you? I said I'd be looking for you. And, I will. Only I'll be waiting and looking for you in Heaven. I'll be having the time of my life praising Jesus, and I want you to come join me when you're through writing books and romancing Miss Harrison. You two will make a fine couple, if that's what you have in mind.

I left a few final thoughts on the recorder you might want to use, or not, in your book. Now that you know the secrets, you can keep them or share them. Whatever you think is best.

With all my love, until we talk again,

Papa Tom

John 15:13

What did he mean by the secrets? I don't remember him telling me more than one. Doc Watson left orders for me to be given some medication to be taken with my evening meal. The nurse insists it has to be taken with food, so if I am to receive the medication I have to first eat my dinner. I eat my dinner and receive the meds.

I awake at 11:30PM. I must admit, I'm not as depressed as I was before getting the drugs. I am also surprised that I slept. I guess the good doctor knew what he was doing. I look over at the recorder on my table. The hand written note from Papa Tom still lies next to it.

There is an ominous sense of finality that accompanies the note. It will be the last communication I have from him, or at least until, and if, I get to Heaven.

There was a time when I purchased a lottery ticket every week. I would keep the ticket in my car's glove compartment and refuse to check the winning numbers for several days after the drawing—the idea being that until I actually checked the numbers, I hadn't actually lost the lottery prize. Well, as long as I haven't actually heard Papa Tom's last words—as long as they haven't been spoken to me—I can still anticipate hearing from him again. It is not hearing from him again that frightens me most.

At 3:30 in the morning, I make the decision to listen to the recording.

> *Tommy,*
>
> *This is the third time I have started over—never used one of these things before. But, I think I have the hang of it now. So, here goes…*
>
> *I want you to know how happy I am at this very moment. I can feel God calling me home and I am anxious to obey. There is no fear of the unknown, of what lies ahead, because I know what's on the other side. He told me in His Word and His Spirit has reminded me over the years of the promise of when I leave this place, I will immediately be in a better place, in His presence. Won't that be wonderful? He was with me when I was buried in the mine. I thought I might die then, but I knew I wasn't alone and He promised to be there with me through all the trials and troubles I would ever face. I could never have dealt with my wife's death without Him*

there to comfort me and assure me she was smiling at His side and not in the burned out shell of her car.

I am glad for the time we had this past week. Has it only been a week? We were apart so much during the last years while you were becoming a man, but you were never out of my thoughts and prayers.

Well, you came to learn about the secret. You have what you came for, I hope you understand it, and do the right thing with this new knowledge. Secrets don't remain secrets once they are shared with others. For that reason it is paramount for you to understand the very nature of a secret is that it contains the truth. If it is not truth, it is false— often gossip and malicious.

What secret or secrets have you learned, Tommy? How will you use your new knowledge?

First, I would like to go over the secrets, the truths, I have shared with you. When you were a child I spoke to you of the secrets contained in the Bible. The Bible contains God's truth, His love for you, His sacrifice for your salvation, and His many promises made especially for you. What makes these truths a secret? They are known only by those who believe in His Son. Oh, He has made the world aware of these truths but the world doesn't understand them. They don't recognize the truth. They cannot know because they do not desire to know. If they were to seek Him, they would discover the secrets about eternity and everlasting life that you know. It is this secret, this truth, which is at the top of the list of secrets I have shared with you.

I suppose you were thinking of the secret of why Morton Podus should have fought to rescue me when I was trapped in the mine collapse—in light of what I had done for him. This was the secret I promised to tell you when you became a writer like your father. Were you thinking it was because I stopped his son Jake from jumping off the water tower? Did old man Podus owe me for saving his son's life or was it for sparing him the embarrassment of the town discovering his son was no hero? Was that the secret?

Bobby Hampton gave his life, a life of honor and fame and took upon himself the life of a disgraced coward who deserted his brothers and ran, leaving them wounded behind to face the enemy and death alone? Bobby Hampton gave up his place of honor so that a brother could have the respect of his father. Was that the secret, Bobby Hampton's sacrifice?

You couldn't have known at the time that Hannah's secret kept her from the respect and love of a whole town that once cared for her and her family. Her secret—she did the right thing and, in doing so, had to hide the truth about herself from the community. Not much different from what Bobby Hampton chose to do. Not knowing her secret, her truth, nearly caused you to miss out on a rewarding relationship.

Knowing secrets, knowing the truth, brings with it a huge personal responsibility. Now that you know these truths, what will you do with that knowledge?

Tommy, I said my goodbyes to your mother and your sister. I said goodbye to Doc Watson, a few close friends, and much of the staff here at Wildflower. The prognosis of my condition was not known to many. I wanted to enjoy their company while I was alive and for them to enjoy mine. It will be up to you to share the secret of my illness along with the joy of my homecoming. I will not put the emotional burden of speaking at my funeral on you. I have already asked my good friend, Randy Buchanan to do the honors. He gladly accepted.

My attorney, Paul Noak, met with me last week and prepared my will. In it, I give you the responsibility of overseeing my things, my resources, and my unfinished work. Besides finishing the writing of my book, you have a lot of work ahead of you. I hope you will accept what I asked of you and make me proud.

Remember me, Tommy Boy, and my love for you… and His love for you.

After playing the message for the third time, I put the recorder safely in my briefcase. Not only have I committed every word to memory but I am determined not to pull the covers over my head and cry over the loss of Papa Tom but to fondly remember him and take comfort in the knowledge of where he is and whom he is spending his time with.

I reflect on my future and because of my grandfather's legacy, will delight in the reality of living each and every minute of my life in his presence as well as God's, both here and in eternity. Papa Tom saw to it.

CHAPTER 21
Two funerals and a...

Where is the courage and conviction I had when I went to sleep? Last night, hearing Papa Tom's voice and reflecting on his words gave me comfort and renewed confidence in myself, God, Hannah, and every dream I ever entertained. But now, this morning, with the light streaming in my hospital room's window, I awake with the realities of physical pain. Whatever and however much pain medication I received last night, my brain this morning is well aware of each wound site, every nerve ending in the vicinity and the muscles affected by the path of the bullet. I struggle to reach the call button.

"Good morning, Mr. Townsend. How are we doing this fine morning?" I recognize Nurse Olinger's voice before witnessing her entry into my room, her rolling computer leading the way.

"Whatever meds I received early this morning to relieve the pain and help me sleep have finished their work. I don't need to go back to sleep but I would certainly appreciate being a little more pain free."

"Often it's the pain in our lives that lets us know we are, in fact, alive." I'm guessing her smile is her way of telling me that more pain medicine won't be forthcoming.

"Oh, I feel alive. I just wish I were dead."

"Dr. Watson left orders for some pain killers as needed."

"Well, alright then. They're needed. And, so is some coffee. And, a shower. Is that me that smells?"

"It's not anything I put on this morning." Nurse Olinger starts the process of checking my temperature, my blood pressure, and my wound sites. "You're healing quite nicely. You need to get on your feet and move around. Doctor Watson will probably release you today."

"That's good news," Hannah says, marching in my room and surprising me with an armful of clothes. "I brought some clothes for you to wear—something besides overalls and Dad's work shirts. I hope you don't mind; I took the keys to your room and went through your things. You didn't pack a lot."

"I travel light."

Hannah sits patiently in the corner of the room while the nurse completes her tasks and registers my progress on her laptop. As the computer rolls out, Hannah comes in for a hug.

"Oh, wow!" She pulls back and her face scrunches up. "You're a little rank this morning. Why don't you brush your teeth and jump in the shower?"

"I can do that—all except the jumping part. Would you find me some coffee and a newspaper and I'll take care of my personal stuff?"

When I finish my daily routine and my shower, Hannah is sitting on my freshly made bed reading the Oklahoma NewsOK and drinking coffee.

"Where's mine?" I say. I'm uncomfortable in these split-in-the -back hospital gowns. Seeing me fidgeting with my gown, she gets up and puts the clothes she has picked out for me on the bed and hands me my coffee.

"I saw Doc Watson when I was getting the coffee. He said you will be getting out today, so go ahead and put some real clothes on. I'll wait outside." She stops immediately and spins back around. Her eyes are full of tears. She wraps me with her arms, buries her head against my neck, and sobs. "I am so very sorry about your grandfather."

"Thank you. I miss him too, but it's all right—I'm all right with it. I've got something from him I will share with you later." I push her back. Maybe I'm not as all right with it as I think. I don't want to completely deal with his death just now. I would prefer to ease into it. She steps outside and closes the door behind her. I slip on a pair of slacks but forego the shirt because I'm sure they will still be fiddling with my wounds. Looking in the mirror, I realize my head wound appears much worse than it actually is. While most of the swelling has subsided, the bruising around my eye has become darker and the white of my left eye is predominantly blood red. Funny, but my pain left the minute Hannah entered the room.

Sitting on the edge of my bed, I sip my coffee and anxiously wait for Hannah to return. And, when she does, she is joined by both Doc Watson and Nurse Olinger.

"I guess you heard you were getting out today," Doc Watson says as he walks up to me and begins inspecting my head, eye, and then the wounds in my chest and back. "I understand you are in a great deal of pain this morning?"

"Not so much now that I've gotten up, had a shower, coffee, and…" I look over at Hannah and smile.

"Better than drugs, isn't it?" Nurse Olinger remarks.

"What is?" I ask. She looks over at Hannah, then back to me and smiles."

"Yes, I suppose it is." I turn to Doc Watson. "I listened to the recording my grandfather let for me."

"Good. Are you okay with everything?"

"Yes. Yes, I am. Thank you for bringing it to me." I put my hand on his shoulder. "I want to thank you for the personal care and respect you gave him."

"Your grandfather and I were very close. I, too, wanted to keep him around as long as possible but I understood the decisions he made about his treatment. I spoke to your mother again last night about your condition. She was very concerned as you might expect. She should be here around noon." He walks to the door, turns and continues, "I'll check back on you before you leave today." Nurse Olinger follows him out, remarking that she will return shortly to put new dressings on my wounds.

"I haven't had a chance to tell you how sorry I am about your grandfather," Hannah whispers as she sits down by me on the bed.

"He left me a sort of farewell message on my recorder."

"I kind of gathered that by your conversation with Doc Watson."

"All this time he was dying right in front of eyes, but he hid it and his pain from me until he could fulfill his promise and tell me the secret."

"And, what was it?"

"I'll tell you all about it sometime, but right now what about you and your family? Is your brother here yet?"

"He's in Georgia right now, caught a military transport from Afghanistan, I think. He'll be here tomorrow. We've scheduled a small family service at the funeral home here in Beaver for tomorrow afternoon. Say, have you seen the story in the paper about Woody's demise?"

"No, I haven't. What does it say?"

"Well, I hope you're not disappointed, but the Federal Marshall and Sheriff Martin got together and released their version of what happened in a press release."

"Why would I be disappointed?"

"Well it depends on what you wanted your role to be."

"Wanted my role to be? What do you mean?"

"It was Marshall Brander's idea. He thought it would be best if the news report didn't say anything about Woody kidnapping me. Instead it just said Sheriff Martin got a tip Woody was headed for Divine to pick me up and head for the Mexican border. It says the Sheriff and his men surrounded Woody outside the farm and that he was killed in a shootout."

"Okay… but what did it say about me?"

"It said an innocent bystander was wounded."

"An innocent bystander? I'm an innocent bystander?"

"They released the story to Oklahoma City's major paper, the NewsOK and made sure it was distributed throughout the prison in El Reno. That's where the drug leaders that were arrested with Woody are housed. They think that if the gang believes Woody and I were still together, they won't suspect I helped set up the bust. And, I don't have to live under the fear of reprisal by the gang anymore."

"Maybe so, but the people of Divine will still think you're associated with the criminal element."

"Let them think what they want. My sister has asked Mom to move down to San Antonio with her family. She could use her help with the kids. Mom's going to lease the farm to one of the neighboring ranchers.

Then, there won't be any of my family living in Divine for them to gossip about."

"Well that makes sense. Guess I won't be writing a book about what happened. No market for books about wounded, innocent bystanders."

"Tommy." She gives me a stern look.

"I'm just kidding. They probably wouldn't have spelled my name right anyway. Guess I won't have any exciting stories about what I did on summer vacation to tell my students back home."

"You can tell them you met me. Don't you find that in itself exciting?"

"Of course I do, Hannah."

Just as I lean over to show her how exciting it can be, Nurse Olinger marches in with a tray of medical supplies.

"I'm going to get you all fixed up to go home. You'll need to see Doctor Watson in a couple days to get your wounds checked and the stitches removed."

"Tommy, I need to get back home. My brother could be here anytime. We have a bunch of family business to go over. I've got to call the clinic in Portland, let them know when I'm going to be back. That is, if I still have a job to go back to."

"You haven't talked to them about what's been going on?"

"What's been going on? My dad's passing, my being kidnapped, my husband's death in a shoot-out, my new boyfriend shot... as an innocent bystander. Who is going to believe all or even any of that? What am I going to tell them? Would you believe it if you hadn't been here?"

"You're right. Sounds like the dog ate your homework. Listen, my mom is going to be here sometime this afternoon, too. Sometime, between funerals, let's try to get together."

Nurse Olinger no longer stands patiently for Hannah and me to finish our conversation. She moves in between us and starts cleaning, swabbing, cutting strips of tape, and opening gauze packages. That exciting kiss I was expecting is going to have to wait. Hannah blows me a kiss from the door.

By 8:30 I'm up, showered, my wounds dressed, and comfortably decked out in the clothes Hannah brought me from my room at the Lodge. I'm groomed and fed. All dressed up and no place to go. Hannah left me the copy of the *NewsOK* and it and my coffee join me in the hospital's lobby. I am not comfortable sitting in my room. The lobby reminds me of a small regional airport; the announcements over the loud speakers are for doctors rather than passengers and the airline uniforms are replaced with white lab coats, but the hustle and bustle puts me at ease. I consume the paper from the nation's headlines to farm and ranch equipment want ads.

Even the huge clock that hangs from the ceiling over the hallway reminds me of an airport. The morning is waning and the little hand and the big hand are joined at eleven. I've scrounged several coffee refills from the nurses' lounge and the paper has been thoroughly read and replaced by an old copy of *Farm Journal Magazine*. I can't believe I am actually engrossed in a Q&A feature, 'Ask an Agronomist,' and wanting to know the answer to, 'Will My Disk Chisel Shatter a Hard Pan Better than an Inline Ripper?' when standing directly in front of me is my mother.

"Mom!"

"Hello, Tommy." She bends down, catching me before I can uncross my legs and get up, and leaves a bright red stain of her kiss on my forehead. "I expected to see you in bed with tubes and wires and such. I didn't picture you lounging with a magazine, uh… the *Farm Journal*? You really are back to your roots."

"I'm glad you didn't see me yesterday in my overalls." I stand and give her a big hug. "When did you leave Atlanta? How did you get here so quickly? I had to fly half a day and then drive several hours. It was almost dark when I finally arrived in Divine."

"Good fortune and good friends. I left Atlanta this morning, first flight out on Delta, and Randy Buchanan met me with his plane at the Oklahoma City airport. We landed here in Beaver just a few minutes ago. Your dad will leave Atlanta once we get Papa Tom's service scheduled. He can't just pick up and leave with his schedule."

"It is really good to see you, Mom. I am sorry it has to be under these circumstances."

"Regardless of the circumstances, I am so glad to see you. The news of you getting shot came as quite a shock. Thank God it was Doc Watson who called. I got the news, *'late breaking and straight from the source'*, as your dad would say, and then Randy called me last night and offered to fly me here. In the middle of what seems like trials, God continues to bless us."

"I have come to see what Papa Tom was always trying to explain to me."

"I am so glad that you were here, Tommy."

"Well, actually I wasn't with him when he… when he passed. I was here, in this hospital."

"But you were here, in Oklahoma, with him. He missed you so much, Tommy. He was so happy you had come, if only to interview him for your book."

"It was stupid and self-centered to have waited until there was something in it for me, before I decided to come. I am so ashamed,

Mom. I got so much more than just a story; I got my life back on track. I got back in his good graces and back…" I look up and point up, "back in His good graces, too."

"Tommy, you were always in His favor." Mom smiles and her eyes fill with tears. "Now you really have made a mess of my make-up. First my lipstick smeared on your forehead and now my mascara running down my face. I must look a fright." She digs in her purse for a mirror and a tissue.

"You look beautiful, Mom." She smiles again and blots her eyes. She dives again into her enormous bag and comes up with her lip color of the day. "Can we go somewhere not so public? You're still a patient, aren't you? Or have you been discharged?"

"Doctor Watson said he would be back and discharge me this afternoon. We can go to my room if you like. Where are your bags?"

"Randy took them on to his house; he has invited your father and me to stay there while we're here. He's sending a driver to take me to Divine and anywhere I need to go. He wants to discuss the memorial service at his house tonight. He said your grandfather discussed with him most of the details earlier this week. You know your Papa Tom liked to take care of everything himself, even his own funeral." She smiled and I nod an agreement.

Nurse Olinger seems pleased that I have returned to my room.

"You know, Mr. Townsend, you are still a patient here and that I am responsible for your care until you are discharged."

"Yes, I am sorry. Miss Olinger, this is my mother. She just arrived from Atlanta. And, Mom, this woman has treated me as though I was her own child while I've been under her care."

"Hello, Mrs. Townsend; what your son means to say is that I have treated him like a child since he has been here." Nurse Olinger moves her rolling computer into position as I obediently sit on the side of my bed and open my mouth to have my temperature taken. "We won't need to take your temperature today. We are confident you don't have any infection. In fact, you seem to be doing remarkably well for a man who's been shot and had his skull cracked."

"As a child, Tommy always bounced back quickly from his little bumps and bruises." Mom added.

"Your lunch will be here soon." She turns to my mother and asks, "Would you like me to request a food tray for you, Mrs. Townsend? Or, would you two like to dine in the cafeteria at a comfortable table and in a more relaxed setting?"

"Mom? What would you prefer?"

"If you don't mind, let me freshen up here first, and then let's find the cafeteria."

"It has been a year and a half since we sat down together and enjoyed a meal." I say, setting my tray down on a table and pulling out a chair for my mom.

"I missed you not coming to Atlanta for Christmas last year. Your sister was there." She set down her salad and iced tea, allowing me to push her chair in as she sat.

"Mom, it was the first Christmas in many years that I hadn't spent with family. A group of my friends, some single, some married, but all without kids, wanted to go skiing over the Christmas holidays. You know, that may have been the last Christmas I spend without family."

"Oh… then you are coming home for Christmas this year."

"I'm not saying that for sure. I'm saying I want to be with family this Christmas."

"Have you talked to your sister about going there for Christmas?"

"No."

"Well, what other family do you have?"

"None, yet." And then things get quiet for a moment and Mom tilts her head and seems anxious to hear more. When nothing more is offered, she snaps, "You aren't planning a wedding are you? I told you I wasn't coming for a wedding."

"No. We actually haven't discussed anything like that. I've just been considering the possibility of getting married."

"Well, when am I going to meet the Harrison girl?"

"Soon enough. How's Dad? He looked good when I caught his broadcast... was it yesterday. I can't remember, but he looked good."

The important stuff was out of the way for the time being. We really hadn't spoken this much... well, since before I didn't show up for Christmas last year. The next two hours were pleasant, not terribly enlightening or productive in solving world issues, but pleasant. We relaxed and let our relationship wrap around us like a warm blanket. It is comfortable and it begins to feel good again, and, as the conversation incorporates the reason for our being together now, the love between a mother and her son grieving the loss of their father and grandfather, our bond surrounds the pieces of our lives and holds them tightly and securely together once more.

CHAPTER TWENTY-TWO
Papa Tom's Memorial

We were invited to dinner at Mr. Buchanan's home the evening Mom arrived. You can't see his home from the highway. The only way is from the sky. We pass several small homes in a cul-de-sac at the front of the property. I am told they belong to some of the staff. No telling just exactly how many acres his property includes. But, for the enormity of it all, it is understated and functional. There are barns and pens for the cattle, enormous metal buildings for the tractors, combines, and of course a hangar for not only his corporate jet but a helicopter as well. The Buchanan compound contains four homes: the main house is the residence of Mr. Buchanan and his wife Elizabeth; two other adjacent homes belong to two of his children, and a fourth houses Mr. and Mrs. Robles and their family. Mr. Robles manages the day to day operations of Buchanan Land and Cattle Company.

For all of his obvious wealth, Randolph Buchanan is a wonderfully gracious and common man. The Buchanan wealth funded most of the altruistic projects in the community as well as met the individual needs of families and situations that were championed by my grandfather. This had been going on since 1963, when God used the tragedy of my grandmother's death to create a relationship between Papa Tom and the Buchanans that would bless many lives and families.

We sit down together in a small intimate dining room. I am surprised to learn Elizabeth has prepared dinner herself.

After Randy says grace over the meal, he starts the conversation. "I hope you don't mind but I would like to discuss Mr. Howard's funeral. I understand this is of course your family's decision but I want to let you know the response I have gotten from the community."

Mom and I glance at each other and nod our agreement.

"Randy, Tommy and I discussed having a small memorial service at Wildflower because we felt that is what he would have wanted. And then a private graveside service at the cemetery where my mother is buried." Mom looks to me for approval and then back to Randy.

"Last week, Mr. Howard asked me to speak at his service and he pretty much indicated the location would be what you have suggested. But, I have been approached by several people as well as some organizations in the community who would like to be able to pay their respects."

"How many people are we talking about?" I ask.

"Well, the sheer numbers we would have to accommodate rules out Wildflower as a venue. You are going to think this rather bizarre, but I have talked with the head of the county school board and she has not only given me permission but thinks it would be a wonderful tribute to have it at the Beaver High School football stadium."

Sitting here now, in the center of the football field, I completely understand why Randy chose this location for Papa Tom's service.

"Your grandfather would be so humbled," Mom whispers to me.

We sit—his immediately family and closest friends—on a raised platform. Across from us, bleachers are filled to the brim. Additional people line the track from goal post to goal post. The parking lot is full. School buses, church buses, and law enforcement vehicles line the fence.

As Mr. Buchanan approaches the podium, my eyes scan the crowd. The entire population of Divine must be here this morning. Three busloads of patients and staff from Wildflower are here. The congregations from four or five different churches are present. Two church choirs have sung a collection of hymns while people were still arriving. The local VFW presented the colors with an honor guard comprised of veterans from Iraq, Afghanistan, Vietnam, Korea and even one member wheeled in representing WWII. The coal mine suspended operations today so that every employee could attend. There is even a broadcast team from a television station in Oklahoma City.

"Good morning friends, family, and citizens of Divine and the surrounding area—welcome all who have come today to pay their respects to and honor the life of Tom Robert Howard. Each one of us has a story of how Mr. Howard touched our lives and we are all better for having known him and having been loved by him. He was not a teacher, but he instructed us all. He gave us lessons on love, compassion, and understanding. He was not a mechanic; however he seemed to fix everyone and everything that was broken. He was not a preacher, but he taught us all about God. He didn't just teach us about God, he showed us God through his life. He showed us the nature and the character of God through his actions.

"I spoke with him two days before he went home to be with God. He knew he was dying but he wasn't afraid, he wasn't sad. Tom Howard was excited and happy, happy like a child looking forward to Christmas morning, happy about being where he is right now—in the presence of God…"

I wish I could feel that happy about being here, right now. Oh, I'm happy for Papa Tom. I am certain he had no regrets. I know he accomplished everything he planned. I am confident his every dream was fulfilled. And, one of those dreams was of me—getting right with God and re-establishing my priorities and goals.

I am grateful to Papa Tom for so many things. He gave me much more than I came for. He gave me the secrets I had been looking for.

Randy finishes. There's not a dry eye in the stadium, but there isn't a sad face in the crowd either. How often do you walk away from a funeral service with a smile on your face and in your heart?

We spend nearly an hour shaking hands with and hugging long lines of people whose lives were touched by Papa Tom in some fashion. This afternoon, I, Mom, Dad, and my sister Susan who arrived yesterday with Dad, will go out to the little cemetery west of Divine. We will gather again as we did thirty years ago. We won't be saying a final goodbye; we will be looking forward to seeing both my grandmother and Papa Tom again.

I realize Hannah and I haven't been together or even spoken to each other in two days. We talked briefly by phone after her father's service. We made awkward, superficial excuses about why we should be with our families now, and it wasn't the time or place to be introducing them to our, what…girlfriend, special person? After all, what were we?

I find a quiet place, away from the crowd of well-wishers, and call her cell.

233

"Hi," she says, knowing it's me from the caller I.D.

"How are you doing?" I say as if it hasn't been two days.

"Oh, fine. You know, under the circumstances."

"Well, what are you doing under the circumstances, anyway?" I try to lighten things up.

"Huh?"

I should have known better. "How is your family? Your brother?"

"He is fine, they're all fine… you know, *under the circumstances*."

"I'm sorry, Hannah. When are you going back to Portland?"

"Tomorrow morning."

"Tomorrow?" My disappointment plain in the tone of my voice.

"Yes, I have to get back to my job. I called them yesterday. They weren't exactly happy about it, but they do seem interested in me coming back."

"What time?"

"What time, what?"

"What time does your plane leave?"

"Well, it doesn't leave Oklahoma City until 1:30 in the afternoon, but I need to leave here at 8:00 in the morning. My brother is going to drive me. Poor guy, he has to turn around and drive all the way back here, his flight isn't for another two days."

"Listen, I need to get back, too. Let me schedule a flight out tomorrow afternoon and you can ride with me to the airport. That will save your brother from making the long, roundtrip drive."

"How considerate of you. You'd do that for my brother?" Her tone gives me a shudder.

"You know that's not why I want to do it. I think the long drive together to the airport would do us some good."

"You really think we can get along together for that much time? You know we have a history… I don't want to be jumping out of your car on the highway and having to flag down a lonely truck driver who's been on the road for several days without any…"

"Without any what?

"Get your mind out of the gutter. I was going to say without any sleep. I don't want to put my life in the hands of a sleep deprived truck driver."

"Good. Let me call and make a flight reservation to Seattle. I'll pick you up at 8:00 in the morning."

"Tom, I am looking forward to seeing you tomorrow."

"I've missed seeing you, too. Good night." She called me TOM!

Mom and Dad are very disappointed about my early departure. My sister, not so much. We need to find time to work on our relationship but a couple thousand miles separation for several years tends to make a relationship wane, even if you are blood related. Younger sisters and older brothers getting along always seems to be a little problematic. I am a writer. I will make a point of connecting with her by email more often. Do I even have her email address? I did promise to spend Thanksgiving this year in Atlanta with my parents. And, I did promise to call Papa Tom's executor, Paul Noak, next week and work out the details of his will.

Sleep is not coming easily tonight. Is it a chapter in my life I'm completing? Is it anticipation of a new chapter about to begin? A lot of promises were made today—to others, as well as to myself.

Is my restlessness about closing the book on my grandfather's life? While I have a huge catalog of memories of our times together—the activities, the talks, the life lessons—there is a somber sense of realizing there will be no more pages, no more events to be added. The book is closed. I will cherish the book.

There is another book weighing heavily on me, Papa Tom's secret. There's the rub. Which secret? Bobby Hampton would likely prefer for his sacrifice to remain untold. I sense he was the kind of man, confident in his choice, who meant to create a new life for Jake Podus. Do I negate his sacrifice with my telling of his story? Bobby Hampton took his secret to his grave, as did my grandfather. There are secrets that deserve to be honored. There are secrets whose truths deserved to be told. What gain will be made by the telling? Who will gain by the revelation of the secrets I now know? Is it any wonder I can't sleep?

My travel alarm clock performs flawlessly. It is 6:00 and I am up. Unable to sleep last night, I got up, showered, shaved, and packed in preparation for the full day of traveling that lies ahead.

Now, faced with two hours to kill and a stomach to feed, I text Hannah.

R U goin to eat brkfst @ home?

Moments later my phone chimes…

on the road

I guess she wants to stop somewhere and get some kind of fast food. My stomach wants some food… fast.

The Spot! opened at 6:30. Coffee and a full breakfast was ordered and consumed. I ate alone but my thoughts of the time spent on top of the water tower keep me company.

Mrs. Ahr at the Lodge wasn't up yet. I'll stop and pay my bill on the way back from Hannah's.

The drive to Hannah's brings back a flood of memories. Was it only two weeks ago I made my first trip down this road? It seems like a lifetime ago.

I pass Wildflower on the right. More memories. The front porch rockers—with Papa Tom—meeting Hannah the first time. Smiles. Tears. Dominoes.

The combines are not parked on the side of the highway anymore. I assume they are at work in some farmer's fields. I still cannot get use to the unending and unremarkable flat horizon. The majestic Mt. Rainier of Seattle's skyline beckons me home. After today, Divine and the Oklahoma Panhandle will have no hold on me.

The dogs announce my arrival, bouncing back and forth across the narrow drive to the Harrison's home. Hannah rises from the porch swing, grabs her luggage and things, and walks out to meet me before I come to a complete stop.

"Pop the trunk and let me put these in the back."

"Sure. Okay." I locate the switch and the trunk swings up.

"Don't get out. Let's just go." She runs around and gets in.

"Why the rush?"

"There was a lot of emotions this morning and…"

"There are a lot of people on your front porch that look a little disappointed." I interrupt and point to the crowd of people standing on the… no, now coming out to the car.

"Okay, okay." She gets out of the car and rushes to meet them. "But only five more minutes of crying and then I have to go."

Hannah's mother comes around to my side of the car. I get out and meet her. She hugs me and I hug her back.

"I want you to meet my son, John, and Hannah's sister, Tiffany."

It was a quick, somewhat awkward collage of hand shaking, embarrassing hugging, and clumsy conversation. I was ill-prepared as was Hannah for all the introductions. Not one person could put an appropriate name to my relationship to or with Hannah. Was it only five minutes? Seem like a lot longer. Hannah is still crying, waving out the back as her mother, pregnant sister and her two children in their pajamas, and her brother return with frantic waves and blown kisses of their own.

"Sorry about that. When I announced this morning that I was going outside to wait for you, the sobbing started again. It has been so long since we all were at the same place at the same time. And now we're faced with life without Daddy, and with John going back into harm's way. I thought it would be easier if I just sat on the front porch alone and waited for you. We all cried all day yesterday, every time we saw pictures of us with Daddy, walked by his empty chair, it was contagious. One would start and then the other would hug that person and then they would start."

"That's understandable. It's painful saying goodbye." I reach across the car and softly squeeze her shoulder, hoping my touch is comforting. What is not comforting is the next several minutes as we both silently sit, eyes straight ahead.

Driving thru Divine, I remember my bill at the Antelope Lodge. This affords me a perfect opportunity to break the silence.

"I've got to stop and pay my bill at the Lodge. Mrs. Ahr wasn't awake when I left this morning." I pull up in front of the office. "I'll be just a minute." She smiles but doesn't speak.

Getting back into the car, I break the ice with, "So, where is this place you want to stop and get breakfast?"

"Just on the other side of Beaver is a truckstop. We can either go thru the drive-thru or go in and sit down, whichever you prefer."

"I'm happy with just grabbing a cup of coffee and a sausage 'n egg biscuit. But, if you'd rather go in, we can do that, too."

"All of that commotion in the driveway at home may have put us behind on time. Let's just grab something at the drive-thru."

And, again, the conversation hits a wall.

I decide not to tell her I already had breakfast. So, I force the breakfast sandwich down and chase it with the coffee.

Now, with a hundred miles to go, I try again, "How was your McMuffin?"

"Fine, thank you." She looks at me and takes a deep breath. "Tommy, we need to talk before we get to the airport."

"Yes, I know we do. I…"

"No, let me start. At first I was upset we didn't see each other these last couple of days but I understand. I had a funeral. You had a funeral. I had family to deal with, you had your family. And, neither one of us made an effort to tell our families what was going on between us because… well, because I don't think we knew… or even know now what is going on between us."

I know I wasn't exceeding the speed limit but the next hundred miles literally flew by. And, we covered a lot of ground, both figuratively and literally. Romantic notions went out the window. We were determined not to let words like fate and pre-destined enter into our reasoning.

Reasoning? There didn't seem to be any of that either in our discussions of what had happened in our lives or what might happen in the future. Let's just say we were in complete agreement that our venue for holding this summit of the minds was ideal. No one was about to jump out of a car going seventy. There would be no fists flying, no tackling, and no running from or into anyone's arms while dodging 18-wheelers and armadillos. There would be logical, calm, and sensible discussions with time permitted for rebuttals and proper consideration and respect shown always—not like a presidential debate. Besides, we agreed there would not be a winner and a loser, only an appropriate and sustainable plan of action achieved.

It was because we were considerate and respectful of each other and seemed to be earnestly seeking a resolution that would be approved and accepted by the opposition that we reached the perfect conclusion.

With the rental car returned, we check in and get our boarding passes at our respective airlines. Her plane to Portland by way of Denver leaves in an hour and twenty minutes. While mine to Seattle by way of Dallas departs in two.

It really isn't necessary we speak anymore. We sit in the passenger's lounge and hold hands and each other's gaze. When the announcement to board comes, she waits to be the last one. She drops her carry-on at the last minute and turns to me, we embrace and kiss.

I watch her walk down the gateway. She turns, waves, and she's gone. I stand at the window in the lounge and watch her plane as it's pushed back. Minutes later, her plane races down the runway, leaps into the sky, banks left, and disappears into the clouds.

My terminal is only a brief jaunt. The incessant clicking of the broken wheel on my travel bag is really annoying—not only to me but apparently to everyone on the concourse. I assume everyone is staring at me because of the clattering of the cracked plastic roller—not because I'm wearing a pin-striped suit with a pair of obnoxious neon orange running shoes. And, of course, my favorite blue and yellow striped rugby shirt.

Thirty-two is a good age to get married.

CHAPTER TWENTY-THREE
Thoughts in Flight

Hannah rests her head against the window and counts the line of planes waiting their turn at the end of the runway. The engines ramp up; the pilot releases the brake, and the giant 727 surges forward. As the plane gains speed, the ground equipment and terminal buildings race by in a blur, and she realizes the things surrounding this soon-to-be-airborne vehicle are moving at the same blurring speed as the other things in her life.

She misses the slow routine of her life in Portland and is anxious to return to it. Has it only been a little over a week? In those few days she has held her father's hand, witnessed him slip away, wept at his funeral, met a man with whom she has established—no make that started a relationship—make that just started, been kidnapped, had a gun held to her head, watched her husband get gunned down, shared her most intimate secrets with a complete stranger—a stranger she is now contemplating spending the rest of her life with. It has all been too fast; too much, too soon.

She releases her white-knuckled grip from the seat's arms and takes a long, deep breath. Relaxing the muscles in her feet as well, she uncurls her toes, lets them reach out to the end of her shoes, and wiggles them to let them know they are free to move about the cabin—

free to rest and relax. She hasn't felt free in what seems like years; not free to come home, not free to walk down the street without looking over her shoulder, and not free to push talk on her cell phone without checking the I.D. of the caller.

She deeply exhales again. At least she is now free of Woody and free of that part of her life that was infected by him. If she could only focus on just the things she could put behind her, but in a plane, not far behind, was a new—a new what? An opportunity? An obstacle? Who was Tommy Townsend and just exactly what was he to her and what role would he play in her future? Somehow she knew these questions were there, below the surface, hidden in the shadows of the events of last week. What was quickly experienced on the surface was his charm, his sensitivity, his good looks, his humor, his shining armor, and his— well; he did have some bad points. He must have had some bad points. Why was she angry with him? Why was he always apologizing?

She thought to herself—things are moving too fast. Now would be a good time for me to sit back and re-think, reconsider, and re-organize my life. My past life had been controlled by a man I barely knew and look how that turned out. With Tommy totally separated from me now and being in another airplane traveling hundreds of miles an hour, thousands and thousands of feet in the air to another airport, I should at least be able to let my head do the thinking and not my heart. Thank God he isn't sitting next to me, my head on his shoulder, and my hand in his, tracing the outline of his thumb. It's that kind of stuff that got me to this point in the first place.

The Sky Mall catalog, a total distraction.

Multi-tasking is not his strong suit. Tommy is focused, a goal-setter and single-purposed—one project at a time. But which project? Priorities mean one before the other but which one? He has a book to complete now and get to his publisher. But he's made other promises, new promises to new people in his life. He struggles to free his Daytimer from the Hemmingway-style messenger back beneath his seat. The tray table comes down, ball point pen clicks and he looks for a fresh sheet, a new plan for his life. Now, list priorities.

His first roadblock. He knows he's prone to list his priorities in order of importance. Bad start. He shakes his head as though to re-shuffle the thoughts in his brain and have them appear in a new random order, an order he could jot down and evaluate later after careful consideration. He starts to write book first as he knew he should but hesitates. Actually Hannah was the first thing on his mind. He reluctantly prints her name at the top of his list of priorities then immediately begins to write book but hesitates and decides to leave a number of blank spaces between action items. It wouldn't be just Hannah. It would be various scenarios related to her. Maybe he should have assigned a full page to each of his action items.

He couldn't help but notice a college student across the aisle. A brightly colored backpack is opened on the empty center seat. A tablet with a connected keyboard is propped on the tray in front of him. His index finger swipes images across the screen. Tommy stops mid thought. He interlocks his fingers behind his head and watches intently. After a moment of observation, Tommy scribbles through the first attempts of ordering his life and scribbles, get an iPad.

The flight attendant affords him the opportunity to continue procrastinating and he orders a ginger ale. Maybe I should think a while before I actually write anything else down.

The book. It isn't turning out to be the mystery he had conjured up when he first considered writing it. There is the gnawing conflict put in his head by Papa Tom; should the secret be kept a secret? However, there seems to be a much larger story which has emerged, a story of character. Papa Tom's life has impacted the lives of all those who have come in contact with him; in a profoundly positive way. While Bobby Hampton's unselfish and sacrificial act toward Jake Podus is extraordinary, perhaps it should remain private, a secret. My grandfather lived his life for a grander purpose. While his life was also extraordinary, it was inspirational and a wonderful story that although told over and over again, can never be told too often.

The girl. You know how a crab boil at the beach is better than the crabs you fix at home or get in a restaurant? Even with blustery winds off the North Pacific, and grit that accompanies every bite—that meal on the sand with friends, both new and old, creates memories that will never fade. You want to keep those memories around and relive them, and revisit them every chance you get.

I should take this opportunity to be objective. I can't resist her when she is close. Why do I feel I can't live without her when two weeks ago I didn't know she existed? Why do I now feel all my future plans need to include her? Her clothes won't fit in my closet. Portland is too far to commute. For either one of us. What will I do tonight when I get home? Where will I eat? With who, uh, with whom? Why do I have to eat with anyone? I used to eat by myself most nights. I've my course outline to complete. What was I possibly thinking? I don't have room in my life for another person—at least not right now.

Although. Although when I had the opportunity I would rather be with her than without. You know, it's like getting a new pair of shoes. At first they look real sharp. No scuff marks. Nice and shiny. But, when you wear them all day, your feet get sore. After they're broke in, they get soft and feel comfy. She was just starting to feel comfy.

What does she watch on the tube? Who does she read? Does she read? What paper? Does she blog? I need to Google her as soon as I get home. No. If she has been hiding out for the last two years, she won't have a profile anywhere. Has she been dating anyone? Next to Woody, I must seem like a real catch.

Maybe she liked the bad boy image? There is something a little fancy about Tommy Townsend. I think I'm going to start calling myself Tom. Yeah. TOM. Everyone always called my Tommy and Tommy Boy because I was the kid, the grandson. Well, not anymore. From now on I'm Tom—Tom the man. My students already show me the respect of calling me, Mr. Townsend. I'll just quietly get my colleagues to begin referring to me as Tom, out of respect for my departed grandfather. I would prefer people thought of me the same way they thought of him. I suppose it would be a great incentive for me to begin acting more like him as well. Worse things could happen. I'll write Mom a long letter explaining how I would prefer if the rest of the family began referring to me as Tom and no longer Tommy. I guess the first person I need to start making the transistion is Hannah. I hope she won't make a joke out it.

"Excuse me, miss. May I have another ginger ale?"

Nothing in Sky Mall I really need. And, do I really need another man in my life now? Yes, I do. I haven't had a man in my life for... well, it has been a long time. I do need a man in my life. I deserve a man like Tommy. He comes from a great family, good background. Good sense of humor, smart, educated. Not bad looking. If he is anything like his grandfather... Yes, I need this man. My children need this man for a father. Why am I not on the plane to Seattle with him? We could drive to Portland and pick up my things this weekend. I could give notice. Give away my plants.

Wait a minute! What do I really know about this guy? We could barely talk for fifteen minutes without having an argument. He probably hogs the bed. I'll bet he has terrible breath in the morning. Probably doesn't pick up his clothes. I'll bet he sits in front of the T.V. in his shorts, watches kick-boxing and drinks beer. And farts!

How did things move so quickly? One minute we were just talking... well maybe shouting... and then the next minute we were rolling in the mud and then we were kissing. Kissing! We were kissing before he even pulled out a chair for me. What was I thinking? I wasn't. It happened too fast. Dad was dying. I was confused, distraught, and lonely. I think he took advantage of me.

He did stick around even after he found out I was married— married to a criminal. Of course, he thought I was a criminal too. But, he did stick around. He does want to still see me. He sees a future for us. He said so.

But, we should take it slow. We should date—maybe every other weekend at first. I drive one month to Seattle. He comes down to Portland the next. It's less than a two-hour drive. What could it hurt? I could always date someone else. We wouldn't have to be exclusive. Wait a minute! He said he wasn't dating anyone before. Why would he have to date someone now? I think we could just focus on our relationship. Take our time. Really get to know each other. Our likes, dislikes. Favorite foods. Something besides Mexican food.

Yeah, we should take it slow and date. Take our time. Get to know each other.

It is several hours later and one plane change for Hannah before both are settled in their respective apartments. Hannah's phone alerts her she has an instant message. She retrieves it.

WILL U MARRY ME?

A moment later, Tommy's phone chimes and displays:

YES!!!!!!!!

*****

Dear Readers,

I hope you enjoyed SECRETS. If you got here by first reading my debut novel, BURIED, you've come to the end of the Tom Howard series. I'm looking forward to starting a suspense series set in Seattle with Tommy and Hannah.

If you haven't read BURIED, I'd like to recommend it although the surprise ending won't be as much an ah-ha moment now that you've explored the sequel. Thanks for being a supportive reader. I'd love to hear from you. You may give me a shout at JohnMillsSATX@sbcglobal.net.

John Floyd Mills
Ezekiel 36:26, 27